EVERYWHERE SHE'S NOT

N. JOHN SHORE, JR.

ISBN 978-1-7336078-0-3 (Hardback)

ISBN 978-1-7336078-1-0 (Paperback)

ISBN 978-1-7336078-2-7 (Ebook)

Cover photo by Cat Shore (www.catshore.com)

To Cat, my Kate.

Also to Lynne Holly, Erin Jorgensen, Dave Bowling, Lauren Danver, David Sinclair, Mike King Moore, and Diane Reischling.

The blues ain't nothin' but a good woman on your mind.

— BLIND LEMON JEFFERSON

ACKNOWLEDGMENTS

This novel wouldn't have been possible without the generous (and patient!) supporters of its Kickstarter campaign. From that campaign, and with all my heart, I'd like to thank: John Penrose, Matt Creed, Laura Bradley, Pete Lefevre, Ann Snyder, Karna Bosman, Dan and Wendy Wilkinson, Ellen Goodwin, Peg Y., Molly Pellettiere, Jayne Trapnell, Cyndy Bailey, Eric Booth, Sue Jordan, Cindi Lee, Melina Vasquez, Donald Gillespie, Teresa Whitfield Bryant, Nancy Greene-Gregoire, Karen Barr, Matt McElligott, Gino Medeiros, Makeshift Me Productions, Beth Luwandi Lofstrom, Darla OConnor, Katrina Corbell, Ryan J. Marotta, Carrie Aldrich, Kate Lucyk, Mitchell Reid, Sheila Janca, Robin Miller, Rachel McCann, Anne Kinney, C. Coker, Bonnie Guy, Sandra Wagner, Dana-Huntington-Smith, Jeremy Myers, Dale Schultz, Rich Lubbers, Janet Ackerson, Sunny Lockwood, Grant McNeil, Russell Mark, Dave Felten, Jenny Kelly, Kristin Prentiss Ott, Jennifer Rahner, Kelly Anderson, Nicholas Leo Carpenter, Craig Waters, Don Burrows, Forrest Clark, Jennie Gillespie, Christine Muller, Chris Lotz, Tom Backus, Shannon Wynn, Neal Washburn, Elizabeth Glover, Shelley Ricci, Lori Sievert, Barbara Tillman, Jana Harrison Currier, Angela Finney, Scottish Bobcat,

Leslie Marbach, Jill Hileman, Ben Husmann, Roger Hooker, Nan Bush, Skip Johnston, Martha Underwood, Patty Simmons, Jason and Cat Fizer-Rau, Budd Hetrick, Wayne Johnson, Shawn Elizabeth Bridgeman, Crystal Pridmore, Cindy Miesse, Albert Kingma, Andrea Targos, Delia Yawnick Hardy, Peggy Odum Thomas, Therese Adamiec, Anne T. Johanson-Wright, William Cook, Sarah Willig, Sheryl Teslow, Michelle Watt and Cathryn Lewin, George Leavitt, Randy Johnson, Bryan Crawford, Dave Stambaugh, Deanna Deville, Robert Elliott, Ruby Arellano, Scott McAuley, Shayne Rasmussen, Ty Duncan, Evan Tysinger, Roisin McCormac, Aliza Worthington, Judith K. Volkar, Julie Lumpkin, Charles Maynes, Ellen Wrona, Wendy Cameron, Lori Olmstead Cipot, Judy Smith, Ryan Blanchard, Phyllis Harbor, Susan Fowler, John Houston, Amanda Justice, Paul Schwager, Alan Herendich, Beth Glover, Christine Kane, Diana Ruby Sanderson, Joanna Brown, Megan Kalb, Juliet Sanders, John Sergent, Kristi Byrd, Reed Bilbray, Becky Everson, Kerry WishIknew, Becky Rogers Wiren, Suzanne Rose, Hillary Spragg, Ray Shawn McKinnon, Donald E. Rappe, Rhonda McIntire, Richard J Laskowski, CJ Emanuels, Jen Henley, Robin127, Leslie Hayes, Jon Larimore, Pam Vitale, Carol Clayton, Dakota John Fox, Christie Landtroop, Rick Brenner, and Karen Connolly.

A special thanks also to my editor, Melissa Gray, whose keen sensibilities and great heart made all the difference; to Bruce Steele, of the Asheville Citizen-Times, for watching over so much of my work; to the manuscript's final proofreader, Katie Treisch; to the brave and brilliant Dan Savage; and to Dr. Kim Flachmann, who, back in the day, said yes.

CONTENTS

1. Man Down   1
2. So Close   4
3. Fly Away   29
4. Wrong Home   48
5. Try or Die   77
6. The Surf   104
7. A Fun Day   125
8. Showtime   144
9. The Idiot   162
10. Lawn Darts   190
11. Wave Goodbye   211
12. Devil's Grip   239
13. The Other Side   258
14. Out and Out   284
15. I Hate You   303

About the Author   313

EVERYWHERE SHE'S NOT

❧ I ❧

MAN DOWN

Back from dropping Kate off at the airport, David took one step into the apartment that was now his and his alone, and stopped.

In a corner across the small living room stood a stack of moving boxes, all packed and taped shut. On the top and sides of each box Kate had written her name.

As his car keys slipped from his hand, David walked to the middle of the room.

"Oh my God," he murmured. "What have I done?"

He turned a slow circle, taking in everything around him.

Kate's boxes.

The behemoth of a '60s-era television he and Kate had come across on a curb with a FREE sign taped to it, which, after wheeling it home, they found still worked pretty well if they wiggled its dials, slapped it just right, and then held their breath as they tiptoed back to their couch. (Kate had named the thing Lucy, because, she said, "It looks just like a TV Lucy and Ricky would have owned—and then I guess just watched *themselves* on.")

The stereo that, on the day they set out to finally buy a real bed (so they would no longer have to sleep on the blankets they rolled out onto their bedroom floor every night), they had suddenly agreed they needed so much more than even a bed.

The door to their bedroom.

The wall furnace that, on the rare Southern California mornings cold enough to require its services, made loud cracking sounds on its way to becoming hot enough to emit the comforting smell that he and Kate both loved, which they called Eau de' Burning Dust.

The pine dining table they'd bought at Sears to christen their new home, in the center of which Kate always took such pleasure in keeping a vase of fresh flowers, or a bowl of fruit.

Their couch, an extravaganza of royal blue velvet they'd found at a thrift store, where they had tried to imagine who would buy it ("The interior decorator for the Munsters?" David guessed. "A seriously backsliding furniture molester?")—right up until they themselves sat down on it.

The wall, entirely blank now save for random nail holes and the evenly spaced picture hooks that had so recently held framed photographs taken by Kate, each one of which, as far as David was concerned, proved her a genius.

And then her boxes again.

"No, no, no," David said. "This cannot be happening. It can't be. It can't be."

But it was, and because it was his legs gave out beneath him. He fell to his knees.

He covered his face with his hands.

"Did I *do* this?" he wailed, rocking back and forth, repeating the question over and over again.

Having no choice in the matter, he surrendered to the shock and grief that coiled itself into a great fist and rhythmically and steadily pounded his midsection.

When that storm finally subsided, he was left curled up on the green shag carpet, perfectly still.

After a long while he rolled over onto his back.

He again covered his face with his hands. Into the infinite black vacuum, he screamed, "What have I done?"

But, strictly speaking, it was a superfluous question.

For he knew perfectly well what he had done.

One week before, standing right where he was now lying, he had told Kate that he wanted to end their relationship, that it was over between them.

And so she had packed her things and flown back to San Francisco, there to resume the rich and rewarding artist's life she had been living before joining forces with him, which she had done because, as she had once put it to him while they were walking on the beach together, "I never dreamed anyone like you actually existed."

His asking "What have I done?" was like a man on a boat who points a cannon straight down, fires it, and then can't understand why he's drowning.

The question to which David needed an answer was not what he had done.

It was why he had done it.

❧ 2 ❧
SO CLOSE

DAVID FINCH AND KATE WOOD HAD MET TWO YEARS earlier, when they were both poor college students living in the dorms at San Francisco State University during the 1978-79 school year.

When the college's five-day Thanksgiving break was fast upon them—which happened about three weeks after the two of them met for the first time at a sparsely attended on-campus showing of Charlie Chaplin's *City Lights*, whereupon they immediately started hanging out almost exclusively with each other—they alone, of virtually all the other students in the dorms, had no home to travel back to.

"Can you believe people still have *families*?" said David. "How retro is that?"

Kate rolled her eyes. "I know. Losers."

"Do you think we should tell someone—like in the dean's office, or whatever—that neither of us has anywhere to go over Thanksgiving?" said David.

"I don't think so," said Kate. "If we tell them we want to stay here, they might tell us we can't."

"Or charge us mucho simoleons to do it."

"Exactly."

"So what're we gonna do? Be, like, student *squatters*? Just hide in our rooms and hope they don't find us?"

Kate shrugged. "I think that's our plan."

"Are you sure you don't have a rich uncle, or somebody like that we can stay with?"

"Pretty sure," said Kate. "You?"

"No. Although, actually, my dad is pretty dang rich. Especially in bitterness, anger, and the certain knowledge that if he ever so much as *thought* about giving me a nickel, his wife, my step-mother, would immediately hijack a Brink's truck and use it to run over his dick."

"Oh. Gosh. Well, that doesn't sound good."

"Trust me, it's not."

Spending five days being the only two people in their sixteen-story concrete high-rise dorm building gave David and Kate a lot of time to get to know each other better—and also to discover how basically impossible it is to tire of eating toasted Triscuits topped with tuna fish and cheese.

"Thank God you have a toaster oven," said David.

"Thank God for canned tuna," said Kate.

"And also for can openers. Before I realized you owned one, I tried prying open a can with my teeth. So thank God for dentists too."

"So much to be grateful for."

"Especially for you," said David, kissing her.

Sitting on her bed cross-legged and facing each other during one of their first nights squatting together, Kate asked David to tell her about his childhood.

David shrugged. "Not much to tell, really. I grew up in Cupertino. Good childhood. Lots of fun. My neighborhood was surrounded by what seemed like endless miles of fruit orchards, which was awesome, since no game in the universe is more fun than Run Around and Cream Each Other With Apricots played in an actual apricot orchard. Plus, I knew that if I ever got permanently kicked out of my house—which I expected to happen to me more or less every day of my life—I could totally live on apricots and water from our hose outside. So I was set."

"Yikes."

"No, it was great. Apricots are good for you. Unless it turns out they cause cancer, in which case I should be dead by Christmas. Anyway, I went to Vista Cupertino High, from which I graduated, more or less."

"More or less?"

"Yeah. Long story. But after high school—or, technically speaking, halfway through my senior year—I left home. After that I had some odd jobs."

"Wait, halfway through—"

"I will tell you that story, I promise. I also promise you'll wish I hadn't, because it's boring. But after more or less getting my diploma from high school I had some jobs, which culminated in my working for a year at the Wrigley's gum factory in Santa Cruz. While I was slaving away at Wrigley's, I started wondering if I was smart. So then I thought I'd go to college to find out."

"And? Are you smart?"

"Who knows? I mean, now I know I'm at least smart enough for college, but I'm not sure that's *actually* smart at all. As far as I can tell, college is just high school without the parents."

"It is!"

"By far the *main* thing about coming here, for me, is that I met you, fell in love, and now only care that I'm smart enough not to do anything that makes you go, 'Wow. I cannot believe that I actually slept with that cretin.'"

Kate leaned forward and gave him a quick kiss. "You don't have to worry about that."

"Well, I know what you don't, which is that you haven't yet heard me sing in the shower. So we'll see how that goes."

Kate laughed. "Okay. Well, in the meantime, please tell me some more about your childhood."

"I'm not sure there's a whole lot more to tell. Like I said, it was good. I was a happy kid."

"But you've told me that your mom left you."

"That's true. She did."

"So, I mean, that doesn't much sound like the stuff of a happy childhood."

"Yeah. No. I mean, that part wasn't great."

"What happened? How long was she gone?"

"Two years."

"Two *years?*"

"Yeah. From when I was ten till twelve."

"Are you kidding?"

"No, that's what happened."

"But—*what* happened?"

David shrugged. "I don't really know. I never knew. That was the whole thing. It came literally out of nowhere. One normal summer afternoon me, my sister, and my mom were at home— this was two years after my parents got divorced—when my mom goes, 'I'm gonna run to the store for some milk and bread.' She picked up her purse from the dining room table, grabbed her keys, and drove away. Then she didn't come back."

"What do you mean?"

"I mean she didn't come back. She disappeared. Vanished. Gone. I didn't hear a word from her for two years. No phone call,

no note, no message delivered by carrier pigeon, no nothing. I
didn't know if she'd been kidnapped, or abducted by aliens, or
murdered, or what. But she and I were really close. So to me it
made no sense that she *could* contact me, but just wasn't. But
every minute of every day, that's what continued to happen. I was
just living in this, I don't know, silence of her absence. And I got
into this really weird thing, where I would see a pattern in just
about anything, everywhere—in the way pebbles were scattered
on the side of a road, or how scratches were on a telephone pole,
or the way a piece of paper or a tin can was set just so in relation
to all the stuff around it—and I'd try to read in those things, in
those patterns, any kind of message that my mom might be
trying to send me. You know? She *had* to be trying to communicate with me in some way, so maybe that was how. I definitely
spent two years reading just about every scrap of paper I ever
found. But I could never get any of it to make sense as a commu-
nication from my mom. I kept looking, though. I think I went
kind of crazy there."

When David saw tears filling Kate's big brown eyes, he put his
hands on her shoulders. "Hey, no. Don't cry. There's no need to
cry."

She nodded her head. "Yes, there is."

"No, no. There's not. It's okay. It worked out. She came back.
She was fine."

Kate pulled a few tissues from the box on her nightstand.
Dabbing at her eyes and nose, she said, "I can't believe that
happened to you."

"No, really, it's fine. A lot worse stuff has happened to a lot of
people."

"No, it hasn't. That's about the worst thing that could happen
to anyone."

"Nah. It's not. But I appreciate—"

"Of course it is. Nobody's mom *abandons* them like that. That just doesn't happen. Ever. Moms ignore their kids; moms make their kids do terrible things; moms beat their kids—but no mom ever just *abandons* her kids. No mom goes, 'I'm going to the store,' and then just doesn't come back. That is seriously, tragically insane."

"I guess. I mean, I know it wasn't *good* or anything. It just—I don't know. I always just thought it was a kind of thing that happens."

"Have you ever known *anyone* else that's happened to?"

"No, I guess not. But it's not like I know all that many people's childhood story."

"David, you will never hear of that happening to anyone else."

"Moms abandon their kids," he said. "I mean, don't you think?"

"Not when their kids are *ten*. And not for two whole *years*."

"Yeah, no, I guess that is pretty rare."

"When she came back, did she say where she'd been?"

"No. I kind of tried to ask her, but, I don't know. She didn't really want to talk about it—or anything else. And, honestly, I didn't really care where she'd been. I mean, I kind of did, of course. But mostly, I was just so glad to see her that I couldn't even talk. I couldn't do anything. I just sat in her car next to her and basically *shook* for however long it took us to do whatever we did. Like, I was actually vibrating."

"I'll bet you were." Her voice broke. "God, David." She hugged him. "You poor thing."

He hugged her back.

That was the most he'd ever told anyone about his mom disappearing.

"Well, what about you?" David said. "Your childhood wasn't exactly a day in Disneyland, right?"

Kate took in a deep breath, puffed out her cheeks for a

moment, and then said, "No, not exactly. Unless it was a day when all the rides were broken."

"Tell me about your life growing up, if that's cool? I'd love to hear about it, of course."

Kate pulled a corner of her bedspread onto her lap and started fiddling with it. "Well, you know I was born in London. My mom was a dress designer. She was also a severe alcoholic."

"Oh, gosh," said David softly.

"Until I was five years old, I was really happy. My mom still had all of her faculties and everything. We lived together in a nice little townhouse in London. It was just the two of us. I never knew my real father."

"Never?"

"No. I've never met him. The only thing I've ever even known about him is that he was an Egyptian physician who was in London for one weekend for a medical conference. I think my mom and him just met up at a local bar one night. The next day he went back to Egypt, and nine months later she had me."

"Yay!"

"So she was a single mother. But this was only eight or nine years after the end of World War II. So there were a lot of single mothers in London. And she had her family and friends, and a whole support network around her. I remember her as being happy during that time. We both were. She used to sew me the prettiest little dresses to wear."

"How lovely," said David.

"It was. That's just the word for it. It was lovely." Kate paused for a moment before beginning again. "I have a memory that's so special to me."

When she said no more, David said softly, "Tell me."

She met his eyes with hers. "It's stupid. But we had this back-yard. I thought it was the most special place there could ever be. It had a tall fence around it, so it was just our little space. We had a wrought iron tea table back there. It was painted white, with two matching chairs. That's where my mom and I would sit together and have tea."

"How great is that?"

Kate snagged herself another tissue. "It was pretty great. And I know it's not a huge thing or anything. But to me it felt magical. We had this teapot. I remember it was made by the Royal Albert company, and had the most perfect little red roses on it. I thought it was the most beautiful thing in the world. My mom would spoon the tea leaves into the pot, and pour the boiling water in just so. Then we'd put the teapot, with the cups and saucers, and maybe a little plate with a few cookies, onto our tea tray, and carry it out to the backyard. And we'd sit there together, at our little table, sipping our tea and just—be together."

"It sounds so wonderful. And so *English*."

Kate looked down at the bedspread. She started picking at it with her fingers. "It was. And then it wasn't anymore. Because then my mom married my stepdad. Things changed after that."

"Yeah?"

"Yeah. He was an American. He was in the Air Force. He'd gotten my mom pregnant. Right after they were married he got stationed in Greenland. Before taking off for Greenland he moved us here, to America. He wanted us to be near his family. He thought they'd take care of us. Which can only mean that he either didn't give one shit about us, or that he'd never met his family."

"That doesn't sound good."

"It wasn't. His whole extended family lived in a trailer park— although 'park' is really stretching the meaning of that word—in this bumfuck place called Lost Hills, Kansas."

"Really? It's called Lost Hills?"

"Yeah. Trust me, it's lost because *nobody* would ever look for it. It's out in the middle of absolutely nowhere. I remember getting there, and thinking it was way too hot for anyone to actually live there. And, suddenly, me and my pregnant mom *were* living there. Our new 'home' was basically just this long tin box that was boiling hot, rusted out all over the place, flimsy as shit, and so filthy that cockroaches and mice were running all around inside it, like they owned the place. Which they did."

"Jesus Christ."

"The whole 'park' was basically just a huge junkyard, with people living in the bigger, hollower pieces of junk. And *everybody* who lived in all the trailers around us seemed related to my stepdad. They were all his brothers or sisters or cousins, or his uncles or aunts, or his parents, or who the fuck knew?

"And they all seemed to live in *all* of the trailers too. It was so weird. It wasn't like these people lived in that trailer, and those people lived in this one. Everybody just wandered in and out of—and slept in, and did *all* the things they did—in whatever trailer they'd last stumbled into before passing out from whatever drugs or alcohol they'd managed to get hold of that day."

"That sounds so brutal."

"It was." Kate looked away for a quick moment before looking back at David again. "My mom was raped there. In our trailer."

"Oh, shit."

"Yeah."

"Kate, I'm so sorry."

Kate fell silent. Then she did a little shrug. "Shit happens." She pulled her knees up to her chest and wrapped her arms around them. "My mom fell apart after that. She had just had a new baby—my sister Jane—and just, I don't know, fell into this completely debilitating depression. That's when she started really drinking."

"This all sounds so unbearable. How long did you live in that place?"

"A little over a year, I guess. Then my dad came back, and we moved to Victorville, which is *way* the fuck out in the desert, east of Los Angeles. And then we moved to lovely Suisun."

"Where's Suisun?"

"About fifty miles northeast of here. You've never heard of it because it's nothing but a huge marsh next to an Air Force base."

"Nice," said David sardonically.

"If you like endless miles of hot and stagnant mush, it's the best. Anyway, after we'd been in Suisun for about two years, my stepdad—who I've really only ever known as my dad-dad—got assigned to Vietnam. He was going to have a job there with a fifty-percent mortality rate. So he quit the Air Force and got a job at the San Francisco Airport. And that's when we moved to Pacifica, right down the coast."

"And how old were you when you moved to Pacifica?"

"Ten."

"How was it there?"

"Well, it was better than Victorville, Suisun, or Get Lost Hills. But, basically, nowhere was good for me."

"Why?"

Kate started picking at her bedspread again. "My home situation was bad. By the time we got to Pacifica my mom had three kids with my dad. Between her depression and her drinking, she basically turned into someone I didn't even know anymore. She was like—I don't know how to say it. She didn't know *me* anymore. And she didn't want to, either. She drank so much that she became incapable of thinking or caring about anyone but herself. And it wasn't like she exactly loved herself. She tried to commit suicide—twice in Suisun and once in Pacifica."

"Oh, God, Kate."

"It was so fucking horrible. She deteriorated into just this completely broken ghost who was in the same space where my mom used to be."

"Was your dad any help at all?"

"Not to me he wasn't. He was as bad a drunk as my mom was. They had that in common, at least."

Kate stopped picking at the bedspread and looked up at David.

"My dad was abusive," she said.

David's *no* got stuck in his throat.

Kate looked back at the bedspread. "But only to me. He treated his other kids—his 'real kids'—just fine, as far as I know. But not me. And abusing me wasn't something he did all the time. He did it just often enough to make sure I never forgot that I didn't belong in his house. That I wasn't really part of the family."

Kate looked up at him again, her eyes now red and wet. "And it's not like I had my mom, or anyone else, to protect me. My mom knew how my dad was treating me. But she didn't care about me any more than he did.

"When I was seventeen, my mom kicked me out of the house. She said I was interfering with her marriage. So I was suddenly homeless. And I barely felt any more alone after I got kicked out of the house than I did when I was living in it."

David took her hand.

"My whole childhood I had no one to talk to," she said. "No one to be with, no one to help me figure out anything about anything. I was just completely on my own. Always. It was so lonely. I hated being so lonely. I wanted someone. I wanted my mom. I wanted to be part of the family." She started crying. "I wanted them to love me."

David quickly moved to her side. She dropped her head into his chest.

He held her as she cried.

By the following Sunday afternoon, students were trickling back into the dorms.

"Your roommate's doing the same as mine, right?" David asked Kate. "Not coming back till tomorrow?"

"Right," said Kate. "And then reality starts again."

David sighed. "I hate reality."

Kate kissed him, and said, "I used to. Now I don't."

———

Later that evening, when David returned to their room from his trip to the little grocery store connected to a nearby mall, he was holding a medium-sized cube of a gift-wrapped box.

"Whoa," said Kate. "That's not from the grocery store."

"No. It's for you."

"Seriously? You got me a present? A real present?" She was as excited as a child on Christmas morning. "I can't believe it!" She took a seat on the side of her bed, straight-backed, her lap ready for receiving. "You got me a present?"

"I did," said David.

"It's so *big*! What is it?"

David set the box down on her lap. "You'll have to open it."

"Oh, I can't. The wrapping paper is so beautiful. And look at this beautiful red ribbon! It's so soft! I'm sorry. I can't open this. It's too beautiful."

"Okay, no problem," said David, like the moment was dead and gone. "What'aya wanna do for dinner?"

"Okay, I can open it," said Kate. But she did so very carefully, folding up the ribbon and laying it aside before moving on to the paper, which she began taking apart like she was performing surgery.

Once she'd laid bare the box inside, she said, "Oh my gosh. It's from Macy's."

When she started opening the top of the box, David went over to the window and stood looking out of it.

From behind him, he heard her gasp.

He turned to see Kate setting the box on the bed beside her, and then reverentially lifting from inside of it a Royal Albert Old Country Roses teapot.

She looked like it might be a while before she could talk again.

She placed the teapot on her lap, wrapping her hands around it as if to ensure that it wouldn't fly away.

Kate's thick and curly dark brown hair was blocking most of her face from David's view. But he did see a single tear fall and splash onto the porcelain.

"This is the one," she whispered.

With slightly shaking hands, Kate slowly unpeeled the two little pieces of tape holding the pot's lid in place. When she lifted it off she saw waiting for her at the bottom of the pot a small gift card.

"Hey," she said.

She lifted out the card and opened it.

It said, *You will never be lonely again.*

She began crying so hard that David came and gently took the teapot from her lap. She released it into his hands. He turned away from her in order to set it atop her desk. The moment he was facing her again, Kate smashed into him with a hug so big and hard it felt like the whole world was wrapping itself around him.

Six months later the school year was nearing its close. Lying on the beach that was a short enough walk from the SFSU campus, David and Kate were discussing their plans for the summer.

"I'm thinking about calling my dad," said David.

Kate rose up onto her elbows. "You *are*? Why?"

Rolling onto his side to face her, David said, "Well, he's a head mucky-muck at that huge corporation down in Long Beach. I figured I might call him, and see if he can get me a summer job there."

Kate looked skeptical. "Really?"

"No?"

"I don't know. It's just so hard to imagine you asking your dad for help."

"Yeah. It's not exactly my thing. But I'll bet he can get me a job with his company that pays well enough for you not to have to work at all. That way you could spend all summer doing nothing but your photography."

"But I don't mind working. I like working."

"Oh! Well, then, change of plans. We'll have my dad get *you* a job, and I can stay home all day drinking and whacking off so much my dick ends up falling off in my hand."

Kate made a mock-excited face. "That *does* sound like a fun summer!"

"I *know*! Then I'll get my fallen-off dick bronzed. We'll treasure it forever."

"No, we won't."

"Of course we will. We'll give it a place of honor on our fireplace mantle."

"No, we won't."

"Yes, we will. What else are we going to do with it? And I know what you're thinking: Christmas tree ornament. But believe me, it's going to be insanely heavy. Just the amount of bronze necessary to—"

"Will you stop?"

David looked scandalized. "You just cut me off at the funny part."

"No, I didn't."

"Humor is so subjective."

"No, it's not."

"Okay, but listen. I really am serious about calling my dad. What do I have to lose? My close relationship with him? I don't think we've talked three times since I left home—what, three years ago? But I could see him helping me out. I'm still his son."

"I just know how you feel about him, is all."

"I know. But it'll be all right."

"If you want to call your dad, it's okay with me. But you've got to promise me that you wouldn't do that just for my sake. Because I'm more than good with us getting summer jobs and just renting something here in the city."

"I hear you. I wouldn't call him just for your sake. I just want us to have as many options as possible. So I'll call him tomorrow, and see whether or not him getting me a job is even a possibility. Cool?"

"If that's what you want."

"All right. Cool." David looked out over the ocean. "I mean, what's the worst that could happen?"

————

"You're in *college*?" David's father said to him on the phone.

"Yeah, Dad," said David, putting his forehead against the wall of his dorm room. "I'm in college."

"What college did *you* get into? Pick Your Nose U?"

"No. I applied there, but couldn't get in. Decided to go to San Francisco State instead."

"Pffft. Same thing. What kind of grades do you get?"

"I have a 4.0."

"You," his dad said flatly. "*You* have a 4.0."

"Is there something wrong with this connection? Yes, Dad, I have a 4.0. I'm on the dean's list and everything."

"What are you majoring in? Navel gazing?"

"With a minor in lint. Listen, Dad, please. I really need to ask you something."

An inveterate interrupter, his father let David talk for maybe fifteen seconds before cutting him off. "Let me get this straight. The first time I hear from you in God knows how long, and you want something from me. Why am I not surprised by that?"

David momentarily considered cracking his head open against the wall. "It's not that I *want* something from you, Dad. All I was thinking was that if you have any kind of opening at your company for which I might be suited, maybe that could be a good thing for both of us."

"Opening? What *opening*? What the hell do you even know how to *do*? In case you're not aware of it, nobody gets paid for sitting on their fat ass all day watching television."

David sighed. "I am aware of that, Dad. But good career tip."

"Jesus Christ. What the hell do you want me to do? What am I, an employment agency? I don't have a job that I can just pull out of my desk drawer and give to you."

"Okay. It's not a big deal. For real. It's just something I thought I'd try. I'll find something else."

His father fell silent, which indicated that he was being thoughtful, which indicated that the world had momentarily swung off its axis. "Are you serious about this? You really want to move down here and work?"

"I thought it might be nice, yeah."

"Just for the summer?"

"Just for the summer."

His father paused before saying resignedly, "All right, fine. Give me your number. I'll see what I can do. Maybe we have something in our Ass Scratching department. You'd fit right in there."

The next afternoon David said to Kate, "Guess what? My dad called me about an hour ago. He's got a job for me."

"He does?"

"Yeah. Working the night shift in his company's apparently gargantuan warehouse. Where I will be—get this—a *Teamster!*"

"You're kidding."

"I'm not. We Teamsters don't have a sense of humor. But you know what we *do* have? Money, honey! Teamsters get *paid*! This is great, right?"

But Kate seemed unsure. "I guess so. *You* seem pretty excited about it. Are you sure this is something you want to do?"

"It is! And it's only for the summer. Although, I think I might actually be able to work there for as long as I want—that part wasn't real clear. But I don't think there's such a thing as temporary Teamsters, do you?"

"I have no idea."

"I think it's a permanent thing. I think I could maybe work there forever."

"But would you *want* to? Don't you wanna come back to school in the fall?"

"I've been thinking about that, actually. I'm honestly not sure that I do. As you know, all I've ever wanted to be is a writer. But I don't think college is the best place to learn how to do that. It removes you from the only thing there is to write about, which is life. Plus, I am *tired* of never having any money. Living in the dorms is great when you're just out of high school. But I was working and living on my own for a long time before I came here. I liked the routine of that life. I liked the *paycheck* of it. I think I'd rather go back to a normal, working life, where I have my own place, pay my bills, eat my own food, don't live in a tiny room with a stranger, don't share a bathroom with forty other people, and don't have to find a new place to live three times a year. Where I just go to work, come home, and do my writing."

"Yeah, I could see you doing that. But do you really want to work for your father?"

"Well, that's the thing. He'll be up in his office—being the *man*, man. While I'll be down in the warehouse, being a Teamster. Corporate versus labor. Whole separate thing."

"Okay."

"Besides, it'll be great in Southern California. Surfers. Volleyball. You in a bikini. Which is *the* best reason for us to move there."

"Could you try being just a little less Neanderthal?"

"Hey, no disparaging of Neanderthals. Without them, we wouldn't be here today. Or we'd be orangutans with fins. Nobody really knows."

Kate laughed.

"What I am afraid of," David continued, "is that if we move to Long Beach, you won't be able to continue doing your photography."

"Why? I can do photography anywhere. Same as writing. The main thing about doing photography at a college is getting to use their equipment. But they have colleges in Long Beach."

"Not like San Francisco State they don't. You're a big deal here, Kate. And this is a huge place to be a big deal in photography. We can't just give that up."

"I'm just not worried about it. This school's good for learning photography. Los Angeles is good for *doing* photography. I'll be fine. Besides, if it doesn't work out there, we can always come back here."

"Yeah. Right. That's true. Okay. So—what? Are we gonna do this?"

"I think we might!"

"I think so too! Let's *do* it! This is very exciting!"

"It is!"

"It'll work! We're not afraid! And why aren't we afraid?"

"Because of love," said Kate.

"That's right," said David, hugging her. "We're unafraid because of love."

Three weeks later David and Kate took a Greyhound bus from San Francisco to Long Beach, where they moved into a one-bedroom apartment they'd managed to rent ahead of time in a complex of apartments so vast that David opined it had to qualify as its own city.

"Seriously," he said. "You put a 7-Eleven out by the dump-sters, and within a month there'd be a Sears next to the mail-boxes. Which, by the way, are we just supposed to *hike* to every day? Shouldn't there be a city bus line to and from Mailbox Village?"

"I kind of like the anonymity of living here," said Kate.

David looked at her with suspicion. "Is there anything about your past you'd like to tell me? Because you're right: Columbo with a hound dog couldn't track you down in this place."

"I know!" said Kate. "I can *finally* return to my life of crime."

"Cool! I hate regular jobs."

Be that as it may, David started working nights in the vast and cavernous warehouse of Premier Foods, Inc., where his job each night, along with fifteen or so other men, was to load six or seven semi-trailer trucks with endless kinds of canned, bagged, and frozen foods, which, each morning, truckers drove to restaurants, hospitals, and industrial kitchens everywhere west of the Rockies.

"The guys I work with get *high*," David told Kate.

"Oh?" said Kate.

"Yeah. And you can see why. Over the course of our shift

every guy there picks up, by hand—and *does* something with—a total of about thirty thousand pounds of goods. So when the night's over they shuffle out, zombie-style, into the parking lot, where they open their tailgates, haul out their coolers, and start drinking beer like it's Kool-Aid."

"They're not worried about anyone seeing them?"

"Nah. It's still dark. They've got a couple of hours before people from the office start showing up. So they just sit around, getting drunk and smoking weed."

"And you?"

"Well, I *am* the new guy. I'm also the guy whose father got him the job that all their dues-paying Teamster pals were in line to get. So I can't afford to offend those guys any more than I already *do* offend them just by being alive."

"So what you're saying is that you have to get high every day after work."

"Hey, if that's what it takes to keep a fifty-pound sack of flour from 'accidentally' sliding off a forklift right on top of me, then that's the price I have to pay. Me and the Bee Gees, baby. Stayin' alive."

Kate rolled her eyes. "My hero."

Kate spent her days keeping their decidedly humble but entirely serviceable abode in order, as well as exploring their new environs looking for photos begging to be taken.

Coming home after one of her first such ventures, she said to David, "This place is such a weird combination of industry and *beach*. You know what I saw in the ocean today, *right* off the shore? These huge, operating—like pumping, real slow how they do?—*oil* derricks! And people were just sitting on their beach chairs, lying on their towels in the sand, and putting on suntan lotion, the same as you'd see at any beach. Except there's *oil derricks* in the water, so close I could hit 'em with a rock. It's un*believable*."

"You must have gotten some great shots."

"I hope so! I went through four rolls of film!"

Throughout that summer, Los Angeles was bakingly hot, and so muggy that, as David put it, "a fainting person wouldn't fall over." Several times a rust-colored liquid rained from the low-hanging red-brown clouds, the little seed-shaped drops of which then had to be scraped off car windshields and windows with a razor blade.

"Is this acid rain?" David asked as he and Kate, waiting for a traffic light to change, watched the maroon gunk falling and instantly freezing on their windshield and hood.

"Well, it's not *rain* rain," said Kate. "Whatever it is, it's fucking nasty. How do people just *live* with this?"

But they lived with it. It could have rained tow trucks, and David and Kate wouldn't have relished any less creating for themselves the nourishing domestic tranquility neither of them had known as children. They festooned their apartment with lovingly tended houseplants, framed and hung Kate's photographs on the walls, mounted shelves in the bathroom to hold the candles Kate liked to burn while she bathed. On weekends they went grocery shopping together, cooked together, cuddled together on their blue velvet sofa, and watched whatever they could coax Lucy into showing them.

They were happy together.

They were also, after a time, poorer than they had expected to be. In the late fall, David's work hours became erratic; boss's son or not, he was still the low man on the Teamster totem pole, and his hours were the first to get cut. Some weeks he worked fifty hours, some weeks twenty, sometimes—and sometimes for weeks at a time—he worked none at all.

"What can I tell ya?" said his dad. "Things are tight every-where. Can't ship out orders we haven't gotten in, son. You'll just have to sit tight."

But David couldn't sleep at night.

"Baby, you worry too much," said Kate. "We're fine. I'll just get a job."

"But I don't want you to have to work."

"Why not?"

"Well, for one, you're doing such amazing photography work. Nobody does what you do. I can't stand the thought of you not doing it anymore."

"But I won't stop taking pictures. I'll just do it on weekends. I *want* to work. It'll take the pressure off us. And it'll mean I can rent more darkroom hours, buy more film and supplies, get my tripod fixed. It'll be great."

"There's just got to be something else we can do."

"I don't understand. I just said that I want to work. You don't seem to hear me when I say that."

"No, I do. I hear you."

"You know, I *have* had jobs before. I've probably had more jobs than you."

"Okay, let's not get carried away. I've been fired from *plenty* of jobs. But—I don't know. Are you *sure* you wanna get a job?"

"I'm positive."

"And are you *sure* that if I let you make your own money, you won't start having all these uppity thoughts about being equal to me?"

"I'm positive that you suck."

David laughed. "All right, then. Cool. Let's do it."

Within a week Kate was the new accounts receivable clerk for a business in Compton called Pete's Pet Supplies.

"Whoa," said David. "You got a job *already*? What do they do there?"

"They sell all kinds of stuff to pet stores. Hamster cages. Cat toys. Flea collars. Stuff for parrots. Dog food bowls. There's tons of it."

"Wow. Think it'll be any fun working there?"

Kate shrugged. "Probably not. It's a job. But it comes with a paycheck. Which means—guess what?"

"What?"

"*We can buy a bed!*"

"Wait, wait," said David. "Are you telling me that you *don't* like sleeping on a pile of blankets on the floor? Because I, for one, love no longer having any feeling on the entire right side of my body. It saves me *so* much time I used to spend scratching. Just the other day I caught fire on that side of me, and didn't even *realize* it, until I was, like, 'Yum. Somebody's barbecuing.' And you want to get *rid* of that?"

"Well, as much as I do enjoy not caring if I catch fire, I still want a bed."

"Okay, fine. If it's a bed you want, then a bed you shall have!"

"Oh my God. I cannot *wait* to sleep on a real bed!"

"Me too. I'll admit it. I dream about, well, being able to fall asleep and dream about anything."

On a Sunday morning one month later, David and Kate were feeling as rich as Roosevelts. Besides an entire paycheck of Kate's that they'd been able to put aside, David's latest check included twenty hours of overtime.

"We are going whole snoozin' hog today!" said David. "Queen-size mattress, box springs, frame, new linens, new pillows—all of it. Right?"

"Right!" said Kate.

"Starting tonight, you and I are going to sleep like Rip Van Winkle in a coma. We'll both lose our jobs, of course, since we'll never get out of bed."

"Of course."

"Bedsores *and* unemployed! I can't wait!"

"A bed, a bed, a bed!" Kate squealed. She jumped up from the breakfast table. "I'll go get dressed!" Halfway to the bedroom she stopped running, turned back to face David, crouched a bit, tensed every muscle in her body, vibrated her clenched fists in the air before her, and said, "A bed, a bed, a bed! *I'm so excited!*" Then she dashed off again.

"You are so adorable I can barely take it!" David called after her.

"A bed!" she cried from the bedroom.

When, minutes later, Kate returned dressed and ready to go, she found David seated at the dining table perusing a colorful insert from that morning's ultra-fat newspaper, to which they subscribed because, according to David, "News comes and goes, but the Sunday *Peanuts* and *Doonesbury* are forever."

"Whatcha lookin' at?" said Kate.

"An ad from a stereo store."

With a hand resting on his shoulder, Kate also read the ad.

When David turned to look up at her, she was already looking at him.

In unison, they said, "Let's buy a stereo."

That day's setting sun found them hours into listening and dancing, and here and there even a little bit crying, to their great old albums played on their great new stereo, for which they paid at least as much as it would have cost them to buy a brand-new bed set, linens and all.

They played Joni Mitchell's *Blue, Hissing of Summer Lawns,* and *Court and Spark.* They played Crosby, Stills, Nash, and Young's *Deja Vu.* They played the Woodstock live albums, Cat Stevens's *Tea for the Tillerman,* James Taylor's *Sweet Baby James,* Sly Stone's *There's a Riot Goin' On,* Aretha Franklin's *I Never Loved a Man.* They played *Sgt. Pepper's, Bridge Over Troubled Water, The Best of Earth, Wind & Fire.*

And they danced until they could barely walk.

Late that night, when they went to bed on the floor, Kate said, "I love you so much."

"I love you too," said David.

And he meant it, with all of his heart.

But that did not stop him from doing what he did to her.

❦ 3 ❦

FLY AWAY

On a Sunday morning six months after their stereo purchase, Kate stood before David in their living room, with tears running down her face.

"You're breaking up with me?" she cried. "Are you *serious*?"

David nodded yes.

Kate said desperately, "*Why*?"

But the feelings that had led him to this moment were too sprawling and undefined for David to put into words. So the words that he didn't have became hand gestures that expressed nothing, until finally he was only standing there, helplessly watching Kate as she struggled to comprehend the bomb that he had just dropped onto her life.

"Talk to me!" she screamed. "Why are you doing this?"

David blurted, "I don't know. I *don't* know. It's just—this isn't —all I know is that this, that we, need to end."

"But I don't understand. What's *wrong*?"

"Nothing! I don't know. Everything. Look, I know people say this. I know it's the ultimate cliché of breaking up. But I can't help that, because in this case, it's actually true. This *isn't* about you, Kate. I'm the problem with us, not you. You don't drink too much. You don't smoke too much weed. You're not a basket case who can't sleep more than three hours a night to save his life. You're *happy*."

"What are you *talking* about, I'm happy? Do you think that just *happens*? I *make* myself happy. I'm happy because I'm with *you*."

"But I don't know what to do with that. I don't know how to handle that."

"There's nothing *to* handle. This is life, David. We're just *living*." She broke down again. "We're being in love."

"I know. I know that's what we're doing. It's just that—I mean, don't you ever think that maybe this has all become just, I don't know, too much?"

When Kate looked too bewildered to even attempt to answer him, David started talking fast. "What we're doing here is basically being married, right? We've got this whole domestic thing going on, where you're the wife and I'm the husband. Even though we're not technically married, that *is* the dynamic we're living. That's who we are. Except for the rings and the certificate and the photo album of our wedding that we could bore our friends with if we had any friends, you and I are married, Kate. And you're okay with that."

"Why the fuck wouldn't I be okay with that? This is what we *wanted*! This is what *you* wanted. We *planned* this, David!"

"I know we did. I know this is what we wanted. I know this is what *I* wanted. And it should have worked. But it hasn't, really, has it? Because we're not happy. We're not—"

"Stop it!" said Kate. "Don't you say *we're* unhappy. Say *you're* unhappy if you have to. But you don't know what the fuck you're talking about when it comes to me. I haven't been unhappy. I like our lives here. I like what we've been doing here." Her chin started to quiver. "I thought it meant something. Something real. Something good. Something we *both* cared about." Her anguish became anger. "But I guess I was wrong about that, wasn't I? I guess I was the only one of us who felt that way. Because until you decided to *break up with me*, you never let me know that you didn't think that what we had was good and working—that it was *great*. No. You didn't tell me that. Until just now, you didn't think to let me know that I was *alone* in thinking we were happy."

"I figured you knew it! We *fight*."

Kate grabbed an apple from the fruit bowl on the kitchen counter. Screaming, "Everyone fights!" she threw it at where his head would have been if he hadn't ducked. Rising back up David found Kate, who was a full foot shorter than he was, charging him. He backpedaled so fast he upended one of their dining room chairs—and then continued moving backwards until Kate had him pinned against the front door.

"What is the *matter* with you?" she screamed. She furiously scanned his face, as if his features might reveal an answer to her question. Finding nothing there she could use, she came down off her toes. She took a step back from him.

"Yeah, David, we fight," she said. "That's what couples *do*. They get in arguments. That's how they work out their problems. We've been together for almost two years, you fucking fool. And *now* you want to leave me? *Now* you've decided that this is all just too much for you? What the hell is the matter with you?"

"Nothing!" said David. He pushed from his mind his sudden awareness of how much might, in fact, be wrong with him. "I just —it's not that I haven't wanted this to work. I *have* wanted it to work. But it's been so hard. You know that's true. You know how often we fight. We fight all the time."

"No, we *don't*. Why would you even say that? We don't fight any more than any other couple does. And every time we *do* fight, something good comes out of it. After our fights, we figure out what went wrong. We *talk* about what happened. We *learn* from our fights. Weren't you *with* me during those talks, David? Don't you remember how we always fixed whatever had gone wrong between us? Was I just talking to myself all those times?"

"No, of course you weren't. And you're right about those big fights. But we fight a lot more often than just the big fights you're talking about."

"We talked about that too! Do you really not re*mem*ber this? Do you really not remember how, *maybe* two weeks ago, we talked about all the things in our life that are causing us so much stress and tension? About how I've stopped doing my photography, and how you haven't written anything in so long? I know you have the attention span of a gnat, David, but you might remember some of those conversations? About how hard it is that your job is so unstable, and your paychecks so undependable? Do you remember us talking about how much you hate having to pay your dad and your stepmom for letting us use their car? Does any of this ring a bell for you, David? We *know* the things that are making it hard for us. We *know* what causes us to be short with each other. How do you not remember us talking about all this? Should we have done a daily fucking recap of our lives, and of all our plans together, so that you'd be sure not to forget who we are and what we're doing?"

"No, we didn't have to do a daily recap. Look, it's not that I don't remember everything we said we were going to do. I wanted all that stuff, same as you."

"No, motherfucker, *not* the same as me!"

Kate went from enraged to shutting her eyes. She took in one long, slow breath, and then another. And then another.

She opened her eyes. "You're serious about this? We're done?"

David hesitated. Something in him was telling him to stop.

But instead of listening to that something he wiped away everything. "Yes. We're done."

Kate looked at the ground, slowly shook her head, and then

looked back up at him. "Fine. I am out of here this weekend. You asshole."

Kate went into their bedroom, slamming the door behind her. Within moments David heard her wailing. It was as sickening a sound as he'd ever heard.

He sat down on the couch.

While staring at the misshaped reflection of himself in the gray television screen of Lucy, he listened helplessly to Kate's crying.

———

When love enters your life, everything changes. When love leaves your life, nothing does. Love flies away today, and tomorrow you're exactly where you were before it left. You wear the same clothes. You drive the same car. You watch the same television shows. You eat from the same dishes while sitting in the same chair at the same table by the same window you did before all the oxygen was sucked out of your life.

Relentlessly and inexplicably, life without love continues.

———

Six o'clock the next morning found David wide awake on the blue sofa, where he'd spent a very long night.

Slowly, he moved himself into an upright position.

That pretty much exhausted his plans for the day.

———

Seven weeks earlier David had been, yet again, "temporarily" laid off from his job. Every weekday since then, he had made Kate breakfast and a lunch to take with her to work, and had dinner waiting for them both when she got home.

And he'd also done all the housework.

Or most of it, anyway.

Or usually at least a minimal amount of it.

But he sure did take responsibility for doing all the housework. Which was not anything that Kate had ever said she wanted or expected him to do. What she was instead repeatedly very clear about was that she didn't care one way or the other if David did any of the housework at all. All she wanted, she told him, was for him to be happy.

"Just enjoy your time off from work," she urged him. "Take it easy. Do some writing."

"No, that's all right," he said. "You're working full-time. Of course I should do the housework."

"But why? Are you *happy* doing housework?"

"Well, I mean, who's happy doing housework? I'm pretty sure even Donna Reed was torturing the family hamster when no one was around."

"Then don't worry about the housework. Do something that will make you happy."

"Like what? Lie on the couch all day eating ice cream and watching the soaps?"

"Exactly! Now you're talkin'!"

But David never take too seriously Kate's urging him to feel free to be just as lazy and non-productive as he ever felt like being. It wasn't so much that he didn't believe that she honestly felt that way. It was that he couldn't comprehend how she possibly could have honestly felt that way.

Of course she wanted a clean house.

Of course she wanted all of her clothes and linens washed, dried, folded and put neatly away.

Of course she wanted him to cook them healthy, delicious

meals.

As long as she was working while he was not, she cared.

She was human.

She had to care.

David knew that a person can love you just because of who you are, just because of how they feel about you, just because of how you make them feel about themselves.

They can, that is, for a time.

And then that time will end.

Because in the final analysis, nobody likes anybody who only takes and never gives.

A person will allow their life to be sapped by a loser for only so long. Then they will find something better to do. Somewhere better to be.

Someone better to love.

And that's when they up and disappear.

One day they're just gone.

So while he appreciated and was even amazed by Kate's unwavering assertions that the absolute last thing she cared to do was judge how he spent his downtime from work, until the call came on any given day for him to grab his leather gloves and tie on his steel-toed boots, David felt compelled to grab his Playtex gloves and tie on his apron.

But in his heart of hearts, what David really wanted to do—what he surely would have done if only he believed Kate when she told him that's what she wanted him to do—was write.

To be a writer was all David had ever wanted for himself. Poems, short stories, novels, plays—he had notebooks filled with ideas, outlines, and characters for them all. And now he actually had the time to do the creative work that never felt to him like work at all. There was nothing stopping him.

Except for Kate.

David loved Kate. And he wasn't about to put his writing

ahead of the relationship he had with her, since, to his mind, doing so would be manifestly self-indulgent, arguably narcissistic, and certainly unlikely to result in his earning any income.

So as much as he wanted to write on the days he wasn't working, David was always driven, first and foremost, to take care of business around the house, to be of some *actual* good in his and Kate's life. To straighten up the apartment, do the laundry, vacuum, clean the bathroom, go grocery shopping, cook meals that were nutritious and delicious.

And every single such day David would have done every single such thing, were it not for one eensy-teensy problem: he *personally* didn't give a moldy sponge about having a clean house or eating only meals made from recipes in *Laurel's Kitchen*.

David starting off his down days from the warehouse determined to tackle domestic chores was like the Creature From the Black Lagoon starting off his days in the swamp determined to tackle knitting. It just wasn't going to happen.

Not that David didn't try to make it happen. Each and every morning after Kate left for work he would tell himself that this day was going to be an extra productive one for him. Today was the day!

And then he would sit down, and have a little more to eat for breakfast. And then he would take a nap. And before he knew it, he had spent the whole of yet another day eating, watching TV, reading magazines, drinking, and entertaining himself doing what since time immemorial all young men have always strongly tended toward doing when left alone for minutes at a time, let alone hours.

And all of this non-activity left David anything but relaxed. He simply wasn't good at relaxing when he felt there were still things undone that he really should be doing. He preferred feeling as if he'd earned the right to relax. But during the long days he spent home from work and avoiding housework, he rarely, if ever, felt that he had earned the right to so much as take up the space that he did.

And at six foot two, and two hundred pounds of muscles that seemed to create a restlessness all their own, David took up a fair amount of space. In their small one-bedroom apartment, he felt like a tiger trapped in a cage. He couldn't seem to take more than two steps in any one direction without running into a wall. It even felt as if the ceiling of the place was too low, like if he suddenly stood to his full height the neighbors upstairs would have to start stepping around his head.

Which would be fine with him, actually. At least he'd be somewhat outside of his apartment for a change. He never went anywhere, for three good reasons: Kate took their only car with her to work every day; the only place that was even slightly worth visiting within walking distance of their apartment was the big-box grocery store about a mile away—which, as David once put it to Kate, "is pretty much exactly like where I work, but with cashiers"; and, most importantly, because leaving the apartment meant possibly missing a call to come in that night for work.

So, there it was. Three strikes, and he was in.

David wanted to go to work every day, but he couldn't. He wanted to write, but he wouldn't let himself. He wanted to take care of the house, but he hated housework. He wanted to go outside, but was stuck inside.

He wanted to like himself.

But he didn't.

What he did do, however, was hide all of this from Kate. He knew that he didn't do a lot of things well. But putting on the kind of personal show that would keep the woman he loved feeling good about loving him? Refusing to let his weaknesses compromise the strength of the life of his beloved? Stopping any of his loser juice from ever spilling over into her life?

That, he could do.

And toward that very end he did, in fact, manage nearly every night to have dinner waiting for Kate when she got home from work—and a breakfast ready for her the next morning, and a lunch to hand her on the way out the door.

It wasn't much. But combined with the general air of contentment he managed to assume whenever Kate was at home (and which her very presence invariably rendered a good deal more genuine; David was truly happier when she was around), it was enough to keep her unaware of just how wretched he mostly was.

And every morning, while David stood there watching, Kate picked up her purse and car keys from the kitchen table, kissed him goodbye, and walked out the front door.

⸻

After spending some time sitting on the couch in the soft morning light, David rose and shuffled into the kitchen, where he started to make Kate's breakfast.

Break-up or no break-up, the girl still had to eat.

Pretty soon he heard Kate's alarm go off. Then he heard the shower running.

Usually after her morning shower, Kate would come out in her bathrobe, have breakfast, and then go back into the bedroom and finish getting ready for the day.

This was hardly a usual morning, though. On this quiet morning, when Kate finally come out of the bathroom she was fully dressed for work, purse over her shoulder and all.

Waiting for her on the table was a breakfast of scrambled eggs, toast, bacon, and coffee. Also on the table sat the lunch David had by then prepared for her: tuna salad sandwich, chips, and an orange, all carefully packed into a little brown paper bag.

Ignoring all of it, Kate headed straight for the front door.

Before David could say, "Have a—" Kate had closed the door in his face.

———————

By quarter till eight that night Kate was two hours late getting home from work, and David was in a panic he could barely control. He had no idea where she was, or what might have happened to her—if she was safe, dead, hurt, or what. All he knew was that he was full of adrenaline, and nearly shaking with a fear he could no sooner rationalize away than he could wave his hand and make the moon explode.

When Kate finally walked through the door just after eight o'clock, David's "Where the fuck have you been?" came out sounding a whole lot angrier than he'd intended it to.

"Sorry," he quickly added. "It's so late. I've been so worried."

Kate shrugged, regarding him as if he had just said to her something like, "I saw a dog today," or "Tomorrow will make today yesterday."

"Well, where *were* you?" David said.

Without looking at him as she walked past him, Kate held up a white, greasy-bottomed paper bag from Angelo's Burgers, their very favorite local eatery. She dropped the bag on the kitchen table and walked into the bedroom. A minute later she was back, wearing her favorite sweatpants and a faded Joni Mitchell T-shirt.

"C'mon, Kate," David nearly pleaded. "You're over two hours late."

"For what?"

"For dinner."

Kate picked up her bag and headed for the living room. "I've got dinner."

"I *made* dinner."

"I see that."

David felt as if he were slipping and sliding down the side of a mountain. "Okay then, just tell me. Are you okay? That's all I want to know."

Kate turned on the TV, sat on the couch, and put her bag on the coffee table. She looked up at him. "What do you care?"

"Whaddaya mean, what do I care? Of course I care. We're still *friends*, aren't we?"

"Are we?" said Kate. She turned back to her food.

David sat at the kitchen table eating the noodles and broccoli thing he'd made for dinner, while Kate sat on the couch eating her cheeseburger and watching *Little House on the Prairie*.

———

Done eating and with the television turned off, Kate sat lengthwise on the couch, her back to the kitchen and dining table. Deep in thought, she was motionless.

After about an hour David came and quietly sat in the space between her feet and the end of the couch.

Her eyes flicked up to him. "What?"

"Nothing," said David. "I was just wondering if you're okay."

"Well, stop wondering if I'm okay. That's none of your business anymore."

"Don't say that. Of course it is. It'll always be."

"No, it's not, and no, it won't be. David, you and I aren't a couple anymore. You probably don't remember it, but yesterday, you broke up with me. That means you don't have to worry about how I am anymore. And if you *do* worry about that, I don't want to hear about it. Keep that shit to yourself."

"Okay," said David. He waited a long time before the next thing he said. "We do need some kind of plan, though."

Kate snapped, "No, *I* need a plan. Thanks to you, all of a sudden *I* don't know what I'm doing with *my* life. I'm sure *you* have a plan. I'm sure you know exactly what you're going to do. I, on the other hand, had to spend my time at work today thinking about what I'm now going to do with my life."

"I know. I *know*. I'm so sorry."

"Don't be. I can take care of myself."

"Do you know what you're gonna do?"

"Yes."

"What?"

"It's none of your goddamn *business*, David."

"C'mon."

Kate sighed. "Fine. I'm going to stay with Lillian."

"You're going back to San Francisco?"

"Yes."

"Wow. So, well, this is weird. I was thinking I'd go back to the city too."

"Why is that weird? Why would I *care*? It's a big city."

"Okay, great. So, I was thinking that, if it's okay with you, maybe I'd see if I could stay at Jerald's motel for a while. See what I might do from there."

"You're going to the Surf?"

"I thought I would, yeah. See if he'll rent to me for a month or two. But, I mean, is that okay with you? Cuz you look like maybe—"

"That's fine with me," Kate said tightly.

"Because if it's not, I can do something else. Jerald was your friend before he was mine, so—"

"I said it was fine. Drop it."

David fell silent. Then he said, "I don't know about you, but I like the idea of both of us being back in the city. In fact, I talked to my mom the other day, and she said—"

"You talked to your mom? When?"

"I don't know. Sometime last week."

"Before you broke up with me?"

"I dunno. I think. Anyway, she asked about you. She invited us to her place for Thanksgiving. She's having a big dinner party, with friends and all that. Since we're both gonna be up there anyway, maybe we can—"

Kate held up her hand. "Stop. No. One of the great things about your breaking up with me is knowing that I'll never have to see or talk to your mother again."

"Oh, come on. You only met her twice. You barely know her."

"Twice was enough."

"What? There's nothing wrong with my mom."

Kate got off the couch. Walking toward the bedroom, she said, "I'm sorry. I forgot. Your mother's a gifted genius."

"Well, I wouldn't say *that*," David said. But Kate had already shut the bedroom door.

The next morning Kate again ignored the breakfast and lunch waiting for her on the table—and also the "Have a good day" that David offered right before she closed the door behind her.

"Fuck," David muttered. Then he choked down the breakfast meant for Kate, donned his standard ensemble of Levi's and a white tee, and walked to the big-box grocery store.

He needed boxes. And tape. And markers. And packing paper.

He got them.

"Take all the boxes you want," the store manager told him. So David flattened a bunch of boxes and walked home with them balanced on his head. Then he did that a couple of more times.

When she returned home from work that evening, Kate said, "All ready to start packing, I see."

"Yeah," said David. "I figured we might as well start. I mean —" But she was already off for the bedroom. She returned a couple of minutes later, having changed into sweats and a tee and tied back her hair.

"Let's do it," she said.

"Okay," said David, "I was thinking that—"

"I'll take half the boxes and work on this side of the room, and you take the other half and pack over there," said Kate. "Sound good?"

"Sure," said David. "Yes."

———

Dividing between themselves the things they'd jointly acquired in their time together proved minimally distressing, as neither of them was especially keen to own anything that reminded them of their coupledom. They also each understood and accepted which items most naturally belonged with whom. They weren't exactly like two dispassionate store clerks taking inventory, but almost.

There was one incident, however.

It started when David came into the living room from the kitchen holding Kate's Royal Albert Country Roses teapot.

"Obviously, this belongs to you," he said.

Kate was on her knees packing a box. She looked up.

"No," was all she said.

David hesitated a moment before taking a couple of steps toward her. "Whaddaya mean? Of course this is yours."

Kate hurried to her feet. "I said no. I mean it. I don't want it."

"Are you serious?"

"Do I *look* serious?"

David went back into the kitchen, where he gently placed the teapot on the counter.

Later that night, while Kate was in the bedroom packing, he quietly carried the teapot back into the living room, setting it on the floor amidst Kate's collection of books by her two favorite authors, Jane Austen and Robert Heinlein.

When she came back out into the living room, Kate saw the teapot and stopped dead in her tracks.

"What the *fuck*?" she said.

She picked up the teapot. She walked resolutely to the front door, yanked it open, and left it open as she headed out into the darkness.

Pretty soon David heard the top of a dumpster swinging open. Then came the sound of the teapot shattering as it was thrown against the inside wall of the dumpster.

Coming back inside, Kate slammed the door shut behind her.

"Jesus *Christ*," she said, crossing back to where she'd been packing. "What part of breaking up do you not understand?"

That was the last time after they broke up and before she moved out of their apartment that Kate showed any anger toward David. Throughout the rest of the week she treated him like he was a pleasant enough roommate whom she was perfectly content to accommodate and work around.

As they sat at Angelo's eating their final dinner the night before her flight back to San Francisco, Kate said, "I miss the city so much. I can't wait to see my friends up there. It's gonna be so great to see Lillian."

David fiddled with his fries and said nothing.

"What?" said Kate.

"Nothing. I dunno. This is just—weird. It's nothing. Never mind."

"Breaking up is always weird," said Kate. "But, listen, I want you to know it's okay that you and I are going our separate ways. I'm fine with it."

David wasn't having any trouble believing that was true.

———

Curbside at LAX the next morning, Kate hoisted her two large suitcases out of the car trunk and onto the sidewalk. When David reached to help her with them, she said, "No, I got 'em. But thanks."

"No problem," he said, stepping back.

When she was all set to go, Kate said, "Goodbye, David. Gimme a call when you get to San Francisco."

"I will. And I'll put all our stuff in storage up there, like we talked about."

"Great," said Kate. "So, I'll see you when I come to get the rest of my stuff."

A smiling, white-haired skycap came up to her. "Take your bags, Miss?"

"You bet," she said. After she and the skycap had exchanged tickets and a tip, Kate headed for the terminal.

David stood there a while, ready to wave her a final goodbye. But he never got the chance, because Kate never turned back toward him before she disappeared from sight inside the building.

———

An hour later David walked into his empty apartment, looked around, and got slammed by the reality of what he had done.

———

When he finally picked himself up off the floor that night, David slowly dialed Lillian's phone number.

"Oh, it's you," said Lillian. "Now, what in this world makes you think that Kate would want to talk to you?"

"I know she doesn't. But please? It'll just be for a moment."

Lillian said, "I doubt that," before, from the sound of it, throwing her phone receiver down onto a steel plate.

When she came on the line, Kate said matter-of-factly, "What is it, David? Is everything okay?"

"Yes. Everything's fine." He felt like he was pushing words out of someone else's mouth.

"So you're calling, why?" said Kate.

Squeezing his eyes shut, David concentrated on sounding like he wasn't on the verge of screaming to her about how he had no idea how he could have done anything so wildly self-destructive as breaking up with her.

"I just wanted to make sure you got to Lillian's all right," he lied.

"Yeah, I did. Is there anything else?"

"I'm sorry. I won't take up your time. I just want to apologize to you. It was—what I did to you—the whole thing is just fucking unbelievable. It was wrong and stupid and unthinkably awful, and something I'll regret for the rest of my life. And I just wanted to say how truly sorry I am for it."

Kate paused. "Tell me that you're not doing this." After waiting for the reply that didn't come, she said, "Yeah, okay. Listen, David. I want to be really clear about this, just so there isn't ever any confusion or misunderstanding about it. You and I will never be together again. You know that, right?"

David found his voice. "Right. I know that."

"I need to hear you say it."

He felt like a drowning man who'd been tossed a block of concrete. "You and I will never be together again."

"*Ever,*" she said.

"Ever."

"Okay. When you have our stuff in storage up here, call me so that I can come get a key to the unit. Okay?"

"Okay."

"Goodbye, David."

Before David could say another word, he was listening to the steady buzz of a phone line gone dead.

"Goodbye," he said, placing down the handset.

4

WRONG HOME

WHEN DAVID WAS EIGHT YEARS OLD HIS PARENTS decided they no longer wanted to be married to each other. Up until that cataclysm, his was the idyllic suburban life. His hand-some, athletic, six-foot-four father, Jack, sallying forth from his yellow-and-white house every morning, briefcase in hand, looking like Captain Dashing in his suit and tie. His divinely beautiful mother, Georgia, attentively caring for Jack, their two children (David had an older sister by four years, Patty), as well as for the family's miniature poodle, Buddy, whose curly, soft *au naturel* fur made David wonder what people who shave their poodles have against cuteness, and Snicklefritz, their black tomcat, who enjoyed getting pet almost as much as he enjoyed suddenly attacking you when you were petting him. Bringing up the rear was the usual menagerie of ancillary pets: hamsters, guinea pigs, mice, turtles, rats, lizards, and, for a while, a huge, floppy-eared gray-and-white rabbit that was supposed to have been a family pet, but that, from the moment their mother brought it home from the pet store, Patty staunchly refused to let David so much as touch, because, as she put it, "Flopsy loves only me."

Before his parents got divorced, David's life was basically

Leave It To Beaver—if the Beav's brother, Wally, had been a girl who seemed to want nothing so much as for her little brother to permanently disappear.

Then, one afternoon in the summer of 1966, Jack Finch sat his two children down on the family couch, pulled up an ottoman, took a seat, seemed lost in thought for a moment, and then sighed, and said, "Patty, David, there's no easy way to tell you this, so I'm just going to come right out and say it. Your mother and I have decided to separate. So, tomorrow, I'm moving out of the house."

David was first to break the stunned silence. "You're what?"

"I'm moving out of the house. Your mother and I are separating."

"Moving out?" said David. His head was suddenly filled with loud fuzz. "You're leaving us?"

"No, son, I would never leave you or Patty. I'm just going to be living somewhere else, is all."

"But isn't that the *same* as leaving us?" said David.

"Shut up, David," said Patty.

David felt like his brain had broken in half. "I don't understand," he said.

"Your mother and I are getting what's called a divorce."

"What's a divorce?" said David.

Patty said flatly, "It's where two married people don't love each other anymore, so they break up."

"No, it isn't," said their father. "Your mother and I do love each other. That hasn't changed. We're just not going to live together anymore."

Patty blurted out, "Can I come live with you?"

"Me too!" said David. He didn't want Patty and his dad living somewhere without him.

"Will you shut *up*!" Patty barked at him.

"C'mon, Pattycake," said their father. "Take it easy."

David looked frantically from his sister to his father. The thought of having to choose between his mother and his father was making a train wreck happen inside of him.

"Kids, listen to me. You're both going to stay here and live with your mother. This is your home, and we don't want either of you to change schools, or have to make new friends, or anything like that. Nothing in your life is going to change, okay? The only thing that'll be different is that I won't be living here anymore."

But to David, that "only thing" sounded like everything.

David had friends whose parents fought and screamed at each other all the time. But, as far as he knew, his mother and father never so much as raised their voices to one another. Every so often one of them would slam a door shut. And sometimes there was a prolonged and definitely tension-packed silence between them. But, fight-wise, that was the extent of what he had ever seen or heard between them.

Which was a big part of why he couldn't make sense of what his father was telling him now.

"Why do you have to *leave*?" David pleaded. "Can't you and Mom just stay here together, in our house?"

"I'm afraid not, Champ. This is something we've both thought about for a long time. We've decided it will be best for us, and for you kids, if I moved into my own place. But I won't be far away. I'll be real close."

When he saw that neither David nor Patty had anything more to say, Jack stood up, bent to pat them both on their knees, and walked out of the room.

Once they were alone, David looked at Patty. Her face had broken into a silent cry.

David felt the impossible, which was his heart breaking even more. His sister never, ever cried in front of him.

He reached out to put his arm around her shoulders. "Don't worry, Patty. We'll be okay."

Patty slapped his arm away, hard.

"Get away from me," she said.

———

The next day, just like he said he would, Jack moved out of the house. For a while, with something markedly less than the hustle his father was always telling him to display, David helped his dad carry out onto the driveway, and then pack into his beloved AMC Ambassador, all of the things in the house that now, and so suddenly, belonged exclusively to him: the lamp and chair from his office, his work files, his clothes, his golf and tennis and fishing equipment. All of it. All of him, item by item, carried from inside to outside.

But eventually David stopped trying to help with his father's move. He wasn't doing much anyway besides getting in the way. He kept dropping boxes, and accidentally tripping over things, and loading stuff into the car in such a way that his dad would have to shoo him off so he could fix the wrong way David had done it.

So, finally, David, who was old enough to at least know how to take a hint, sat on the front lawn as close to the car as possible, and silently watched as his father efficiently and resolutely packed up his car for the beginning of the whole new life he was going to start living somewhere else.

More than ever, David was awed by his dad's sheer physical strength. The man carried from the garage, and placed down right in front of him, a bulging box so heavy with the weights from his barbell set that, after marveling that it hadn't snapped his dad's back in two, David worried it might do the same to the driveway, if not to the earth itself. When his father strode back inside the house, David put both his feet against the box, and pushed. The thing didn't budge.

"Well, son, that's it," said his dad, arching his back a little to stretch it out. "Got everything packed. I'm on my way."

David got up off the ground. "You're leaving?"

"That's right."

David looked at the stuffed car. Between all the boxes and clothes in the backseat, he thought he saw just enough room for himself. "Aren't you gonna wait for Mom and Patty to come back from the store?"

"Nah, this works out. I already said goodbye to Patty. They'll be back in just a minute, okay? So I want you to stay right here and wait for them. And you're having hot dogs for dinner tonight! Pretty great, huh? Hey, now. C'mon, son. Don't look like that. I told you, I'm not moving far. I'll be back to see you kids all the time. You know that, right?"

David nodded yes.

But he didn't really know that. At all.

"And you're gonna be my strong little guy, right? You have to be, son. Because from now on, you're the man of the house. And that's a lot of responsibility. Your mom and your sister will be depending on you. So you've gotta be tough for them. Can you do that? Can you be my tough little man?"

David looked down at the ground. He was pretty sure he couldn't. But he knew he had to try. So he shrugged.

David's dad tousled his hair. "Of course you can. Because you gotta be. So you will. All you have to do is stop worrying so much." He turned to get into his car. "You're one of the world's great worriers, son."

Once he'd backed his car out of the driveway and into the street, Jack braked, slipped his car into drive, waved to his son, and started on his way.

David the Worrier stood in the middle of the street, waving goodbye to the back of his father's car as it drove away.

He watched as, far up the street, his dad signaled, braked, turned a corner, and was gone.

And then he was just a kid standing in an empty street waving at nothing.

David looked at his house.

He looked back down the street.

He dropped his hand.

He thought maybe he'd keep standing right where he was until a car ran him over.

No cars came, though.

The curb in front of his house looked miles away.

But it wasn't, as it turned out. It was just the usual amount of steps away.

His legs and feet felt like lead.

But he kept moving them forward.

Off the street, up the curb, along the long, long pathway to the two front porch steps of his house.

One step, two steps, three steps, there.

The door there.

He watched his hand reach out and take hold of the doorknob he used to know so well.

He made his hand turn it.

It turned.

He pushed.

The door opened.

And then he couldn't move.

He just couldn't.

From the threshold of the open door, he could see that this was not his house.

No.

He knew his house. He knew it like he knew his name. He knew what it felt like. He knew all of its dimensions. He knew what it was.

But this wasn't that place.

This was a place larger by far than any place he'd ever imagined.

This was a place filled with dark shadows, waiting voids, winds that would whip down from above and pull him up into nothingness.

This place wasn't his home.

This place didn't care for him.

Here was no friend of his.

Here was no love for him.

Here was a place that would swallow him whole the moment he stepped inside it.

He took a small step backwards.

He heard the winds from inside the house moving, stirring, wanting him to enter.

If whatever was hungering for him inside there came out for him, it would get him, he knew. Because he couldn't move.

All he could do was wait.

So he did.

And while he was waiting he heard a voice coming from behind him.

"Son?" It was his mother. "Are you all right?"

Then he heard Patty say, "Move it." She pushed him on her way inside the house.

He collapsed to the ground like he was made of nothing but broken dreams.

Within a month of his father leaving home, David's mother enrolled as a full-time student at San Jose State University.

"Why would you want to do that?" David asked her, worry-ingly, as she was puttering around the large bedroom that used to belong to both of his parents but was now occupied by her alone.

"Because I want to learn about psychology," said his mom.

"What's psychology?"

"It's the study of why people are the way they are, why they do the things they do."

David thought for a moment.

He loved his mother, but didn't understand why she was okay with her husband going to live somewhere else.

He loved his father, but didn't understand why he wanted to live anywhere but in his own house with his own family.

He loved his sister, but didn't understand why she didn't love him.

And that was just for starters. Basically, he didn't understand why anyone—and especially adults—did half the things they did.

"I wanna learn—what's it called again?" he asked.

"Psychology."

"I wanna learn that too. Can I go to college with you?"

Georgia smiled lovingly at her son. "No, honey. You've got your own school to go to."

"But all we ever learn about is math and spelling. What's *that* teaching me about why people do stuff? Why don't I just come to your school? I could carry your books. That won't be hard for me, you know. I carry stuff a lot heavier than books all the time."

"I'm sure you do, sweet pea. But college is for grown-ups. The school you go to is for people your age. Besides, you don't want to be away from your friends all day, do you?"

"Yes."

She laughed. "No you don't. You'd miss them."

"No, I wouldn't." He turned his attention to something on her bedspread that needed picking at.

"What's the matter, baby?"

"Nothing." He never wanted his mother to know if something

was bothering him. He knew that she had enough troubles of her own now that she was a single mother.

"C'mon. What is it?" said his mom. Receiving only silence in reply, she sat down beside him on the bed. "Talk to me, sugar. What's bothering you?"

David shrugged. "I don't know. I just think that maybe—I don't know."

"What?"

"It's just—you're starting college."

"I am. Is there something wrong with that?"

David was silent for a moment. Then, seeming to have resolved something within himself, he looked back up at her. "Never mind. I'm being stupid. Just forget I said anything. It's okay. I understand, Mom. Sometimes things just change a lot, that's all."

David had no idea how right he would soon be proven about that.

Within two months of starting her classes at SJSU, Georgia Finch transformed from a conventional fifties housewife into a fervent social radical. She started listening to Bob Dylan, Simon and Garfunkel, Joan Baez, Peter, Paul and Mary. She took her place in the front lines of students protesting the war in Vietnam —and held her position, battling with the best of them. She burned incense throughout the house. She rolled her own cigarettes, ones that smelled completely different from the cigarettes she'd always smoked. She took to wearing oversized dark sunglasses.

She also began hosting at her home gatherings of liberal intellectuals, mostly men who were unfailingly happy, if not distractedly twitterpated, to welcome into their circle the witty, long-legged, and decidedly buxom beauty with the easy laugh and the dark hair styled like Marilyn Monroe's. And, naturally enough, the bolder amongst these men began to court Georgia.

One such suitor, Dr. Dan Wilcox, a wildly popular SJSU psychology professor, began staying overnight at the house, sleeping in the same bedroom on the same bed on the same sheets that David's *real* dad used to sleep on.

David was extremely wary of "Dr. Dan," as he more or less insisted everyone call him.

Sure, the guy could spin a funny yarn. But so could Bozo. Besides, *nobody* was funnier than Jack Finch, and that was just a fact.

Not at all helping his case was that Dr. Dan also wolfed down his food like a starving wild boar. His eating sounded like an over-stuffed garbage disposal trying to work. David didn't know how his mother could stand it.

David kept his eye on Dr. Dan. The guy was bound to trip up sooner or later. And when he did, David would be there to let him fall.

Between Dr. Dan, her classes, studying, protests, cocktail parties, and all the "rap sessions" she went to, Georgia was away from the house most of the time. This left David free to enjoy a life of doing pretty much anything he wanted, such as spending countless hours watching television while eating breakfast cereal; bathing no more than he himself deemed absolutely necessary (which was pretty close to never); doing just enough homework to stay out of trouble, and not one fraction problem more; staying up as late as his eyelids and nodding head would allow; and, in general, leading exactly the sort of life that he felt more than justified him being nicknamed Huck, which he *would* have been if his stupid friends had ever cooperated with his determined efforts to get them to call him that.

Fairly soon into this new phase of her life, Georgia began to drastically change how she related to her children. Before her divorce, her demeanor toward David and Patty was generally calm, controlled, imperturbable. As the time following her divorce went on, though, she became erratic, mercurial, and, at least for David, almost impossible to predict.

Sometimes she was nearly overcome with an inexpressible love for her children; other times simply being in their presence seemed to fill her with rage. Sometimes David was a brilliant boy genius who could do no wrong; other times he was a loathsome disgrace who couldn't do right if his life depended on it. Sometimes Patty was "a beautiful goddess of light"; other times she was, as Georgia once put it during a rare dinner that the three of them were eating at home together, "a fat pig who lives to stuff her fat piggy face."

David became increasingly proficient at immediately adapting to his mother's moods. Once he had learned to identify, and even, in some measure, to anticipate her emotional states, he learned to positively affect those states, mostly by saying and doing whatever at best made her happier or calmer, and at worst deflected her ire away from him.

It was his knack for, essentially, emotionally manipulating his mother that led David to the mistaken belief that he and she enjoyed a uniquely close, and even rarefied, relationship. They did, but mainly in the way that an animal trained to perform knows how it must act and react in order for its handler to provide it the nourishment it craves.

It was on a Sunday afternoon, two years after her divorce, that David's mom slipped her sunglasses on, picked up her car keys and her purse from the dining room table, and said, "I'm going to the store for some milk and bread."

By seven thirty the following morning Georgia had still not returned home, and her children, who had suffered through a night fraught with fear and anxiety, had heard nothing from her.

Looking exhausted, but dressed for school, Patty came out of her bedroom to find David curled up on the couch, where he'd spent the night.

"I'm leaving," she said.

David lifted his head. "You're going to *school*?"

"Yeah, David. Not all of us are babies."

"But what about Mom?"

"What about Mom?"

"She's still *gone*."

"What am I supposed to do about it?"

"I don't know. But don't you want to wait here for her?"

Patty went into the kitchen to find some food to take with her to school. "No. I'm sure she'll be back sometime today."

Though he tried hard not to, David began to cry. Coming back out of the kitchen carrying a lunch sack, Patty said to him scornfully, "Will you grow up? I'm sure Mom just got busted at a protest, or is with Dr. Dan. Maybe she's at a sit-in."

"But we didn't see anything like that on the news."

"Not *every* protest is on TV, dummy. Just get dressed and go to school."

"No. I wanna be here when Mom gets back."

"You're just making things worse."

"How?"

"Goodbye."

"Please stay!" said David.

But he heard the front door open and then slam shut.

David lay back down on the couch. Pulling the blanket he'd taken from his bed the night before over his head made him feel a little safer. Through the blanket's open weave and the heavily smudged sliding glass door across the room from him, he looked out at the brilliant morning mist hovering just above the unkempt lawn of his backyard. He imagined his mother emerging from out of that glowing, golden light and walking toward him.

Five hours later David was still on the couch, half-heartedly eating a bowl of cereal and staring at a game show on TV that he'd watched countless times before but now couldn't seem to follow.

He heard a key turning in the front door.

He hurriedly set down his cereal bowl and bolted for the entranceway. "Mom!"

Just as he reached it, the front door pushed open.

David stopped, flat-footed and wide-eyed.

"*Dad!*"

———

Dressed for work and looking like a million bucks, Jack Finch reached down and placed his giant hand on David's skinny little shoulder. "Hey, Champ. How ya doin'?"

David knew he was practically screaming, but he couldn't help it. "I don't know! Good! *Mom's gone!*"

"Calm down, son. I know she is."

"You do? Where is she?"

"I have no idea. But I'm back. That'll have to do for now."

David seemed to freeze, while his overloaded system recalibrated itself just enough to allow him to speak. "Did you say you're back?"

"You catch on fast, boy." Jack turned to reveal the woman standing on the porch behind him. "Son, you remember Karen. She's going to be moving back here with me."

David looked at the woman whom he'd barely ever seen

outside of his dad's apartment—and who, for the previous six or so months, had been at his dad's apartment just about every time he was over there. He liked her. Sometimes. She was crazy pretty. But whatever. He looked at his dad again.

"You're *back*?" he said.

"For the twentieth time, yes. C'mon, let's go inside."

"Where's *Mom*?"

"I just told you, I don't know."

"You're moving *back* here?"

"Not if you don't get out of the way, you lump. Move!"

David hurriedly stepped aside. "Hi, Karen," he said with a little wave as his dad's girlfriend stepped through the door.

The executive secretary to Palo Alto's commissioner of city planning, Karen was wearing a tight knee-length navy skirt, matching high heels, and a long-sleeved floral polyester blouse with a huge bow at its neck. Atop her head was her usual perfectly coiffed helmet of golden hair.

With a cold and perfectly manicured hand, Karen reached out, cupped the bottom half of David's face, and squeezed. Sticking her bottom lip out in an exaggerated pout, she said, as if commiserating with him, "Hello there, my dear little David."

"Hewo," David managed. "Howawoo?"

Karen let go of his face, stood straight again, and pulled his head into the only bosom he'd ever seen that could realistically compete with the size of his mother's. With his face buried deep between her perfumed breasts, David heard Karen say, as if she were in another room, "I'm just fine, honey. But the really important question is, how are *you* feeling? Oh, you must be so scared. And so *confused*."

The moment his head was back out of Karen's boobs, David turned to his father.

"Are you guys *married*?" he said.

Jack nodded. "We are, son, yes. We got married just this morning, as a matter of fact."

———————

And so David, age ten, began living with the woman whom, that very night, his father asked him and Patty to start calling Mom. After finishing their very first dinner together as a brand-new family, Jack said, "I want you kids to call Karen Mom because she wants you to call her that. And it's the least you two can do, since she's sacrificed so much to come here and take care of you both. Okay?"

Patty shrugged. "I don't really care. Sure."

"David?" said his father. But David was still struggling to wake up from whatever dream world he seemed to have stepped into.

"Son," prompted his father.

"Sir?"

"Don't you want to thank Karen for coming here to take care of you?"

David looked at Karen. "Thank you."

"Thank you, what?" said his dad.

"Thank you, Mom," said David.

———————

Within four months David was not only calling Karen "Mom," he was calling her—at least to himself, or while screaming at the top of his lungs into his bed pillow—every curse word he knew.

Living with his dad's second wife turned out to be, in a word, hell. Every day. All day. Seven days a week.

Hell.

Karen was born and raised in a tiny rural town in northern Minnesota, where she had been so severely impoverished that, as a child, she and her family had at times been reduced to eating snow and boiled tree bark. Growing up that kind of poor had left her, as an adult, almost savagely ferocious about money.

Her obsession with money did not serve Karen well in her new role as stepmother to two children who had not only never known want, but who, for two years prior to her sudden entrance into their lives, had been free to do most anything they pleased, given how often their mother was away from home.

Immediately upon moving into their house, Karen placed David and Patty on strict daily food rations: one cookie, one bowl of cereal, one piece of fruit, two pieces of bread, three slices of lunch meat, and so on. She kept her neatly written list of their daily food allowances prominently affixed to the family fridge. All food beyond what was absolutely necessary to keep in the pantry, Karen packed into travel trunks, which she kept padlocked and stored underneath her and Jack's bed.

"Under your *bed*, Dad!" David cried to his father. "*C'mon!*"

But Jack, who had started staying in his office like it was a bomb shelter in an air raid, said, "When you're starving to death, come see me. Until then, you and your mother figure out your problems yourselves. I've got work to do here."

That became Jack's sole response to the fact that the other three people in his house were constantly crying and screaming bloody murder at each other: "Solve your own problems. I've got work to do."

If either David or Patty, brushing their teeth in the bathroom they shared, forgot the rule and kept the water in the sink running while they stood there scrubbing away, Karen, if she was home at the time, would start pounding on the bathroom door and screaming at them to turn off the water. If they left a room without turning off the light; used too much soap to wash their clothes or the dishes; failed to shut every window in the house before turning on the heating or air-conditioning; showered for too long; hastened the ruination of their socks by wearing them without slippers—if they did anything at all that wasted so much as a penny, Karen's fury would be unleashed upon them.

While outside of it she was the very model of cheerful conviviality, inside of their house Karen violently raged about the money or resources that David and Patty were forever wasting, about the unfairness of her being the only person in the family who seemed to care about financial security, and about the "ridiculous expense" of keeping their dog, Buddy, and their cat, Snicklefritz—both of whom she so unabashedly despised that one day David returned home from school to find that she had, in her own words, "Gotten rid of those little beasts"—about which she refused to say another word, no matter how desperately he and Patty pleaded with her to tell them what she had done with their beloved animal companions.

Most of all, Karen raged at her husband—screaming and fuming, and at times wildly hurling whatever object was nearest by—for his steadfast refusal to come out of his office to help her fight the war she was ceaselessly waging with *his* children, whom, she constantly reminded them all, she had never asked for, or wanted.

David was on his school's playing field during recess, surrounded by a crowd of fellow sixth-grade boys.

"Okay, *fuck* this," he said impatiently. "Gimme the football." One of his friends did so.

Spinning the ball in his hands, David said, "Listen. We do

this every fucking recess. We spend so much time picking teams, figuring out who's gonna play what position, and where the goal posts are, that by the time we start actually *playing* football we're out of time. It's bullshit. Recess is only twenty minutes long—and every day we waste fifteen of 'em. Fuck that. I *love* football. We all do. But we need a better game. And I've got one."

He didn't, actually. But anything would be better than rarely getting to have any real fun for more than about three seconds before the end-of-recess bell went off. *That* had to go.

By way of buying himself a quick moment to think up a new game for them all to play, David started with, "Here's the game that we should be playing instead of football. Okay. So what we do is, whoever has the ball runs. Everyone chases the guy with the ball, and tries to tackle him. The guy running with the ball can hang on to it for as long as he wants. But whenever he wants to—and for whatever *reason* he wants to—he can get rid of the ball, just by tossing it away. He can throw it up in the air to nobody—*or* he can throw it right to somebody, like maybe to the guy who was just about to tackle him. Then *that* guy becomes the guy everyone's trying to tackle."

"The old switcheroo!" said one of the boys.

"Exactly."

"What happens if the guy with the ball gets tackled?" asked a boy.

"Yeah, *before* he throws it away," added another.

"Well," said David, "if you keep the ball till you get tackled, then you stand up, and can do whatever you want with it. You can keep the ball, and start running again—but you *can't* do that more than twice. *Mostly* what you do is throw the ball to someone else. You can close your eyes and toss the ball behind you; you can lob it right into the middle of the crowd; you can throw or kick it as far away as you want to; you can hand it to somebody right next to you, and then tackle them. It's up to you. But whatever you do, the game starts again right then."

"So there's no *teams*?" said a boy.

"That's right," said David. "No teams. It's every man for himself."

"What's this game *called*?" one boy asked suspiciously.

"Suicide," said David. "It's called Suicide."

The boy screwed up his face. "Why's it called *that*?"

"Because it's suicide to have the ball," said David. "Watch." He tossed the ball to the kid.

"*Get 'im!*" cried one of the boys, and before the kid with all the questions knew what hit him, everyone had. He disappeared beneath a pile of bodies.

Once the boy had dragged himself back up to his feet, David said to him, "Now you throw the ball."

Smiling wickedly, the kid tossed the ball to David.

"Ha!" cried David, and he was outta there like a racehorse on fire.

Once he'd dashed down the field, David stopped and faced the bloodthirsty stampede charging toward him. Glancing quickly toward the school building, he saw, standing together at the edge of the playing field, three of the prettiest girls in the sixth grade.

They all waved to him.

He smiled and waved back. They turned to each other and giggled.

Immediately—not that he had a choice, since the mongrel horde was already upon him—David got down to the business of showing the girls, and all of his friends who tried in vain to tackle him, why exactly it was that he so fully expected to be drafted by the 49ers by at *least* the end of that school year.

He dodged. He leapt. He spun. He feinted one way and cut the other, leaving so many jockstraps on the field they'd need a grass Zamboni to collect them all.

Those boys might touch him, but they wouldn't tackle him until he let them. And then he would go down howling, screaming, and having all the fun in the world.

Nobody inside his home ever considered David anything but a pain in the ass, a pest, a waste. There, he had no power, no influence. There, his will meant nothing.

But outside of his home? In *his* world, amongst his friends and schoolmates, in his territory?

Out in that world, where nobody knew much if anything about his home life, he was too smart, too funny, and too damn hard to tackle to be anything but a king.

Georgia Finch came back into David's life in August of 1970. During the two years she was gone, David heard nothing whatsoever from her. No note, letter, phone call, telegram—never a sign of the ingeniously cryptic messages for which David spent those years feverishly searching.

Never anything but the impossible and infinite silence of nothing, where once his mother had been.

And then one day, when David was twelve years old and just home after a long and hot afternoon playing baseball with his friends, he was unexpectedly met by his father, who had stepped out of his office to meet him.

David had never seen his dad looking so troubled.

He froze. "Hi, Dad," he said cautiously. "What's up?"

"Son, there's something I need to tell you."

"Okay." David waited.

Finally, his dad said, "Your mother is back. She wants to see you. Tomorrow afternoon."

Instantly David's legs turned to jelly.

What fluttered out of his mouth like a broken bird as he dropped down to his knees was, "Oh my God."

———

The next day, in a new white Volkswagen van, Georgia pulled up to the curb outside David's house.

With her engine softly idling, she sat rigidly still, both hands on the steering wheel, looking straight ahead.

From inside the house, David breathlessly watched her through the kitchen window.

Karen stood beside him. "So that's Georgia, huh?"

David said softly, "It is."

Karen looked at him. "So what are you still doing here? Don't you want to see your mother?"

Without taking his eyes off the mirage come to life on the curb outside, David said, "Yes. Of course I do."

"Go, then," said Karen.

"Okay," said David.

But he didn't move.

Karen said, "Come to think of it, I guess I can see why you might want to make her wait a while."

"Whaddaya mean?"

"Never mind. Listen, honey, don't forget: she's probably more nervous than you are."

David looked at his stepmother. "Do you think?"

"I know," said Karen.

———

Once he had silently opened the door and climbed up into the passenger seat of his mother's van, David tried to say something. He tried to say anything. But for the life of him, nothing would come out. So he busied himself putting on his seat belt. Then he sat looking straight ahead out the windshield, the same as she was doing. He felt like his brain was exploding.

The woman he'd been desperately yearning to see every day for two years hadn't even turned her head to look at him yet.

And except for the quickest glance when he first opened her car door, David hadn't looked at her, either. He couldn't. Seeing her so close would be too much for him.

So the two of them just sat there, side by side, silently looking forward.

Finally, Georgia turned her head toward her son.

"Look at you," she said contemptuously. "You're so furious at me you can't even talk."

David nearly spun in his seat to face her.

There she was.

"Oh, God, no, Mom. No. It's just the *opposite* of that. I swear. I'm so happy to see you I can't even talk."

But she only looked back out the windshield again. Shifting her van into gear, she said, "You're lying."

David felt as if he were disintegrating. "No, you're wrong," he pleaded. "Please believe me." As the vehicle pulled away from the curb, a cry that he tried to muffle burst out of him—and as quickly as it escaped, he silenced it. He used his hands to quickly wipe his eyes and nose.

Looking straight ahead, he kept himself silent.

Wordlessly, his mother drove for about twenty minutes before pulling into the driveway of a modest three-bedroom home on a peaceful tree-lined street in San Jose.

"Here we are," she said.

She got out. David got out. He walked behind her up to the front door of the house. When she unlocked it and went inside, he followed her.

"Dan's not here today," said Georgia.

"Who's Dan?"

"Dan Wilcox," she said, closing the door behind him. "The man I live with. You remember Dan, don't you?"

David flashed back to a morning when he was ten years old and walking down the hallway on his way to getting some breakfast for himself. As he passed the open door of his and Patty's bathroom, he saw Dr. Dan in there, sitting on the toilet, naked, reading a newspaper.

"Hey, Davey-boy!" the man called to him. "Come on in! Let's rap for a minute!"

David had just made it past the bathroom door and was exactly one step into bolting for the front door when he pulled up short.

He knew that, as a kid, he was basically stuck having to obey adults. That was a given. But he wasn't sure if that general rule applied in this particular situation. Rapping crapping adults had simply never come up in his life before. Seemed to him like this might be a situation where there was a little wiggle room in the Always Obey department.

"Come on, pal," came Dr. Dan's voice. "Let's spend a little time gettin' to know each other."

But there was no one in the world David wanted to know that well.

By then Dr. Dan had become a fairly regular presence in David's life. The man was at their house all the time—sleeping over in his mom's bed, with his mom. And his mom had obviously greatly failed to explain to the interloper which of the two bathrooms in the house it was okay for him to use, and which it was absolutely not.

David didn't see that he really had much choice but to try and act like it was perfectly normal for him to stop and have a little chat with a grown naked man who was sitting on a toilet.

He slowly backed up two steps.

"Hi, Dr. Dan," he managed—and then, burned into his memory forever, was the image of Dr. Dan's pasty side-butt.

"Davey, my main man! How's it goin'?"

Staying resolutely in the hallway, David tried to casually look around the bathroom that had once been his. "Fine."

"Do you follow sports at all?"

"Yeah," said David. But the stench in which Dr. Dan was sitting felt like it was melting his face.

"You like the Giants?" said Dr. Dan.

David nodded. Quickly concluding that it would be less rude to get the hell out of there than to projectile vomit, David said, "Okay, well, talk to you later," and strolled the step or two it took for him to clear the bathroom doorway—whereupon he picked up his speed so fast he thought he might blast right through the front door and not slow down until he was on the other side of the Rocky Mountains.

"I do remember Dr. Dan," David said to his mother. Looking about her living room, he said, "Are you married to him?"

Georgia walked across the room to her dining area, where she dropped her purse, keys, and sunglasses onto her table. "Would it make a difference if I was?"

David shrugged. "No, not at all. I was just wondering. Where is he?"

"Today is his day for visiting his children."

"He has *kids*?"

"Of course he does, David. He was married for thirteen years. He has four children. Becky is eleven, Noah is nine, Joan is seven, and little Sally is four."

David let his mouth do what it did best, which was run with

only minimal input from his brain. "Wow. What great age-spacing. College professors are so *organized*."

"Each of Dan's children is a pure delight," said Georgia. "Getting to know them has been one of the great joys of my life."

This time David's mouth failed him.

"Oh," was all he said.

After that first visit with her, and throughout his high school years, David had lunch or dinner with his mother a couple of times a month. Whenever they were together, he would play the student to his mother's teacher, the devotee to her guru. She dispensed wisdom—about people, about psychology, about spiritual enlightenment—and he soaked it up. This worked for the both of them.

Periodically he would spend the weekend at her house. Every night, about fifteen minutes after they'd all gone to bed—he in the guest room, and she and Dr. Dan in their bedroom across the hallway—David would then have to endure listening to the shouted moans and groans made by Dr. Dan in response to whatever apparently extraordinary thing his mom was doing to please him sexually.

Though he endeavored to hear as little as possible of the inevitable goings-on across the hallway, David never once heard so much as a sigh from his mother. Except for how obviously he wasn't, Dr. Dan could have been in their bedroom all by himself.

When he was about halfway through his senior year of high school, David's father and stepmother informed him that his father had accepted a position as Vice President of Sales for

Premier Foods, Inc., a company Karen described as "the kind of place where, if they offer you a job like they've offered your father, you don't say no."

David looked at his dad. "You got a job with the Mafia?"

"Funny," answered Jack. "You're a funny kid."

Karen said, "As you know, David, you're free to live under our roof until you graduate from high school. Your father and I talked about it, and we've agreed that you can move with us to Los Angeles, and continue living with us there until that happens."

"Until what happens?"

"Until you graduate from high school."

"Down there? In *L.A.*?"

"Yes."

"But I only have half a year of high school to go."

"But your father's new job starts in two weeks. So that's our offer. Take it or leave it."

David left it. He wanted to spend six more months living with his dad and Karen before getting turned out onto the streets of Los Angeles like he wanted to be the Bearded Lady at a carnival.

The time had come, he knew, to strike out on his own.

———

Vista Cupertino was one of the top ten schools in the nation in the National Forensics League, the organization that oversees high school speech and debate competitions.

During the first half of his junior year of high school, a friend of his who was on Vista's debate team cajoled David into entering a local N.F.L. contest.

"For a guy as funny as you," said his friend, "it shouldn't be any trouble at all to win the Humorous Interpretation event."

"I should say not," said David. "What's Humorous Interpretation?"

"It's where you take a ten-minute selection from a play—in this case a funny play, obviously—and you act out the whole scene."

"Like, play all the parts? With different voices and all that?"

"Exactly. Humorous Interp is the most popular event in N.F.L. They end every speech contest with its final round, because it's the one event literally everyone wants to see. It's an hour of live comedy as good as comedy gets. Packs 'em in every time."

"Cool. And good to learn that you speech dorks have at least a rudimentary understanding of the general concept of humor."

"Well, we're no David Allen Finches, of course."

"Of course," said David. "But who is?"

"Tell you what. If you enter the speech contest that's coming up in two weeks, I'll buy you dinner. If you make it to the finals in Humorous Interp, I'll buy you dinner *and* give you twenty bucks."

"Done," said David. "Where's the contest gonna be?"

"San Jose State."

"My mom went there!" said David. "But the point is, you're going to feed me."

When it came his turn to speak in the final round of the Humorous Interpretation event at the speech contest that he did, in fact, enter, David was so nervous that when the judges called his name he could barely get his legs to walk him out onto the middle of the stage.

Once there, he stopped, looked up, and saw, just as his friend had told him that he would, an auditorium packed to capacity. When the tidal wave of energy rolling off the five hundred or so people focused on him hit him, it immediately wiped clean his brain.

He went totally blank.

What brought him back into something like normal

consciousness was the deafening roar of the auditorium crowd, which was giving him a standing ovation.

It took him a few long moments to realize that the object of the unbridled affection of the ocean of people before him was himself.

And then he knew that what he *thought* had happened really had happened: he had made it—and apparently successfully—through his speech.

An hour or so later, to another great ovation, he was handed a first-place trophy that just about reached his waist.

David won the first speech he entered with his rendition of the famous "You Call That An Insult?" scene from *Cyrano de Bergerac,* the 1897 play by Edmond Rostand about a man who has all the confidence in the world, except when it comes to the woman he loves.

By the end of that school, year David was one of the top N.F.L. competitors in the country.

He took to acting like a fish to water. All he had to do was stop being himself, and become someone else. Doing that wasn't a huge problem for him.

When they learned that he was determined to drop out halfway through his senior year, Vista Cupertino's powers that be cut David a deal. In exchange for giving him a 3.8 GPA for the classes he was supposed to take in order to graduate along with the rest of the class of '76, he agreed to compete for the school in the six biggest N.F.L. contests still to come that year.

The school would get to maintain its prestigious ranking in the N.F.L., and David would get great grades for a semester's worth of classes that he wouldn't even have to take.

"Are we really doing this?" David asked Mr. Carr, the guidance counselor who had been empowered to actually do the deal with him.

Mr. Carr, whom David had always liked, shrugged. "It would

seem so." He stood up from his desk and put out his hand. "Congratulations, David. You're graduating from high school early."

Shaking his hand, David said solemnly, "I want you to know that if I *had* taken those classes, there is no question at all that I would have gotten a much worse grade in trigonometry than the one you guys are giving me. You all caved like a Potemkin house in an earthquake."

Mr. Carr laughed. "It's because you can even *say* those types of things that I will sleep tonight."

5

TRY OR DIE

AS DAVID STOOD ON THE PORCH OF HIS FATHER'S AND Karen's palatial home in the monied Los Angeles community of Sherman Oaks, he thought about simply leaving in their driveway the car he'd come to return, and taking a cab back to Long Beach. Or catching a bus there. Or walking.

Or crawling. Crawling would be fine, he thought. Anything would be better than doing what, sighing, he finally forced his hand to do, which was reach out and ring the doorbell.

A few long moments later, Karen opened the door.

"David!" she cried.

Once David was literally no longer costing her anything—and also because she felt more secure in her relationship with her husband, since there was no longer anyone in the house competing for what there was of Jack's affection—Karen had been meticulously amiable, if not downright convivial, toward David during his previous couple of visits to their home.

Now she held him at arm's length, looking him up and down. "I still think of you as a boy! But that's not you at *all* anymore, is it?"

"No, I guess not," said David.

"Not by a long shot! Come on in! Your sister is here from Hawaii!"

"She *is*? I had no idea."

"Oh, we're just having the most wonderful time you can imagine! Now, what's this about you wanting to return our car?"

Stepping into the house, David saw Patty standing at the opposite edge of the foyer, her arms folded beneath her chest like a bouncer outside the least fun nightclub ever. "I need to return the car because I'm moving back up to San Francisco," he said. "Hi, Patty! I'm so surprised you're here! Nobody told me! How are you?"

Staying right where she was, Patty held out her open arms to David, inviting him to come and receive a hug. Her eyes were showing the same glassy redness they pretty much always had since the summer between her freshman and sophomore year of high school, when she had first started smoking pot.

"I'm in such a good space," said Patty serenely.

"You look great!" said David, walking over to hug her.

"Let's go sit in the kitchen," said Karen, putting her hand on David's back. "We'll enjoy half a beer each, and you can tell us all about what in the world is going *on* with you, Davey! I know all of us want to hear so much about anything you might be *writing* these days!"

The two siblings fell in behind their stepmother as she led them past the formal living and dining rooms and into the large, sensibly decorated family room, which extended into the everyday dining area just outside their kitchen.

Along the way, David gave Patty a silent two thumbs-up. With a broad expression of mock-excitement on his face, he mouthed, "Half a beer!" He needn't have wasted his time, though. In return for his jocularity, he received a look from Patty like he was waving around a huge booger that he'd just pulled out of his nose.

For the millionth time in his life, David wondered why Patty had decided that Team Parents was the only team she wanted to join. Why, even during the worst of his and Patty's years together—when, for instance, Karen was so relentlessly demolishing both of their young lives—did Patty never seem to *once* so much as entertain the idea of forming a team with *him,* her sole sibling, her natural ally, her would-be comrade in arms, whom she knew perfectly well would do anything in the world for her?

Why wouldn't Patty want to bond with the only person on earth who understood and could fully commiserate with her over the bizarre and painful nightmare that so much of her childhood had been? Wasn't the primary greatness of having siblings knowing that someone besides you not only witnessed, but actually *experienced,* what it was like to grow up in your house?

Try and try and try though he did, David was never able to understand what Patty gained by insisting, from as far as he knew the very day he was born, that he did not, or certainly should not, exist.

Because he did, after all, exist.

So why wasn't Team Siblings the one to join?

"Once again, Mom," said Patty, "I have to say how *beautiful* your house is."

"It really is," said David agreeably. "It's so *huge.*"

Completely unsurprisingly, David's father was kicked back in his recliner in the family room, watching a golf game on TV. When he saw David, he raised his hand. "Hey, Champ."

"Hey, Dad. Watchin' golf?"

"No, I'm outside mowing the lawn."

David laughed. Say what you might about his dad, but the man really was funny.

Karen had walked over to their round oak dining table. Rolling back one of the four oversize padded dining chairs set around the table, she said, "Davey, you come sit here. I'll sit here—and,

Patty, you sit here to my right. And Jacky will sit in the chair he always sits in, because that's the chair he likes."

As the children unhurriedly took their assigned seats, Karen, already in her seat, folded her hands on the table. "I'll get us our beer in a moment. But first, tell us, David, what's this about you moving back to San Francisco?"

"Well, I—"

Karen held up a hand. "Wait!" she said. "You know what? Let's get our financial business out of the way first. You two kids have a nice chat here for a moment, while I go into Jack's office and get the paperwork for the car. Then we'll all go out and inspect the car, and make sure that everything is okay, and that we don't have anything that we have to figure out or discuss before we can all just relax. And once all that's done, you'll tell us all about what's going on in your life, Davey, just like Patty has been catching us up on all the goings-on in *her* life. So let's do that! I'll be right back with that paperwork."

As Karen hustled off down the hallway, David turned to his sister.

"It's so good to see you, Patty. How ya doin'?" Then he settled back in his chair to wait out what he knew would be her interminable answer.

Patty sighed wistfully. "I miss Hawaii." (Which, native-style, she pronounced *huh-VIE-ee*, which is where she had moved some seven years earlier.) "I love coming back to the mainland, where I know so many people, and have so many friends and memories and good times to reflect upon and cherish. And I do cherish it all; there's nothing like friends—real friends, David, the kind you know you can count on forever, you know?—to give your life real meaning, depth, and everything that makes life worth living."

Speaking as fast as he knew he'd have to in order to squeeze it in, David said, "Friends are great."

"But the longer I'm away from the lush island greenery," Patty continued, "and the clean beaches, and the white sand so fine it's like running silk through your hands, and the longer I'm away from the crystal clear water you can see straight through to the bottom—so teeming with life, so full of coral and fish showing off every color of the rainbow, with so many wonders and miracles of nature your mind simply fails to take in the gloriousness of it all —and especially, truly, the longer I'm away from the amazingly fresh, *amazingly* clean island air, air that—and I know you'll find this hard to believe, David, because I'm not sure that I could have believed it myself before I moved to Hawaii and experienced it firsthand—you *can't* see, air that *doesn't* hang in the sky like the aftereffects of a nuclear disaster, air that you *don't* have to smell every time you go outside, until you feel like you're living in the middle of some huge, disgusting ashtray."

"Yeah, in Long Beach, we've had this acid r—"

"I miss it all. I always do. Every time I come to the mainland, it never takes very long at all before I'm looking back toward the setting sun, longing to return to the land where I belong, and where I am happiest. And it's not that I don't understand how people living on the mainland can feel like there's no real reason for them to have any more nature in their lives than they do. Especially people living on the coast of California, which, if I was going to live anywhere on the mainland, is certainly where I would live, because there are stretches of land and beach all up and down the California coastline that, in their own way, are every bit as beautiful as what we have in Hawaii. So I understand how people can feel that they're communing with nature, wherever they are. And everyone *should* spend as much time as they possibly can in the holy presence of the Earth Goddess; that's so important to do, no matter who you are, or where you live. Every tree, every flower, every bird that flies in the sky should be seen as the inspiration that it truly is."

"For sure. In San Francisco—"

"But what I miss most when I'm away from my island home are the people. Oh, how to even begin explaining to a mainlander the magic, the wonder, the sublime spiritual majesty that lies at the heart of the native people of Hawaii, who have welcomed me into their *ohana*—that means family—with such open arms. That the Hawaiians have embraced me as one of their own is something which never fails to make me feel *ha'aha'a*, meaning humble. And when I am away from the place where the spirit of *aloha* lives and thrives in the hearts of my Hawaiian brothers and sisters, I actually feel as if I am suffering. You would know what I mean if you yourself had ever experienced true *aloha*, David. I won't try to explain all that is meant and expressed with that simple word, *aloha*, the true meaning of which is beyond all words. The spirit of *aloha* is a philosophy, an attitude; it's truly a way of life—of a generous, warm, spiritually harmonious life. It's something special to Hawaii, because it comes from the very heart and soul of the Hawaiian people. And when I am away, I hear them calling—"

"Got the suckers!" cried Karen, coming down the hallway waving a sheaf of papers. "I couldn't *find* the darn things. But here they are! Now, let's all go outside and inspect the car, shall we? Jacky, we're going outside to take a look at the car now. Why don't you come and do that with us, sweetie?"

"What in God's name are you jabbering at me about?" said Jack.

"I'm not jabbering," Karen said curtly. "I'm asking if you want to come outside to inspect the car that David is returning to us today."

Jack said, "Son, have you been in any accidents with the car?"

"No," said David.

"Have you driven it into any lakes or telephone poles?"

"No."

"Has anyone *kicked* it?"

"No."

"Well, then, I really don't see a lot of work to be done here." He returned his attention to the television, making a bit of a show of pointing the remote control at the thing to turn up its volume.

"I swear," said Karen, "sometimes I think I'm just going to kill that man in his sleep. Patty, do you want to come out with Davey and me to inspect the car?"

"No, I've got to start packing for my return to Hawaii tomorrow."

"Oh, did you move to Hawaii?" asked David.

Jack snorted a laugh. David quickly said to Patty, "I'm sorry. I'm just goofing around. Of course you want to start packing to get back to Hawaii."

"Of course you do," said Karen.

"And to my house there," said Patty. "With my two spare bedrooms."

David didn't hesitate to give her what she wanted. "Let me stay in one of them! C'mon, Patty. Invite me to your home. I've never seen it! I promise I won't eat much, *or* make a lot of obnoxious jokes. Plus, I'm super handy around the house."

In a tone that made it perfectly clear she wouldn't, Patty said, "I'll think about it."

"Looks like it's just you and me, Davey," said Karen. "Let's go! This should only take a minute." Pretending to admonish him with a stern wag of her finger, she added, "Unless you're trying to hide something about the car from me! I'm kidding you, dearie. C'mon."

Kidding or not, David knew that border guards wouldn't inspect a car driven by Hunter S. Thompson any more thoroughly than Karen was about to inspect the green 1971 two-door Datsun 1200 that, when David and Kate first moved to Long Beach, she had arranged for them to lease from her, with an option to buy, for two hundred dollars a month.

A half hour later, putting a check in the box next to the final item on the car inspection form she was using, Karen said, "And we're done! You took such wonderful care of the car, honey!"

"I really appreciate your letting me lease it from you."

"Isn't it just the best little car *ever*?"

"It really is," said David sincerely.

"Now let's go have us that half a beer! Oh, I just *love* the weekends!"

Once they were back inside the house, Karen said, "Jacky, won't you turn off the television now, and come sit with us, and have a little afternoon refresher with some pretzels? David is going to catch us up on what's happening in his life." She then charged down the hallway toward the bedrooms, returning moments later with Patty in tow.

"It's so *nice* to have all of us together again," she said. "C'mon over here and join us, Jacky." Surprisingly, Jack clicked off the television set, and got up from his chair.

"Now, you three sit down at the table," said Karen, "and I'll get the beers out of the fridge." She disappeared into the kitchen, returning moments later bearing four glass tumblers. As she was setting down a glass at each of their places, Jack said, "Son, can I get you a real drink?"

"A whiskey on the rocks would be nice," said David.

"Sure thing, Dean Martin." He turned to his daughter. "Patty?"

"Whatever Mom's having is fine with me."

"Now I'll get the pretzels and some paper plates," said Karen.

"I'll help you," said Patty.

Watching the others as they busied themselves and then settled back down into their chairs, David felt like it was the first time that the four of them had ever sat at a table together. It wasn't, of course. But, almost to the point of crying, he suddenly felt nostalgic for something he'd barely ever known at all.

Once everyone's drinks and pretzels were before them, Karen, taking her seat, said, "So, Davey, sweetie, tell us everything about what's going on with you. Why are you moving back to San Francisco?" The gleam of delight in her eyes at the prospect of his living far away from her again was enough to make David look down at his pretzels, and then take a sip of his whiskey.

"Well, I guess the main reason is that I broke up with Kate," he said.

Patty was first out of the blocks. "Oh, David," she said mournfully. "Not another girl."

"You broke up with *Kate?*" his dad asked, in about the same way he might have asked him if he'd drop-kicked a three-legged puppy. "How the hell could you do something like that?"

David said, "Well, see—"

"And I suppose this means you're going to quit your job?" said his dad.

"Well—"

"The job I *got* for you? *That's* the job you've decided to quit?"

"Yeah," said David. "Dad, I'm so sor—"

"The job I leaned over *backwards* to get you, even though it meant bumping guys who'd been paying their union dues for *years?* Guys with families, who would murder their own *mothers* to have that job? *That's* the job you no longer want?"

"Actually, Dad, the job was—"

"Oh, clam it," said Jack, dismissing his son with a wave of his arm. "I don't wanna hear it. Fine. You're quitting the job I got you. I don't care. Go. Move. Do your thing. I'm sure I'll hear from you the next time you need something."

"Dad, I kept getting laid off. You know that. So—"

"I told you I don't want to hear it."

"I got the impression from Mom and Dad that you were going

to marry Kate, David. Is that what Kate was expecting, too, you think?" Patty asked concernedly.

"That's what *would* have happened if he had half the sense God gave a houseplant," interjected Jack. He pointed a finger that to David still looked big enough to him to do chin-ups on. "*Kate* was a keeper. She was a rare one, that girl. Good as gold. You mark my words: you'll never find another like her."

"I agree," said David. "And I'm—"

"Well, dearie, we're all so sad to hear that you and Kate have broken up," said Karen. "And now you're moving back to San Francisco, where you have so many friends and people that you've known for years who love and care for you, and who will be so glad to have you in the area again. And just think of the writing you can get done there, in that *city* of writers. Of course, this means that you won't be coming here for Thanksgiving after all."

"No, I guess not," said David. "Georgia's invited me to her place, so that's where I'm gonna go."

"Oh, how wonderful!" said Karen. "Thanksgiving with your mother! That's just the way it should be."

Standing up, Patty said crossly, "I need to finish packing." She stormed off down the hallway. They all heard her bedroom door slam shut.

"Your sister misses Hawaii," Karen intimated to David. "She's ready to go home now. I'm sure she misses her life, teaching swimming at the YMCA near her home, and doing all the other wonderful and fun things that she does."

"Like smoking pot," is what David barely chose not to say. If his parents didn't know by then that Patty was a round-the-clock stoner, they didn't want to know it.

"Oh, but *gosh* we're going to miss having you here for the holidays, Davey," Karen continued. "But you're not going to want to come all the way back down here once you're home in the Bay

Area. You'll be so happy to be there! And I'm sure Georgia is looking so forward to having you living near her again. And she has that magnificent home in Pacific Heights! What *money* she got after she divorced her husband—oh, what was his name again?"

"Dan Wilcox," said David.

"Yes, Dr. Wilcox. He wrote that best-selling book. The title of it is right at the tip of my tongue."

"It was something like, *I'm OK—You're a Fathead*," said David.

Despite himself, David's father laughed. *"I'm OK—What the Hell's Your Problem?"* he offered.

Despite *him*self, David also laughed. *"I'm OK—You Have Halitosis."*

"Ha!" said his dad. *"I'm OK—You're a Mime."*

"I'm OK—Your Dog Has VD," David said.

"Oh, you *boys!*" said Karen. "Whatever it was called, his book was such a *success*, wasn't it? It's not the beautiful kind of writing that *you* do, David, of course. What you do is *real* writing—what you do is *art*, isn't it, Jacky? But that book Dr. Wilcox wrote was *everywhere*. In the grocery store, in the drugstore, at the airport—just everywhere. He's so *famous*. Remember that one time, Jacky, when we saw him on the Johnny Carson show?"

"No," said Jack. "I must have fallen asleep."

"You and the rest of America," said David.

"Oh, you do too remember," said Karen. "And he wasn't boring at all. He really was a witty and charming conversationalist. I wonder if Georgia ever regrets divorcing him?"

"I doubt it," said Jack. "His next two books hit the shelves like ten pounds of rotten mackerel."

"I'm Still OK—Where'd Everybody Go?" said David.

"Anyway, David," said Karen, "you must be looking so forward to spending Thanksgiving with your mother. From what Jacky tells me, she is a wonderful cook. Now, didn't you once tell me, Jack, that instead of turkey for Thanksgiving, Georgia prepares little Cornish game hens, or pheasants, or something like that? Isn't that true? Didn't you tell me that?"

"As usual, I have no idea what the hell you're talking about," said Jack, taking a drink from his glass.

"Yes, you do," said Karen. "You told me that Georgia never serves turkey on Thanksgiving. She serves little Cornish game hens instead. Which I am sure are delicious. You'll enjoy every bite of your Thanksgiving dinner with her, David. Especially the dessert. Oh, *yum!* I know how much Georgia likes her dessert!" To Jack, she said, "Georgia makes wonderful pies, doesn't she, dearie? It's hardly any wonder that she's put on a few pounds. And she carries it so well, I'm sure."

"Will you stop already?" Jack snapped. "What the hell is the matter with you?"

Karen sat bolt upright in her chair. "There is nothing the matter with me. And I'll thank you not to imply that there is, Jack. All I was saying is how nice I think it is that David is going to spend Thanksgiving with his mother. I don't see why you have to jump down my throat for that."

"Oh, Jesus—here we go," said Jack, dropping his napkin on the table. "Here we goddamn go again."

"Oh, yes, here we go, *again!*" said Karen. "Here I go again, saying all the *crazy* things I say, just being such a terrible pain in the ass that it's a wonder anyone can stand to have me around at all, *isn't that right, Jack?*"

It wasn't the loudest David had ever heard Karen scream, but it was within range of it.

Jack stood from his seat like a mountain suddenly rising from the earth. "I'll be in my office," he intoned. "David, let me know when you want a ride back home."

"Sure," said David softly.

As Jack walked away, Karen let out a scream that it was possible she'd been holding in since 1945, slammed her hands down on the table, jumped up from her seat, and stormed off down the hallway.

And then it was David sitting all alone at his father's and stepmother's dining table, with ringing silence everywhere around him.

It was then that David flashed back to a memory from his childhood.

He was sitting at his desk in his bedroom. With the use of a Sherlock Holmes-style magnifying glass he had saved up for and bought for this very purpose, he was examining every last detail of what was, as far as he knew, the only photograph of his mother left in the house after she vanished. Since discovering it in a box of her old things out in the garage, David had kept the picture hidden in his room, and told no one about it.

The black-and-white photo was three and a half inches square. It showed his mother, wearing black Capri pants and a crisp white sleeveless blouse, sitting alone on the front porch of her then brand-new home in Cupertino. She was looking straight into the camera and squinting one eye shut against the sun, which rendered her smile cockeyed. It looked a bit like she was winking, or maybe keeping a secret that she ever so slightly enjoyed the photographer not knowing.

Studying the picture, which he does for hours at a time, makes David crazy in a way that he cannot help and can barely control.

At the moment he's been staring at the photo for so long that his mother within it starts to stir, and then to grow. She gets bigger and bigger—until, finally, she steps out of the picture and is standing before him in his room.

Hurling himself into her arms, David cries, "Where have you *been?*"

Hugging him and softly running her fingers through his hair, his mother says, "Silly goose. What have you been so worried about?"

And then none of it had ever happened. Not the divorce, not her disappearance, not her replacement by Karen, who hated him so much and had found a way to make his dog and cat disappear forever.

All of it was gone.

Everything was back just the way it had been.

Then it was just him, hugging his mother, holding on to her as tightly as he could.

———————

David slowly rose from the table and headed down the hallway. He passed by his father sitting at his office desk looking over some papers. When he reached the end of the hall, he paused for a moment before softly tapping on the door of the guest bedroom.

Patty opened the door barely more than a crack. "Yes?" she said impatiently.

"Just wanted to say that I'm headin' out—or will be soon, anyway. It was good to see you again, sister."

"You too," said Patty. She closed the door.

David heaved in a quiet sigh and spent a long moment standing right where he was, his head hung low. Then he turned and started back down the hallway.

He stopped to stand in the doorway of his father's office. He wasn't surprised when Jack did not look up from his work.

He said softly, "Hey, Dad. Anytime you're ready."

When his father still didn't look up, David turned his gaze to the office itself. The whole room looked exactly as it had back in Cupertino: literally the same black executive chair at the same expansive corner desk; the same mini-TV and black rotary telephone on the same places on that desk; the same low wooden bookcase holding the same set of Encyclopedia Britannica that David had spent so much of his childhood poring over; the same oak credenza, across the surface of which were proudly marching the same besuited phalanx of golden salesmen—each mid-stride, swinging a briefcase, and wearing a fedora—topping the same Salesman of the Year trophy that his father had been awarded by the B.T. Rickoff Foods and Supplies Company every one of the thirteen years that he and his family (in whichever of its configurations) had lived in Cupertino.

All of it was exactly as David had always known it. Standing there watching his father work in his office could have been any moment from his childhood.

Just then it felt like it was all the moments of his childhood, rolled into one.

Finally, his father looked up at him. "*What?*"

"What?" said David.

"You're standing there in that *fog* you're always lost in. Jesus, it must be nice in whatever place it is you spend all your time."

"It varies," said David.

"Look at you. You've heard of *grooming,* haven't you? It's a concept you're familiar with? Shaving? Shampoo? Laundry detergent? These are things you've heard of, right?"

David looked puzzled. "Detergent. What a weird word. Did you make it up?"

"Get out of here."

"But—"

"Go wait in the kitchen. I'll be there after I finish this work." As David was walking away, his father called from behind him, "Work? You've heard of *that,* haven't you?"

"Yes!" called David. "It's a Chinese cooking pan, right?" Then he mumbled to himself, "Good one, me. I still got it. Sort of."

But David was more than aware that if there was one thing to be said about his father, it was that the man worked. His whole life was built around his work.

One time, when David was in seventh grade, he'd asked his dad why he worked so hard.

"Because you're a sucking vortex of needs," said his dad.

David had deadpanned, "Promise me right now you'll put that on my tombstone."

David had learned very early in his life that his father's constant derisive comments toward him hurt less if he laughed at them—usually an easy enough and even natural response, given that Jack Finch was essentially a taller, less manic, and much better-looking Don Rickles.

But this time his father's words had stung him hard. He hated to think of himself as the reason his dad had to work as hard as he did.

"Seriously, though, Dad," he said. "I can need less. I really can."

"What's that?" said his father. "You're needless? Finally, we agree on something."

David's smile was weak.

"Finally," he said.

———

David was sitting at the table sipping the last of his whiskey when his father strode into the room.

"*Vamanos*," he said.

"Right on," said David.

They were halfway to Long Beach before David broke the silence inside his dad's tan 1978 Cadillac DeVille. "I enjoy this so much."

"You enjoy *what* so much?"

"Sitting in the passenger seat while you drive. Driving with you while you went on your sales calls was such a huge part of my childhood. I loved it. It's nice to be doing it again."

"It must be wonderful being so easily pleased."

"It must be wonderful having a *car* like this. What a boat."

After a few miles, David reached to turn on the car's radio. His dad slapped his hand away.

"Ah, memories," said David.

After driving five more silent miles, Jack said, "So how'd you manage to screw up yet another one of your relationships?"

Rather than answer, David looked out the window at the freeway, which was just like every other brutally grimy Los Angeles freeway.

Three miles later, his dad adapted a slightly more conciliatory tone. "What the hell's going on with you?"

"Nothing."

With just enough prissy childishness to make it funny, Jack said, "Okay, fine. I didn't want to talk to you anyway."

David turned to his dad. "Could we maybe really talk about this?"

"Talk about what?"

"About Kate."

"What about her?"

"Well, can I talk to you about it without you being, you know, *you*?"

"What kind of a thing is that to say to me? If you want to talk about something, we'll talk about it."

"Okay, well, the truth is that I *did* screw it up with Kate, Dad. She didn't do anything wrong. She's great. I mean, really, truly great."

"So what happened between you two?"

"That's just it. I don't *know*."

His dad looked over at him. "What are you talking about, you don't know? You were *there*, weren't you?"

"Yeah, I was there."

"*Well?*"

"Well, I mean, in a way that I'm just now starting to realize might actually be, I don't know, critical, I think I maybe sort of basically *wasn't* there. Do you know what I mean?"

"Right," said Jack, "because I speak Vague. How in the hell would I know what you mean? Jesus, it's like English isn't your first language."

"Okay, like with Mom. When you two got divorced, did you feel like you just *knew,* the whole time, what was *really* causing the breakup of your marriage?"

His dad looked over at him like he was a lunatic. "What are you talking about? Of course I knew why our marriage broke up. There wasn't a lot *to* know. Your mother was crazy, and she wanted out. That pretty much wrapped up the details."

"And she just came right out and told you that?"

"That she was crazy? I figured that out for myself."

"No, that she wanted out."

"Yeah, she just told me that. How the hell else would I have known it? Who am I, Carnac the Magnificent?"

"And her telling you that took you completely by surprise?"

"*Yes*, it took me by surprise. What the hell? Is this about me or you?"

"Me. Sorry. I guess in the relationship between me and Kate, I played the role of Mom. I'm the one who just suddenly, sort of out of nowhere, ended it."

"And you're telling me you don't know *why* you did that?"

"I am telling you that. And I know it sounds so extremely stupid. But I honestly *don't* know why I broke up with her. And that's not the worst part of it. The worst is that right after I got back to our apartment after dropping Kate off at the airport, so that she could, you know, fly out of my life forever, I realized, down to my bones, just *how* stupid breaking up with her was."

"You always did have excellent timing."

"I'm serious. It hit me like a ton of bricks. I was just, I mean, suddenly *dazed* when I saw, all at once, how—I don't know how to say this—how shockingly, unimaginably *wrong* it was for me to break up with her."

"Whaddaya mean, *wrong*? Wrong how?"

"Wrong in every way. Phenomenally wrong. As wrong as wrong gets. Kicking Kate out of my life was just a massively wrong and crazy thing to do. And knowing that I did it has been killing me since I got back from taking her to the airport."

His dad glanced over at him. "Whaddaya talking about, 'killing' you?"

"I mean, I feel like I'm dying. I feel hollowed out inside. I feel empty."

"And you don't think maybe you're being a little melodramatic?"

"I wish I were."

They drove for five more miles in silence. Then Jack said, "Where did Kate go?"

"Back to San Francisco."

"Isn't that the same place *you're* moving to?"

"Yeah."

"So?"

"So—?"

"So are you a complete fungus?"

"Most of the time. But what are you talking about?"

As he moved the car into the exit lane for David's place, Jack said, "I'm talking about you trying to win Kate back."

David's laugh was short and bitter. "Yeah, that's not gonna happen."

"Why not?"

"Because the only reason to try for something is if you have *some* chance of success. Trust me, Dad. I am the last person on earth Kate would ever want to be with again. That ship has really and truly sailed."

For the rest of the drive, Jack said nothing. After pulling into David's apartment complex, and then swinging into a parking spot near David's apartment, he did just about the last thing David would have expected him to do. He turned off his car.

After a long silence, he took from his shirt pocket a soft pack of Lark cigarettes, pushed on the bottom of the pack so one slid out the top, pressed the car's lighter, pulled open the crammed ashtray, waited for the lighter to pop out, and used its red, glowing end to light his smoke.

Jamming the lighter back into the dashboard, he exhaled a plume of smoke. "Lemme ask you a question, son."

"Sure."

"Do you love Kate?"

"Like I didn't think I could love anyone."

Jack turned the key in the ignition far enough to allow him to lower his window halfway down. "You're serious about that? Because you change girlfriends like I change socks."

"No, I don't."

"Okay, you don't."

"I *don't.*"

"*Anyway*, Kate's not just another one of your girlfriends. That's what you're telling me, right?"

"That is definitely what I'm telling you. And I think it's safe to say Kate's not a 'girl' at all. She's a woman. And I think part of my whole problem is that I've never been with a woman before. I've had girlfriends, as you say. But I've never been in a relationship that was anything like the one I had with Kate. It was so, I don't know—"

"*Real?*"

"Yes. Real. I have no idea how you know that, but—"

"I know that because I met Kate, that's how."

"Right. Well, you understand her right now better than I ever did. She's a *really* serious person, Dad. And honestly, I think I just kind of choked around that. I didn't, I don't know, step up, in a way."

"And now that she's gone, you wish you had stepped up."

"Yes."

"You feel like you know now what you didn't know then."

"God, I really do. Yes."

Jack took a long pull on his cigarette. "Lemme ask you something. Are you listening?"

"Yes."

"If you got Kate back, would you *keep* her back this time?"

"Yes, I would. But—"

"If she trusted you again—if she *loved* you again—would you ever betray that love?"

David's thought train was momentarily derailed by the wonderment of his father having somewhere along the line turned into Dear Abby. "No, I would not betray that love. But—"

"And you'd give her your *word* on that?"

"Absolutely."

"Would you marry her?"

"Yes."

Jack tapped his cigarette ash into the waiting tray. "Then you have to try to win her back."

The thought of it actually being possible to be with Kate again jerked David into an involuntary outburst halfway between the explosion of crying and the implosion of immediately choking that crying off.

"Sorry, I'm sorry," he said, quickly swiping at his eyes and nose. "I don't know what that was."

"Jesus Christ. Are you okay?"

David nodded. "Yeah. Listen, Dad. You have to understand. There's just no way that Kate would ever take me back. Ever."

"You didn't listen to me. I didn't say you have to win Kate back."

"Oh. But I thought—"

"Gee, what a surprise, you *didn't* think. I swear, talking to you is like talking to a retarded monkey whose ass is on fire. I didn't say you have to win her back. I said you have to *try* to win her back. Not win—*try* to win. Grasp the difference there, Jocko?"

"No." David took a moment to think. "Yes."

"You've got to try. You've got to go up to San Francisco, and get your goddamn act together. Either go back to college, or get a job that you can turn into a career that has some substance to it —something real, something decent, something that puts some folding money in your pocket, so you can take Kate out on the town every once in a while. Become a journalist. Publish some short stories. Write a novel. Do *something* to show her that you've changed from the boy she knew, to a man she might care to know. As soon as you get to San Francisco, start dressing better, combing your hair, *shaving*. Tuck in your shirt every once in a while. Polish your shoes so you don't look like a farmer. Take care of the things a man takes care of. I know that right now you don't think she can—but trust me, son, if Kate loved you once, she can love you again. Nothing's really over till it's over."

David did a quick internal check to make sure his mouth wasn't agape. The most advice he could remember his father ever giving him was, "Dress for the job you want, not the job you have," and "Stop eating like a feral badger." So this was stunning.

Jack took a drag on his cigarette. "But whether or not she takes you back really isn't the point. Are you listening to me now?" David nodded. "The point is that if Kate is the woman you love, then you have to try your best—and you have to *know* that you tried your best—to win her back. If you don't do that, you'll regret it for the rest of your life. And the reason you'll regret it has nothing to do with Kate. It has to do with *you*. It has to do with your self-respect. Because if you don't try to win—or in your case win back—the woman you *know* you love enough to marry, then you know what that failure of effort would mean to you? You know what you'd be telling yourself if you didn't even *try* to win Kate back?"

"What?"

Grinding his cigarette butt into the ashtray, Jack said, "That you're not good enough for her. That you don't deserve her. That you're just not man enough for her. And that's not something you *ever* want to think about yourself. Because that cuts deep into your self-respect. And in the end, your self-respect is all you have. It's what you *are*. When you have self-respect, nothing can hurt you; when you don't, everything can. A man who doesn't try his best to win the woman he loves isn't a man at all. He's just a guy going through life thinking he doesn't deserve what he wants. And that's about the saddest thing a man can be. If you try to win her back, and you lose—then screw it, that's life. But if you don't even try? That's no life at all."

Finished with his disquisition, Jack silently looked out the windshield for a while before turning back to David. "Capiche?"

David slowly nodded. "Yeah." After a minute or two of letting the totality of what he'd just heard sink all the way in, David said, "That was some high-octane advice, Dad."

"I'll send you a bill for it."

"I'll pay it. Thank you."

"You're welcome. We done?"

"We are. But, seriously, thank you. I've heard what you said. And you're right. I'll do it. I'll try to win Kate back. I won't just give up on her. Or on me."

"Atta boy," winked Jack. "Now get out already."

Back inside his apartment, David grabbed a stack of flattened boxes, found a tape gun, cleared the kitchen table, and got to work.

While taping together boxes, he started talking to himself.

"Why would I wait three more days to leave this place? Just because my rent's paid through October? Who am I, Karen? Three more days here is three more days I'm *not* in San Francisco. And that's where Kate is. So completely screw that. I am going to pack up everything left in this apartment. I'm gonna call Mom, and tell her what's happened to me and Kate. I'm gonna tell her that I want Kate *back*. She's gonna say something weird and unhelpful about that. I'm gonna ask her if I can stay at her place tomorrow night through October thirty-first. And then, on November first, I'm gonna go to Jerald's motel, because that is when he's expecting me, and I am a responsible person. Therefore and henceforth, come the morn of tomorrow, my butt is *outta* here, and that's all there is to that."

He stopped his work on the boxes.

"And where the hell has *that* dad been all my life?"

Then he set himself back to work on the boxes.

Five hours later, everything in the apartment was packed, stacked, and ready to go.

Standing in the middle of the living room, his hands on his hips, David said, "Okay. Time to call Mom."

Then he quickly wondered if there was any booze in the house.

It turned out there was not.

So David grabbed his wallet and keys, and left for the grocery store. He'd phone his mom once he'd returned and refreshed himself with a drink.

Back home with his giant bag of Halloween candy and a fifth of Jack Daniel's, David soon recalled that he had already packed away all of his drinking glasses. Resolved that for such an occasion no regular glass would do, he carefully cut open the top of the special U-Haul box in which Kate had so lovingly packed her wineglasses.

He uncovered and then slid from its snug and padded compartment one of the elegant pieces of stemware. Delicately holding its long neck between his thumb and index finger, he remembered some of the times that he and Kate had enjoyed wine from it or one of its mates: in either of their dorm rooms at SFSU; on the shore of Lake Merced, where they had sat on the lawn chairs they'd carried on the short walk between there and the college; while picnicking in Golden Gate Park; while sitting together on a blanket at the beach; on the sofa in the very room in which he was now standing and pretty damn near crying.

Kate had a genuine appreciation for wine. Before he met her, David didn't know a Cabernet Sauvignon from a jar of grape jelly. Now he did. He also now knew more than he ever thought he would about ballet, in which Kate had taken classes for years.

As much as anything else, Kate had taught him about photography, which he now loved almost as much as she did.

As he stood staring at the shining bowl of the wineglass, David tried to think of a single thing he had ever taught Kate. He finally came up with two things: that Batman doesn't actually have any superpowers, and that, while certainly a challenge, it's not absolutely impossible for a person to burp the entire alphabet.

He wondered if, in any way whatsoever, Kate had benefited from their time together.

But he couldn't think of a single way that her life had gotten anything but worse for the time she'd spent with him.

"Motherfucker," he said softly.

He slipped the wineglass back into its cocoon, properly recovered it, and taped the box shut again.

He sat at the kitchen table.

He cracked open the Jack Daniel's.

He took a sip straight from the bottle.

He grimaced at the harshness of it.

A minute later he took another sip. That one wasn't quite so harsh.

The third sip went down even easier.

He never did get around to calling his mom.

Three days later, David was sprawled on his couch, dumbly staring at something he wasn't really watching on TV, when he had three realizations in rapid succession that bolted him into alertness: it was Halloween; it was almost dark outside; and he'd eaten all the candy he'd bought at the store along with his recently emptied bottle of whiskey.

He stood up off the couch—too quickly, as it turned out. The moment his boozy dizziness subsided, he gingerly stepped around his coffee table. He snapped off the television. He then moved quickly throughout the apartment, turning off all the lights, shutting all the windows, and closing all the curtains. Finally, and as quietly as possible, he locked the front door.

Managing not to trip over anything in the darkness, he felt his way back to the couch.

As a kid, Halloween was hands-down David's favorite holiday. On that night he left his crazy family behind, and then the whole neighborhood—*all* of the neighborhoods, everywhere in the world, it felt to him—were his for the taking.

On Halloween he was finally allowed to cut loose and move as fast as he seemed designed to—which, when there was free candy to be had, was so fast that on that night he practically left scorch marks on every sidewalk and lawn within five miles of his house.

Everyone thought Christmas was the big deal holiday for kids. And when it came to purely hauling in the goods, Christmas was the best, and no two ways about it. But for his personal money, nothing could touch Halloween.

Minimal to no adult involvement; full nighttime liberation; candy literally free for the asking.

"*Let's go!*" he'd cry to his friends, none of whom, on that night of all nights, stood a chance of keeping up with him.

Lying on his couch, David heard from somewhere out in his apartment complex the excited shrieks and hollers of the night's first trick-or-treaters.

As it grew still darker outside, he lay on his back on the couch, and pretended that nobody was home.

And for the next three hours, as he stared up into the blackness and ignored the frenzied knocks upon his door, it was almost like nobody was.

❧ 6 ❧

THE SURF

FOUR NIGHTS LATER, DAVID WAS ON THE EDGE OF SAN Francisco's two-lane Great Coastal Highway, walking through fog so thick it was achieving the impossible, which was to make the pitch-darkness of the night even more impenetrable. He could barely hear his teeth chattering over the thunderous ocean waves pounding so near him, and the air through which he was making his way smelled like ten thousand nearby crabs had all just farted at once.

Over a mile behind him was the U-Haul store where he'd dropped off the rumbling truck he'd driven that day all the way up from Long Beach. There also was the storage unit, where all of Kate's stuff, along with everything he owned that wasn't inside the bulging denim sack he was then carrying over his shoulder, was safely behind lock and key.

Over a mile ahead of him was the Surf Motel, owned and operated by his friend Jerald McCormick.

Kate had been friends with Jerald for two years before David met him. For some two years before she left to become a student at San Francisco State, she had worked with Jerald at the downtown branch of the local bank, of which his father was chairman of the board and the major stockholder.

In January of their college year together, Kate and David had gone downtown on a weekday to meet Jerald at a casual Italian eatery near the bank, a place where, Kate told David, "We used to eat lunch so often that if we ever skipped a day, the owner of the place would practically come over to the bank to make sure we were okay."

Kate said, "I heard somewhere that when you introduce two people for the first time, you should say a little something about each of them. So, Jerald, this is David. David's an outgoing, brilliant writer who thinks I'm the most incredible person he's ever met. David, this is my dear friend, Jerald. Jerald is unfailingly kind, extremely intelligent, and thinks I'm the most awesome person he's ever met."

Laughing, David and Jerald hugged. "We have so much in *common!*" said David.

"But do we, really?" said Jerald.

"Yes, shut up," said Kate.

At the bank, the duo of Kate and Jerald was made a trio with the addition of one Ken Dillingman, an affable if piercingly perceptive gay man who was out and proud of it. The three of them were thick as thieves (of the non-bank-robbing variety, of course).

Soon into their mutual friendship, Kate noticed a special spark in the air between Jerald and the handsome Ken. This didn't surprise her particularly; for the longest time she had simply assumed that Jerald was gay. Later on, she learned that he was more doggedly than devotedly married to his wife, Paula, while at the same time clearly adoring their toddler son, Brian.

Kate didn't positively know one way or the other if Jerald was gay—or, if he was, whether *he* knew it. But she was certain that if anyone could clear up that issue for him, it was Ken Dillingman.

On a Saturday morning six months after Kate and David moved to Long Beach, Jerald called their apartment. David could see from Kate's face as she spoke with him that something bad had happened.

Hanging up the phone after their long conversation, Kate was at a loss for words.

"What *happened?*" asked David.

"Paula caught Jerald and Ken kissing in the parking lot of a gay bar, and now she's divorcing him."

"*What?*"

"It happened last night. Ken's leaving the bank. He's moving somewhere. It was his last day at work. He and Jerald and a bunch of people from work went to a huge bar in the Castro. After everyone but Jerald and Ken left, the two of them ended up in the parking lot, inside Ken's car."

"No," said David.

"Yeah. And it was their first time ever together."

"Oh God."

"Yeah. Jerald said he was just so sad, and drunk, and *sad* that Ken was leaving, that he ended up having his first actual gay experience ever."

"I can't even believe this."

"Well, apparently neither could Paula."

"What was she even *doing* there?"

"Jerald had told her what bar they were going to. He said he'd be home by ten, or whatever. When it got to be one o'clock, or whatever time it was, Paula went out there to find him."

"She drove all the way from Burlingame to get him?"

"Yeah. Maybe it's because she knew he was in a gay bar. I don't know. All I know is that she found him and Ken in Ken's car. And that was that. By the time Jerald got home, half his shit was piled up by the door. She threw him out."

"Jesus Christ. So he's coming here, right?"

"I hope you don't mind my inviting him."

"Of course I don't. Is he driving down today?"

"Yeah. He's got nowhere to go. And I guess Paula's being crazy as hell. She's telling everyone what happened—her family, his family, everyone they know. She's also threatening to leave with Brian and go back to her family in Bakersfield. Jerald's hoping that maybe if he just gets out of there for a while, she'll calm the fuck down."

"He can come down here for as long as he wants, as far as I'm concerned. But does he have any plans for after that?"

"I don't think so. He's just reeling. Poor thing."

By the time Jerald arrived at their apartment that night, though, he did have a plan.

Less than a year earlier Jerald had purchased, on a short sale, as an investment, a run-down, recently foreclosed motel called Surf. It was located in the outer-outer Sunset district of the city, essentially right across the Pacific Highway from the ocean.

On his first night at Kate and David's, Jerald said, "I had a lot of time to think while driving down here. What I've decided is that I'll let Paula have everything: the house, the money, all of it. I need to keep her as happy as possible, and that will go a long way toward doing that. What I will have left is the motel. It's got an attached residential unit, where the manager usually lives. I'm thinking that's where I'll live. My father's already let me know he's going to disown me. I can't work at the bank anymore. And I'm not going to have enough money to buy another house. One of the reasons I bought that motel was just because I so love old motels like that. I really couldn't stand the thought of that place being torn down. So I've been thinking, why don't I move into it, renovate the whole place, open it back up, and make my new life being the proprietor of a quaint little motel by the beach?"

After a pause, Kate said, "That actually does sound like a pretty great idea."

"It does," said David.

Jerald said, "Are you sure it's okay if I stay here long enough to put all that together—which I believe might be just as simple as remembering where the keys to the motel are. And getting the water and electricity turned on there again, which I think I can do from here. So it won't be long. But I really don't want to interfere with your lives."

"You're not," said Kate. "We want you to stay here for as long as you want to."

"That's real," said David. "Plus, we don't have lives. But with you here, we just might get one. Please stay."

"You two are so sweet. I'll only be here for maybe two days."

"Fuck that," said Kate. "Listen, Thanksgiving's only a week away. Stay here through Thanksgiving, Jer."

"Yes!" said David. "Do that."

Kate turned to David. "You're not working until when?"

"They said there's no way they'll call me in for another three weeks."

"So here's an idea," said Kate. "Jerald, right after Thanksgiving, David can return with you to San Francisco. He can go with you to the motel, and help you at least fix up the residential unit so it's suitable to live in." She turned to David. "Right?"

"Hell yes."

"Oh, now that *is* interfering in your life," said Jerald. "And it's not necessary. I think the living unit is in pretty good shape. It needs some work, I'm sure. But I can take care of it."

"But David can help you with that! He's really good at fixing stuff. And I'm sure he'd rather go with you up to the city than stay cooped up in this apartment all that time. Right, baby?"

"That is so true," said David. "And I am super good at fixing stuff. I own a flathead *and* a Phillips screwdriver."

"No. I mean, it's such an amazing offer. But I couldn't think of—"

"You can, and you will," said Kate. "I can't stand the thought of you all alone in a place that, for all I know, is overrun with snakes, or whatever."

"Beach snakes *can* be a problem," said David.

"With everything all rusty or moldy, then," said Kate. "I just need to know you're okay, Jer. If you go up there with David, and I know the two of you are cleaning and putting your new place together, then I'll be happy. Otherwise I'll just be upset and worried about you. And we don't want that, do we?"

"No," said David.

"No," said Jerald.

"Then it's settled," said Kate.

Nearly a year had passed since David and Jerald had spent two weeks of long days fixing up and then moving Jerald into his new home at the Surf. David hadn't been back to the motel since. But Jerald had indeed renovated the place, and reopened it for business.

As he walked along the darkness of the highway, David tried to imagine what the Surf looked like now. But he failed at that, because he was too cold to imagine anything besides being warm again. He was also distracted by his awareness that the thunderous ocean would keep him from hearing any car coming up from behind him, while the soupy fog would keep him from seeing any car coming toward him until he'd become part of that car's front grille. Even in broad daylight, a vehicle coming from either direction would have a decent chance of mowing him down, since the Great Coastal Highway wasn't so great that it possessed any shoulders to speak of.

Anyone walking that narrow ribbon of road had to choose between staying on the pavement and maybe getting hit by a car, or walking in the fine, deep sand just off the pavement and maybe collapsing from exhaustion. David was making the choice most do, which was to walk on the pavement, while remaining ever cognizant that the sand was right there, should the need arrive to suddenly bail into it.

At the moment, though, David had nothing to worry about from cars. No one was driving that lonely highway so late at night. It felt to him like no one had ever driven on that road at all, as if no one but he was even aware it was there.

As he trudged along, shivering, David began talking to himself, the sound of his voice immediately before him in the buffering thickness of the air.

"Could it *be* any darker out here? Or colder? This is how I'm gonna die. Right here, on this road. And it won't be from getting hit by a car. It's too late at night for that. I'm gonna get attacked by a pack of wild dogs. Wild beach dogs. They're the worst kind. They're so tired of eating washed-up jellyfish and seaweed. They crave meat. I won't be *warm* meat for them, but I'm meat none-theless. The only reason they haven't jumped me yet is because they want me to baste in this salty air just a little bit longer. Shit. Now I really am scared. C'mon, David. Get a grip. There's no wild beach dogs. And even if there were, all they'd ever do is surf and smoke weed."

He walked another quarter mile or so in silence before he started talking to himself again.

"It's so goddamn motherfucking *cold*. How can I *be* this cold? What the fuck am I even doing out here? Why didn't I take a cab from the U-Haul place? This is insane. If I were a psychotic ax-murderer, I would set up shop right here on this road, and never

EVERYWHERE SHE'S NOT 111

go anywhere else. It's the perfect place. For one, no one walking out here in the middle of the goddamn night like I am right now is someone anyone's gonna miss real quick. For two, you couldn't hear a fucking bomb going off right here, let alone anyone screaming. For three, what could be easier than murdering someone who's already half frozen to death? It saves so much trouble. They can't run. They can't fight back. They're already frozen, so they're not gonna spoil in the car on the way home. There's no way travel agencies all over the world aren't selling special travel packages at this moment for the ax-murderer who's tired of working so hard. The brochure is super gross, for sure. But the trip sells itself."

He imagined the text of the brochure.

Tired of chasing down people who aren't frozen? Whom others nearby can easily hear screaming? Tired of trying to attack people who can see you? Of course you are! And that is why we have just three words for you, you deranged maniac: Great. Coastal. Highway.

Come. Live the dream.

————

When he discerned the blue-and-white glow of the Surf Motel sign materializing from out of the depths of the impenetrable mist ahead of him, David said, "Oh, please, God, don't let that be a mirage. And if it is, I'm begging you to make it such a great one that I've taken a hot mirage shower, or sat by a hot mirage fire, or in any way experienced any warmth at all, before I'm suddenly right back out here again, where I know the only reason I'm still alive is because the vacationing ax-murderer closest to me right now can't see me through the fog. And is also deaf."

A few long moments later, David stepped onto the small plot of lawn in front of the non-mirage Surf. Across the grass he saw the tall fence he had helped Jerald build in order to hide from view the little patio and sliding glass door of the two-bedroom living quarters that his friend now called home.

Through the curtains drawn across the sliding door, David could see the lights on inside of Jerald's.

He stepped across the grass and went to the Surf's front office. There, having realized what felt like his lifelong dream of dropping his sack from off his back, he cupped his hands against the glass-paneled door of the office, and peered inside.

What he saw made his frozen jaw drop open. A year before the office looked like it had been abandoned by zombie squatters for being just too rundown and depressing. Now it looked like a blue-ribbon county fair exhibit, one titled, perhaps, "Ready for the Morrow," or "Orderly and Tranquil."

Positioned just so atop the shining, mustard-colored front counter was a postcard rack, a business card holder, two thriving houseplants in bright glazed pots, a telephone, a telephone book, a guest book, and five copies, neatly stacked, of the *San Francisco Examiner*. In one corner of the room was a round tea table covered with a ruffled floral linen tablecloth, flanked by a pair of comfy-looking easy chairs. Here, guests could sit and relax while reading their paper and enjoying the complimentary coffee that Jerald set out each morning at the little table located in the opposite corner of the room, upon which a large and gleaming stainless-steel coffee percolator stood ready to help propel guests into full consciousness before they headed out to explore one of the greatest and most exciting cities in all of the world.

The only things David recognized in the room were the front counter, the wall cabinets, and the door behind the counter that opened into Jerald's living room.

Pulling back from the office door, David thought how beautiful it all looked.

Beside the door was a little sign, framed and neatly hand-painted. It said, "Press to ring manager after hours."

But David hesitated to do that. While the lights in his place told him that Jerald was probably still awake, the clock behind the front desk told him that it was nearly midnight, which seemed a little *too* after hours.

David turned and looked up the coast toward the Cliff House restaurant, where, on weekend mornings, he and Kate had so often come up from school to sit together, eat warm croissants with butter and strawberry jam, sip coffee, and gaze out over an ocean that seemed to go on forever.

But the fog allowed him no view beyond the Surf's parking lot —and barely that far. So he surveyed the lot for a minute, and then ambled over to stand in its middle. From there he looked at the two floors, of seven rooms each, that constituted the motel itself.

The curtains were drawn in all of the rooms, with the lights still on in a couple of them. Given the number of cars that were in the lot, David guessed that eight or nine of the rooms were occupied. Seemed pretty good.

When David had first laid eyes on the motel, it was a color for which he and Jerald had had some fun coining names, such as Feeling Down Brown, Disengage Beige, and (David's favorite) Fall of Man Tan.

But that was then. Now the place was painted an ebullient blue, with each of its numbered doors, along with the wood railing running across its second floor, done in sunshine yellow.

"Fantastic," David whispered. He imagined the Muppets delightedly and permanently occupying every room in the place.

He shuffled back to the office, where he stood staring at the buzzer below the sign. He sighed, knowing that he was trapped either bothering Jerald then, or bothering him a whole lot more the next morning, when the poor guy would have to drag his frozen body into whatever sun he could find and hope for the best.

David pressed the buzzer, stepped back, and waited.

Within moments he heard Jerald's back door sliding open— and then, from around the corner, came the man himself, looking just as David remembered him: like a trim, bespectacled, thirty-something farmer with thinning red hair whom you just somehow knew you could trust with your life.

Beaming a broad smile and throwing his arms in the air, Jerald spoke exuberantly—though at a volume mindful of his guests. "David! You made it! It's so great to see you!"

"You too!" said David. When they embraced, David felt how taut Jerald was beneath his tucked-in, long-sleeve flannel shirt.

"My gosh, you are freezing," said Jerald. "And *wet!*" He stepped back a bit, the better to see David. "Did you *walk* here?"

"I did."

"From *where*? Why didn't you call me?"

"It was just from the U-Haul place. It was only about, I don't know, eighty miles, as it turned out. I thought it was closer."

"We need to get you inside and warmed up, pronto. My goodness, buddy. How are you only wearing a *jeans* jacket?"

"I've been asking myself that same question."

Pointing at David's sack, Jerald asked, "Is that all you've got with you?"

"Yeah," said David, hoisting the beast back onto his shoulder. "It's from the Homeless Sailor collection of soggy luggage."

"Ha! Well, you're not homeless anymore, Sailor. C'mon. I've put you in room 101, closest to the office."

As soon as Jerald started forward, David stopped. "Jerald, I have to tell you something right now."

"What is it?" said Jerald, now looking concerned.

"This whole place looks amazing. I can't even believe it."

Jerald smiled his mile-wide smile. "It is looking pretty good, isn't it?"

"It *is*! You should have sent pictures!"

They started walking again. "Well, I wanted to wait until it was *done* done. It's still a work in progress." In a moment Jerald had stopped outside room 101, and pulled out a ring of keys you could drop on a charging mastiff to stop it. "Here we are."

He opened the door, flipped on the wall switch, and said, "Welcome to the Surf Motel."

David was one step inside the room when, once again, his jaw fell open to somewhere around his waist.

"No. Way," he said.

Jerald closed the door and then bent to the heating unit beneath the room's window. "Let's get some heat in here."

Gazing about the room, David said in an awed voice, "Seriously. Did I die on the Great Coastal Highway, and get sent to motel heaven?"

"I *hope* that's not what's happened. Now, c'mon. Put down your bag."

"On this carpet? I don't think so. This thing is soaked." David walked back to the bathroom, flipped on its light, momentarily marveled at how nice the accommodations were, and then dropped his sack on the floor and headed back.

"The bathroom is amazing. Jerald, I cannot believe what you've done here. Last time I saw this room, it felt like the kind of place strung-out drug addicts come to either kill themselves or find God. And look at it now! This could be where Mr. Rogers lives!"

"That's the look I was going for!"

"Well, you hit it. This place makes me *calm*. It's soothing."

Grinning broadly, Jerald softly and rapidly clapped his hands together. "Okay, okay, okay. Now, listen. You warm up, take a hot shower, get into something warm and cozy, and I'll go get us some tea and cookies—unless, are you hungrier than that? You must be."

"I'm not. I promise. Tea and cookies would be so great I can't even tell you."

"I got the Mother's taffy cookies I know you love so much."

"Oh my God. Marry me."

"Okay, well, speaking of that, are you wondering why I'm not inviting you over to my place?"

"No. I hadn't even—"

"It's because there's a *man* there."

David's eyes opened wide. "Are you kidding me right now?"

Clasping his hands together and holding them to his heart, Jerald said, "I am not. His name is Franklin. We're in love."

"*What?*"

Jerald was beaming. "Yes. That's what's happening. He's asleep right now in my bed."

"You have to tell me everything right this very second."

"I will. But we'll do it in fifteen minutes. Okay? Get warm."

"Okay. But don't make me wait sixteen minutes."

Once alone in the room, David looked around again at his new digs.

"Holy cow," he whispered. The room was decked out with plush navy-blue carpeting; a new queen-size bed, replete with a Mission-style headboard and footboard; matching nightstands that held matching lamps—one with a phone beside it, the other with a clock radio; a sturdy six-drawer dresser; a writing desk and chair; a spacious closet behind sliding doors; and a waist-high formica counter spanning an inset space between the main room and the bathroom, on which was sitting a coffeemaker, two ceramic cups, and a full napkin holder. Beneath the counter was a gleaming mini-fridge just waiting to be filled.

"Wow," muttered David. "Just—wow."

He went into the gleaming white bathroom. While undressing for perhaps the most welcomed shower he'd ever taken, he began to softly sing.

Trailer for sale or rent,
Rooms to let, fifty cents.
No phone, no pool, no pets . . .

———

After placing a plate of cookies on the desk, and pouring a cup of steaming mint tea for a clean, warm, and extremely grateful David, Jerald poured his own cup, sat on the bed, and said, "Before we talk about anything else, tell me what happened between you and Kate."

David sighed. "Okay, well, the short story is that I'm an idiot. The long story is that I'm a fucking idiot. As I'm sure you're already aware. Kate must have told you what happened."

"Not really. She called and said you two were breaking up, and that she was going to move back up here, and stay with Lillian. But that's about all she said. We haven't even gotten together since she's been here. But now *you're* here. So talk to me, buddy. What went wrong between you two? You were so happy together when I was there last year."

"What went wrong is me. You're right. We *were* happy. We were great. She's great. She's incredible. But I sure didn't let that stop me from completely fucking it up with her."

"Tell me."

"There's not much *to* tell. I broke up with her, for fucking no good reason at all. I just, out of *nowhere,* bailed, on the best thing that's ever happened to me, or probably ever will. It was insane. It was absolutely the worst, most destructive thing I've ever done to my own life. Not to mention what I did to *her* life, of course."

"I don't—I mean, I don't understand."

"I don't either. That's the whole bitch of it, Jerald, right there. I have *no idea* why I broke up with Kate. The fact that I don't know how or why I could have done something so wrong, and so stupid—something that I know I'm going to spend every day of the rest of my life regretting—is where the train in my head just runs out of track. Kate was the best. Kate's *always* been the best. You know that. I know that. Lillian knows that. My own *father* knows that—which is a whole other story. Kate is everything anyone could dare ask for in a partner. So, of course, I did the only thing I *could* do with her, and kicked her out of my life."

"Oh, David."

David sighed again, and took a sip of his tea. "And then, what happened was—I mean, are you sure you want to hear all this?"

"Of course I do."

So David told Jerald about how, upon returning to their empty apartment after driving Kate to the airport, the full magnitude of what he'd done hit him like a ton of heart-shaped bricks.

"You called her that very night?" asked Jerald.

"Yeah."

"What'd she say?"

"Not much. We didn't talk long. I apologized for what I'd done to her, for breaking up with her—for all of it. And before I could say anything more—because I think she sensed where I *wanted* to go next in the conversation—she said, 'You and I will never be together again.' And she made me repeat those same words back to her. I did. Then she hung up."

"Oh. Ouch."

"Yeah. To say the least. But what else could she do? She'd be insane to even think about taking me back."

"No."

"Yes. No one gets back into a car that's already suddenly steered all by itself—with them *in* it—right off a cliff. But I'm going to tell you one more thing, and then I want to hear about this man in your place. Okay?"

"Okay."

"As crazy and stupid as it is, I'm going to try to win Kate back. I know it's like I'm a six-hundred-pound guy who hasn't left his bedroom in four years saying that in a week he's gonna climb Mount Everest. But what can I do? When you've made a mistake as cataclysmically horrendous as I made with Kate, you have to try to undo that mistake. I *have* to figure out what it is inside of me that is so broken that I would push someone as perfect as Kate out of my life, then fix whatever that motherfucker is, and see if I can't get Kate to do the one thing that I, of all people, have no right to even consider asking her to do."

"Take you back."

"Yes. That. I can't even say the words. But that's what I'm gonna do while I'm here." He reached for a cookie. "Speaking of my being here, let's talk about my paying you for this ultra-awesome room."

"Oh, let's not."

"But I insist."

"We'll talk about it. But not tonight. And listen, this motel isn't so packed that I can't afford to let you stay here for as long as you want. Especially right now. It's winter in San Francisco. This is the off-season. And a lot of people don't even know the motel is open yet. So we're more than good."

"All right. But I still want to pay you whatever you'd charge anyone to stay here for, I dunno, two months—if that's even a thing. But Kate and I split the money we had. And I'm getting unemployment from my Teamsters gig. So, money-wise, it's not a problem."

"We'll work something out, okay? But please, no more about that tonight. Now, have you been doing any writing?"

"I was going to. But then I thought to myself, 'You know what would be even better than writing? Ruining my life, and the life of the woman I love.' So I went with that. Which kind of cuts into my creative time, as it turns out."

"Well, I've got plenty of pens and paper in the office, if you ever feel inspired to write while you're here. And I hope that you do."

"Thank you. And I mean it. Speaking of feeling inspired: Franklin! Tell me, tell me, tell me!"

From behind the hands he used to cover his face, Jerald said, "Oh my God!"

"Spill. Now."

Jerald put his hands flat on his thighs. "I met him about four months ago."

"How? Where?"

"When I went with Lillian to a benefit show for the dance studio he'd just opened in the Fillmore."

"He's a dancer?"

"He's an *amazing* dancer. He was in the Harlem Dance Company."

"Wait. No. I *know* him!"

"What? *How?*"

"I mean, I don't know him. But Kate does. She's talked about him before. She's always, like, 'I can't believe I actually know someone who was in the Harlem Dance Company.' That's *your* Franklin?"

"Who else! And it makes sense that Kate would know him. He's friends with Lillian. That's how I met him."

"And he hurt his knee, right? That's why he's not with Harlem anymore?"

"Yes, he did. It was just awful."

"Is he okay now?"

"Oh, yeah. It's healed. He can't dance at the level he used to, but his knee's all better."

"Well, that's good. I can't *believe* this. Kate *loves* that guy! And not just because of his whole dance thing, either. She says that he's just the sweetest person ever."

"Oh, then that is *definitely* my Franklin. Because that's exactly what he is. From the moment I met him, I was just—gone. I went with Lillian to this fundraiser for his studio, and the minute he walked into the room, it almost felt like I couldn't breathe."

"Whoa."

"David, he is *so* beautiful. And he moves like—I don't even know what. Like he's in a whole other world. And he puts *me* in a whole other world. And I'm telling you, when he came into my life, I really *was* in a whole other world. And it was not a good world to be in."

"No?"

"No. You know what happened to me. It was so terrible. When Paula caught me in my first ever gay *anything*, she went ballistic. And I don't blame her, really. She thought I'd been lying to her for years. And she really punished me for it." He took a deep breath. "Anyway, I ended up out here, which was just—well, you know what this motel was like. Not exactly cozy. And I was out here all by myself, just sort of existing day to day. I had no idea what to do with myself. Ken was in town for another week or two, but I couldn't see him, even though I wanted to so badly."

"Why couldn't you?"

"Because Paula had guaranteed me that if I so much as *looked* at a man, she'd make it so I would never see my son again. And later, in our divorce settlement, that's exactly what happened. The judge ruled that I could see Brian every weekend, but that all my visitation rights would be immediately revoked if I ever 'cohabitated' with a man, or 'engaged in any homosexual activity whatsoever.' Those were his exact words. They were so shocking to me, and made me feel so ashamed."

"Oh, Jerald."

"It wasn't a good time for me, to say the least. I'd lost my marriage. I'd very nearly lost my son. I'd lost my home. My parents disowned me. Paula's family disowned me—not that that was such a loss. The career I'd spent years working so hard to build for myself was gone. All I had in the world was this motel, which I had no idea what to do with. I'd certainly never planned on living here—until that was my *only* plan. And then, here I was. And I knew I was gay—but I also knew that I could never, ever do anything about that. I was like some wretched ghost, haunting this boarded-up old motel out by the sea. I spent half my time numb, and half my time crying."

David reached out to put his hand atop Jerald's.

"But, you know, a person can only remain in deep despair for so long. At some point, I began to realize that this motel really *was* all I had in life. It had nothing to do with my past, but everything to do with my future. And slowly, but surely, I started fixing it up. I would just hammer straight a little section of gutter here, or oil a doorknob there. Maybe do a little sweeping, or whatever. Nothing big. But when you have nothing—when you're *doing* nothing—anything is something. And every day that little something became a little something more. And pretty soon, I did what I told you guys I was planning on doing during Thanksgiving last year: I got a loan to renovate the place. And before too long at all, I was a whole lot busier than I had been in months."

"It definitely shows."

"And then, this past summer, just as the major renovation work was wrapping up, I met Franklin. And the first thing I thought—after, you know, *Oh my God!*—was, no. No. I can't do this. I can't feel this way. I won't feel this way." He sighed and took a sip of his tea. "But how do you say no to love? How do you shut down everything that's happening inside of you—when there isn't even anything left to actually do the shutting down? Do you know what I mean? *All* of me loved him. *All* of me wanted to be with him. There was nothing left to resist. And the craziest, most unbelievable, most impossible of all things happened. He wanted to be with me, too. I mean, when you see Franklin, you'll understand why the *last* thing I could have imagined was a man like him being interested in a man like me."

"What are you talking about? You're amazing."

"Thank you, but no, I'm not. I'm just a regular, pretty shy, and definitely forced-into-the-closet gay man. What I *most* was when I met Franklin was sad. And scared. And so, so lonely. And then, suddenly, I just—wasn't anymore. Franklin was so sweet, and so smart, and so funny, that I felt everything that I'd completely shut down inside of me waking back up. It was like I'd come back from the dead. I found myself remembering that life isn't supposed to make you feel terrible all the time. That, at least sometimes, life is supposed to feel good."

David put down his cup, and stood from his chair. "I have to hug you right now."

Jerald stood, and they hugged.

After, both sniffling and wiping their eyes, they had resumed their seats, Jerald said, "Of course, what's not at all good is that I have to hide Franklin from Paula—and even from Brian."

"Oh. Right. How does that work?"

"Fine. Awful. It's just something we have to deal with. I am always so, so glad to see Brian. But it also means having to say goodbye to Franklin for a couple of days—which I don't like at all. You'll see why when you meet him."

"Let's go wake him up right now!"

"No! Stop. He's sleeping. And you should do the same. And me too. So I'll go now, and we'll all get some sleep. First thing in the morning, you come over and meet Franklin. Does that sound good?"

"It sounds great. I can't wait."

The two stood and hugged one more time.

Jerald said, "Don't worry about anything, okay? You're a good person, David. I know how much Kate loves you. What she saw in you before she can see in you again."

"No," said David. "I've shown her that what she saw in me before wasn't really there at all. But thank you. I love you, brother."

"I love you too, David. I'll see you tomorrow."

❧ 7 ❧

A FUN DAY

Peeking through his curtains early the next morning, feeling surprisingly buoyant after a long and dreamless sleep, David was surprised to see that he could see anything at all. The previous night's fog had disappeared.

"It's an omen," he muttered. "Except that I wouldn't know an omen from an omelet." Turning from the window, he clapped once and then rubbed his hands together.

"It is time to *do* something, Davey-boy," he said. "Time to get strong, be positive, be a winner." He started pacing about his room. "No more acting like the world just kicked you in the cajones. Like it says in the Good Book—or, probably, in some reasonably good book somewhere: Where love is, hope is. That strange man in my dad's car the other day gave me great advice. I can win Kate back to me—or at least, and more importantly, I can *try* to win her back! I can do it! And the first thing I'm gonna start right off doing is *grooming!*" He cut his volume level in half. "Or at least, you know, getting dressed. Let's not get crazy."

When David walked into the Surf's office a few minutes later, he found Jerald behind the counter, carefully watering one of his plants with a little brass watering can.

"Oh my gosh," said David. "It's like being on Fantasy Island."

"There's the man! How'd you sleep last night?"

"Like you drugged my tea. Last time I slept that well was three minutes into *The Way We Were*."

"Oh, I love the song from that movie."

"Me too! And I'm sure the movie's wonderful. Especially if you're in need of an anesthetic." Looking around, he said, "I cannot get over what you've done to this place. This office is wonderful. You *rescued* it."

Jerald moved to his other plant. "It rescued me."

"Can I help you put out the coffee, or anything like that?"

"No, thanks, I've got it. I've done the morning set-up here so often I can do it in my sleep—and believe me, sometimes I do." He gestured toward the door behind him. "Why don't you go on inside, and meet Franklin? He's just having his morning coffee, so this is the perfect time. I told him all about you. He's dying to meet you."

"Really? Dying? Awesome. Let's wait till he's dead. I find it so much easier to talk to people when they can't talk back."

"Oh, you are in a lively mood today, aren't you?"

"It's all that *sleep*—which I now realize I never get nearly enough of."

"Tell Franklin you're to have no coffee this morning. Now go in and meet him."

"Is he decent?"

"He's the most decent person I've ever met. And good-looking too."

"Oh, and I'm the lively one. Okay. I'm goin' in."

He went around to the back of the counter, opened the door to Jerald's place, and stuck his head inside.

Across the room, seated at Jerald's dining table, cradling a coffee mug in his two large hands and reading the newspaper spread open before him, David saw a black man, his hair buzzed on the sides and longer on top, wearing a grandly ornate red-and-blue silk kimono.

"Hello," he said. "I'm Jerald's friend David. You must be Franklin."

"I am!" said the man. He rose from his chair, and opened his long arms wide. "Come in, come in!" Tall and broad-shouldered, Franklin flowed across the room toward him with such assured gracefulness that David had to stop himself from stepping back-wards like an awed child. "I am so very glad to meet you!"

"I'm so glad to meet you," said David. He then had the fairly unique experience of hugging a man exactly his height.

"Man," said David. "It's not hard to believe you're a dancer. You cross a room like Nijinsky taking over Moscow."

Franklin took a step back, as if to more fully appreciate David's overall physicality. "Do you dance?"

"Me? No, I just shoehorn the names of famous dancers into conversations whenever I get the chance. It's charming, don't you think?"

Franklin boomed out a laugh. "I do! Oh my. Jerald told me that you have a marvelous sense of humor."

"As you'll know soon enough, he lied. But his heart's in the right place."

Franklin laughed his deep and rich laugh again. "Jerald's heart *is* in just the right place, isn't it?"

"Absolutely."

"Here, now, let me take your jacket." After hanging David's Levi's jacket in the small closet near the door through which David had entered, Franklin said, "If you'll have a seat, David, I'll go get us some coffee and muffins from the kitchen, and then we

can sit and chat, and get to know each other a little. Does that
sound good to you?"

"It sounds great," said David.

A few minutes later the two new friends were settled into
Jerald's couch, their coffee and muffins on the shellacked bamboo
and glass coffee table before them.

"So," said Franklin, "Jerald tells me that you're a writer—and
an actor!"

"No, no," said David. "I *like* to write, yes. And I did some
speech stuff in high school. But I'm afraid that's it."

"I could definitely see you as an actor. You have a lot of presence."

"Only at Christmas—ha-ha. No, I'm kidding. I never get
anything for Christmas. Because I have no friends. But that's
really a whole other problem."

"Oh, my *Lord!*" Franklin laughed. "So, how long have you
been a comedian?"

"Since the day my mother first saw my face, laughed, and said
to the doctor, 'What is this, a joke? Get me one that won't give
me nightmares.'"

While Franklin cracked up, David looked down at his coffee.
"Sorry," he said. "I'm babbling." Then he looked back up at
Franklin. "I'm just happy to meet you, is all. Jerald has so many
wonderful things to say about you. And I *would* say, by the way,
that you, too, have a *lot* of presence, but that would be like saying
that the universe is a fairly decent size."

"Oh, so you're a flatterer, too."

"Hardly. When Jerald said you'd been a member of the Harlem
Dance Company, it was basically impossible to believe. By the
time you had reached me just before we hugged, it was impossible *not* to believe."

Franklin reached for his coffee cup. "Well, I don't know about
all of *that* kindness. But yes, I was with HDC for five years. And

then, one day, my knee thought, 'You know what, Franklin? I think it's time for you to make a great big change in your life—starting *right now!*'"

"Yeah, your knee, right? Jerald told me. That must have hurt —literally and otherwise."

Spreading the thinnest bit of butter on half a muffin, Franklin said, "Oh, it hurt all right. The moment it happened, I knew that it was all over for me, that I was finished. It was really unbearable. My entire life—everything I had, everything I was—was dancing in that company. And then, a simple *grand plié* one November morning—and *pop!* It was all gone. Suddenly I could no longer bring what dancing demands."

"I can't even imagine. How do you go on from something like that?"

Franklin shrugged. "You go on because you go on—because it is, after all, just a knee. It took me a while to really see it that way —to realize that I hadn't *actually* died. But one day just kept on following the next, and somewhere along the line, I found myself wondering, 'Okay, well. *Now* what?'" He took a sip of his coffee, and silently returned his cup to the table.

"I've never had anything in my life that's meant to me what dancing has meant to you," said David. "I've never been that committed to any one discipline, and certainly not for as long as you gave yourself to dancing. Dancing was—and largely still is, I believe?—your *life*. The only thing that's ever been *my* life is— what? Trying not to fart in elevators. Endeavoring to not accidentally brush my teeth with Ajax. Not getting hit by a car. My life actually *is* just not dying—and that's about it. It's sad."

Laughing, Franklin said, "It's not sad. It sounds to me like you're just living your life. There's nothing at all wrong with leading a normal, happy, balanced life. *Balance* is what I'm after, if I'm being honest."

"I think that's what everyone's after. I think just *knowing* that's what you're after puts you halfway to home."

Just then Jerald came into the room. "There's my two favorite guys in the world." He shut the door behind him. "So, what do you think of my beau, David?"

"I think you must have done something to please God, Jerald." He crooked a thumb at Franklin. "I mean, *look* at this guy. I am no longer worried about winning back my ex-girlfriend. You know why? Because now I'm gay, that's why. That's how impressive Franklin is."

Franklin almost spit out his coffee.

"Oh, so you're *gay* now, are you?" said Jerald.

"Yes, I am," said David. "I'm ready to take the gay pledge. And I believe there's some sort of club T-shirt that one of you now bestows upon me? Along with the secret handshake all gay men know?"

"I am afraid that you have misread some of the literature," said Franklin. "It's not exactly a handshake."

"Also," said Jerald, "you have to promise to swear off orange juice."

"I can do that," said David.

"It's easier said than done," said Franklin. "Believe me, the Anita Bryant—which, as a new gay, you should know is made from vodka and apple juice—is *not* a screwdriver. And I, for one, am in mourning for mimosas."

"The first mimosa I have once that terrible woman is in her grave," said Jerald, "I'll use to toast to the memory of Harvey Milk."

"Amen," said Franklin.

A woman stepped into the room through the office door. With her long, jet-black hair pulled back into a ponytail, she wore blue jeans, a black T-shirt, a blue hooded sweatshirt, and a pair of black and white Converse sneakers. Built solidly, she had a pretty, broad face, with skin so smooth a butterfly trying to alight on her cheek was likely go skidding right off.

She was one of those people David sometimes met with whom he felt immediately comfortable, for no reason he could ever put his finger on or name.

"It's Erin!" said Jerald.

"What's going on?" said Erin.

"You've arrived at a very important moment," said Jerald. He pointed to David. "This one here just went from being as straight as a laser beam to being, just like the three of us, gay as a cockatoo."

"Well, technically, I'm gay like a *no* cock'll do," said Erin.

"Ha!" said Franklin. "Brilliant!"

Erin regarded David. "So you just now turned gay, huh? How'd that happen?"

David pointed at Franklin. "I met him, that's how. I *might* have had a chance, if he wasn't wearing that Confucius At Studio 54 robe. Look at that fabric! What choice did I have?"

David grinned happily while the three people laughed.

"Erin, this is my very good friend David," said Jerald. "David, this is Erin. She helps me run the motel. She's been with me since before we opened the place. She watches over the front desk, she does the books, she helps with the rooms—without her I'd be out of business in three days."

"Two," said Erin.

David got up from the couch. "It's nice to meet you," he said.

"Nice to meet you," said Erin. As she was shaking his hand, she added, "Fag."

Once they'd all collected themselves after laughing so hard, Jerald said, "Okay, back to work for me." Heading for his kitchen, he called, "Anyone want a baked treat before I bring them out front?"

"Already got ours," said Franklin.

In a moment Jerald was on his way back from the kitchen, holding a big tray piled with muffins. "Okay, you three. Behave yourselves."

"I'll be right out," said Erin, closing the door behind him. Turning to Franklin, she said, "Brian's coming this morning, right? Isn't this Jerald's weekend to have him?"

Franklin sighed. "It is. And well before the young prince arrives I will have skittered back into the shadows, lest his mother, Queen Paula, sees me, and has a heart attack."

"Wouldn't be the worst thing in the world," said Erin.

"Now, now," said Franklin.

David spent the rest of that day and the next living like a cross between Jack LaLanne and his all-time favorite TV hero, *Kung-Fu*'s Kwai Chang Caine.

He did yoga (on the beach, no less).

He ran for miles (also on the beach).

He meditated in his room, on the beach, on a secluded bench in the rose garden in Golden Gate Park, and sitting high atop the cliffs of the park's Lands End, which overlooked as much of the Pacific Ocean as he guessed it was possible to see from any location in the world.

He read the first half of Mark Twain's *Roughing It*.

He also took the bus to the famous City Lights bookstore, where, besides trying not to be wildly intimidated by the sheer volume of successful writers in the world, he purchased *A Coney Island for the Mind*, a collection of poems written by City Lights' founder, Lawrence Ferlinghetti. One of Kate's favorite books, he'd never read it until she introduced him to it. Now he wanted a copy of his own to replace the one that was first hers and then became theirs.

But for all the things he did that weekend, what David *mostly* did was resist his almost constant desire to call Kate.

He did, however, call his mother.

First he tried her at her house, but she didn't pick up. Next he called the office where she worked as a mental health counselor. But he only got her answering service, as he mostly expected to, given that he was calling on a Saturday.

"Would you please tell Georgia that her son David called?" he told the friendly answering service lady. "Tell her that I've moved back here to the city, and would love to come to her house for Thanksgiving. Tell her that it will just be me, by myself."

After giving the lady the phone number of the Surf's front desk, which, he told her, his mother could use to get a message to him any time, David said, "Please convey to my mom that I'm looking forward to hearing from her. And please also tell her that I'm looking forward to, if you'll excuse my grossness, hogging out on her mincemeat pie on Thanksgiving. Okay?"

The service lady laughed. "Will do," she said.

⸻

That night in his room, David was thinking about some of the guys he had worked with in Long Beach, when he found himself almost desperately wanting to write. After quickly locating a pen and a legal pad, he sat at the desk in the room, remained motionless for a time, and then started.

He wrote a loosely structured short story about a guy named Rocky, a gigantic and uproarious Mexican with a glass eye, whom some of the guys at the warehouse got a kick out of startling by suddenly leaping out at him from his blind side.

He wrote a story about another of his former coworkers, who, hanging his head, and speaking in a barely audible voice, once told him of the time in Vietnam when he and four other soldiers were being led by their renegade, drug-maddened sergeant on a jungle reconnaissance mission they were sure would get them all killed. After a whispered meeting between the soldiers, the two of them who had drawn the shortest straws lured their sergeant into the jungle, where they shot him in the head, claiming later that the man was the victim of an ambush.

He wrote a third story about one Edwin Bunker, a snaggle-toothed, red-headed, barrel-chested man who spent his every waking hour off work sitting at home with his ear glued to the fire-alert channel of his emergency-band radio. Whenever he heard a call going out for fire emergency personnel, Edwin would run out of his house, hop into his trusty white 1957 Chevy panel van—on the sides of which, in big bright red letters, he had neatly stenciled RESCUE 1—and take off driving.

Once he screeched to a stop at the scene of the fire, Edwin would hop out of RESCUE 1, throw open its back doors, and start pulling out sundry road cones and traffic flares, with which he would then attempt to help the real fire emergency personnel redirect traffic around the scene of the conflagration.

This was not something that the local firefighters appreciated. At all. Ever. But that never stopped ol' Edwin from doing it—or trying to, anyway.

———

After about three hours of writing just about as quickly as he could get his hand to move across the page, David dropped his pen, grabbed his jacket, and nearly lurched from his motel room out into the foggy night.

A minute or two later he was at the ocean's edge.

As he stood on the velvety sand, listening to the crashing waves of the sea he couldn't see through the darkness and the fog, David turned up his collar.

He wondered about what he'd just written. Why those stories? Why those characters?

From somewhere along the coastline miles north of him he heard the lowing lamentation of a foghorn.

When David walked into the motel office the next morning, Jerald, from behind the counter, said, "Happy Sunday, David! There's a blueberry muffin and a cup of coffee over there calling your name."

David smiled. "Really? You actually heard them saying, 'Yoo-hoo! Loser!'?"

"You stop that. Today is a beautiful day, and you are a beautiful man."

"I would totally pay you to do nothing but follow me around, saying those two things. Can you start today?"

"Not today, I'm afraid."

"Why? What's going on?"

"Well, Charles—the man who watches the front desk for me at nights, and always when I have Brian—can't show up today. Which means that I'm stuck here at the front desk—and will be for a while, since guests will start checking out pretty soon. Which means that I can't play with Brian the way I'd like to. Which makes me so sad." He turned and looked downward. "I love playing with my best pal, don't I, Sport?"

Raising up on his toes, David leaned over the counter to see a fair-haired, rosy-cheeked tot sitting contentedly at a little plastic table in the play area Jerald had set up for him back there. Besides the Barrel of Monkeys he was fiddling with, David spotted among the other distractions available to the boy a Wooly Willy, a Sock Monkey, an Etch-a-Sketch, a bendable Gumby and Pokey, a Mr.

Potato Head, Tinkertoys, a bucket full o' Legos, and a set of wooden Lincoln Logs.

David waved. "Hey, there. My name's David."

The boy returned his wave. "I'm Bwian."

"Hi, Brian," said David. Then he stood back down on his side of the counter. He said quietly to Jerald, "Oh my gosh. Could he *be* any cuter?"

"I don't see how."

"Me neither. Listen, Jerald, if you'd like me to keep Brian entertained this morning, say the word. I'd love to do that. I don't have anything else to do. I wasn't going to start hiding in the bushes outside of Lillian's house until at least tomorrow afternoon."

"Are you serious? About watching Brian, I mean?"

"I am. And you might not have a choice here. I seriously want to play with those toys."

"If you're *sure* you wouldn't mind—and I mean absolutely sure, David—then yes, honestly, it would be fantastic if you could keep Brian company until my business here is over."

"Great! Let's do it."

"You're a godsend," said Jerald. "Hey, Brian. Is it okay if my good friend David joins you for a little while? He wants to play with your toys. Would you share your toys with him?"

David leaned over the counter, so Brian could see him again. "Hey, buddy," he said.

Brian looked at David for a second, and then back at his dad. "Okay," he said.

David let out a little squeak. "Yay!"

"Great!" said Jerald. "And good timing, too," he said to David, "because here comes my first checkout of the day."

In moments David was sitting cross-legged on the low-pile carpet across the play table from Brian.

Brian looked up from the little red monkeys whose tails he

was hooking together. "You can play with any of my toys. It's okay."

"That is so kind of you, Brian. Thank you. Now, let me see. Oh! How about Mr. Potato Head here?" Brian nodded. "And it looks like ol' Spudsy here has all of his parts!"

"Yeah!" said Brian. "He has a, a—" In lieu of remembering what it was called, he pointed to his own upper lip.

"An ear?" said David.

"No!" said Brian, pointing with an increased vigor. "*This!*"

"Oh, *right!*" said David. In the hole beneath Mr. Potato Head's nose, David inserted one of Mr. Potato Head's arms. "There. Yes. I see what you mean. That's perfect."

"Noooo!" howled Brian, literally falling out of his chair laughing.

Jerald, just then between customers, looked over at the pair, and beamed a smile.

After an hour or so, during which time the two of them had as much fun playing together as two friends have ever had playing together, David asked Brian, "Do you think we can go outside and play some soccer?"

Brian nodded enthusiastically. "Yes! Let's go!"

"Wait! First let's ask your dad." David lowered his voice to a near whisper. "He's with a guest right now. But after the guest checks out."

Brian whispered back, "Good idea."

David put his elbow on the table, dropped his chin into his hand, and with a great, finger-tapping show of exasperated impatience, rolled his eyes skyward. Brian copied him exactly.

After a minute or two, David said, "Okay, the customer's gone."

"*Dad!*" cried Brian. "Can we go outside and play soccer?"

David added, "Yeah, Dad. Can we?"

"You sure can. That sounds like so much fun!"

As the two boys were bustling their way out the front door, Jerald mouthed to David a silent thank you.

On the same little plot of grass that David had welcomed a few nights before as eagerly as a shipwrecked man would welcome dry land, David now lightly kicked the ball to Brian. Through the office window he gave a happy thumbs-up to Jerald, who merrily waved back before returning his attention to the guest who was checking out.

David said, "Now, Brian, you *do* know all the rules of soccer, right?"

After thinking about it for a moment, Brian solemnly shook his head no.

"You *don't*?" said David.

Brian shook his head again.

"*Whew!*" said David. "Thank *goodness*! I don't know the rules of soccer, either! Let's play!"

About twenty minutes later—during a moment of sheer athletic deviousness, when Brian had stolen the ball *back* from David—Erin appeared on the edge of the grass.

"I'm makin' grilled cheese sandwiches for lunch," she said. "You two want one?"

"*Yeah!*" said Brian.

"*Yeah!*" said David.

"With pickles!" said Brian.

"With pickles!" said David. "Please?" Nudging Brian, he said out of the corner of his mouth, "Say please."

"Please?" said Brian.

"Pickles it is," said Erin.

"Wahoo!" said David.

"Wahoo!" said Brian.

Suddenly David became very thoughtful. Softly tapping his chin with his finger, he said, "You know, I wonder if I might like some *boogers* on that sandwich?"

Brian immediately collapsed onto the ground. "Noooooo!" he cried.

"And how about some clipped toenails on that? Mmmm. Crunchy."

"Noooooo!" Brian wailed.

Erin rolled her eyes.

"I'll see you two kids inside," she said.

———

On a typical day, the Surf's office would fall quiet after lunchtime, leaving Jerald free to spend time with Brian if he were there. But on this particular day, Erin, who had exited the office after lunch in order to tend to a few of the rooms, quickly returned to Jerald's quarters.

"Room 106 is trashed," she said. "And there was a leak coming from under the bathroom sink. I turned the water off, but the carpet is soaked."

"Oh, that's not good," said Jerald. "David, would you mind staying with Brian for a few minutes more, while I go see what's happening?"

"Of course not," said David.

"Erin, watch the front for me?"

"Yeah," said Erin. "Go."

"Be right back, Brian!"

After Jerald left the office, David said to Erin. "Wow. I wanna be like that when I grow up."

"He's the man," said Erin.

"What happened to the room?"

Erin shrugged. "Stupid people happened to the room."

"Stupid people do break things," said David.

———

It was nearly two hours before the plumber and, as David put it to Brian, "The man in the van with the big hot fan" drove away.

"And that ends all of *that*," said Jerald, behind the counter once more, and closing the big binder from which he'd just cut two checks. He turned to David and Brian, who were sitting beside each other in Brian's play area, their backs against the wall, a large book lying open across their legs. "Now, what are *you* two doin'?"

"We are reading about the greatest bear ever," said David. "I'm talking about, of course, Winnie the Poop."

Brian cracked up and toppled over. "No! It's Winnie the *Pooh*!"

"Are you sure?" said David. He looked quizzically at Jerald. "It's Poop, right? Winnie the Poop?"

"You are so silly," said Jerald.

"Now, come on," said David earnestly. "I think we can all agree there's nothing silly about poop." He reached out, pulled a squiggling Brian onto his lap, and started tickling him. "No matter *what* this poopyhead says!"

"Dad! Dad!" squealed Brian. "Help!"

David stopped tickling him. "Okay, fine. I'm gonna go now. But before I leave, I want you to promise me something, Brian."

"What?"

"I want you to promise that you will always call that cute little bear by his right name: Winnie the Poopyhead."

"It's Winnie *the Pooh*!" cried Brian.

Getting up off the floor, David said to Jerald, "Kids. Whaddaya gonna do?"

Jerald opened his arms to hug David. "Thank you so much for today."

"Of course," said David, walking into the embrace. "One of the funnest days I've had in a long time. It did me a world of good."

"Well, you saved my day."

"And everything's okay with that room?"

"It is." Jerald sighed. "I swear, I'm just going to quit renting to anyone under thirty. Present company excluded, of course."

"No, no. If I were you, I'd kick me out right now. God only knows what I'll do to that room before I leave. Get rid of me while you can."

"What? And lose the best babysitter I've ever had? No chance."

"All right, then," said David. "But don't say I didn't warn you." He turned to Brian. "Bye, buddy."

Brian ran over to David and hugged his legs. "Bye," he said.

Jerald walked David to just outside the office. "Brian had such a good time with you today, David. Thank you for that."

"I had at least as much fun as he did. When is Paula due to pick him up?"

Jerald looked at his watch. "Criminy. She'll be here in half an hour. Well, shoot. I'm hardly gonna see Brian at all today."

"Can't you ask her to come later tonight?"

"Oh, she would never say yes to that."

"Even though you had that emergency today?"

"She wouldn't care. If I asked her for more time with Brian, she'd laugh in my face."

"Wow. For sure?"

"For sure."

"Yikes, man. Tough girl."

"That's one word for her," said Jerald.

Back inside room 101, David sat down on the edge of his bed, and got lost in remembering a moment from his childhood.

He was sitting on the edge of his parents' thrillingly gigantic bed. His mom was standing at her closet hanging up some of her clothes.

He is planning to crack his mom up—with a joke *he* thought of.

He starts off with an innocent, "Hey, Mom, guess what?"

"What, sweetheart?"

"During recess at school today, I hit a home run."

Busy with her clothes, his mother remains silent. But he has prepared for this very contingency.

"Do you *believe* me?" he says.

"Of course I believe you. Why wouldn't I believe you?"

Nonchalantly, he says, "Oh, just checking."

He kicks off his shoes, and scoots backwards on the brown and gold paisley bedspread. Once in the middle of the bed, he flops down onto his back.

"What am I doing right now?" he says to the ceiling.

"You're lying on the bed," says his mother.

Lifting his head, so as not to miss her reaction, he delivers his payload. "I thought you said you believed me!"

He wasn't really expecting his mom to laugh; the most he usually got out of her was a smile. But that never kept him from trying another joke later. More than just about anything else in the world, David wanted to crack up his mother.

And this time it worked.

While looking right at him, Georgia let out a loud and deep laugh. The power, the volume—the *bass* of it—took David by such surprise that his own laughter was snatched right out of his mouth.

He sat up on the bed and stared at his mother, as if her laughter was a sound he'd never heard before. Then, laughing harder than he'd ever laughed in his life, he fell backwards on the bed, his hands on his stomach, his feet kicking the air. His laughter blended so completely with hers that, for a fleeing moment, it sounded to him like they weren't two different people laughing, but one.

David slid along his bed toward the nightstand, picked up the phone, and dialed the number to his mother's house.

He listened to one purring ring following another. He pictured the phone on her end, sitting on its elegant little cherry wood stand in the corner of her dining room, plaintively calling out into the vacant house, over and over again, to no avail.

❧ 8 ❧

SHOWTIME

AT 9:30 THE NEXT MORNING, DAVID ANSWERED A knock on his door to find an anxious-looking Jerald.

"Are you free to come to the front desk, David? I have a situation on my hands."

"Let's go," said David, closing the door behind him. "Is everything all right?"

"No, it's not," said Jerald, walking rapidly. Stepping into the empty office, he said, "I got a call from Paula. Just a few minutes ago."

"Is Brian okay?"

"He is—and thank you for asking that first." Jerald stepped behind the counter. He was talking fast. "And speaking of Brian, guess what?"

"What?"

"He loves you. He *really* loves you. He loves you so much that I guess he hasn't stopped talking about you since Paula picked him up last night. He's been talking about all the great things the two of you did together, all the fun you had. He's been talking about you so much, that guess what happened?"

"What?"

"Paula's decided that you're my boyfriend."

"*What?*"

"Paula's decided that you must be my boyfriend. She thinks that's why you and Brian spent so much time together yesterday —she thinks you must, like, *live* here with me, or just spend a suspicious amount of time here. Because, you know, a straight guy and a fag like me can't possibly just be friends. She's convinced that since you and I are so obviously close—close enough for Brian to have spent the whole *day* with you yesterday —we must be lovers."

"But—"

"I told her that you're just a friend of mine who's staying here, and that, when a room needed emergency repairs, you volunteered to help watch Brian, since Charles wasn't coming in. But she didn't care about any of it. She wouldn't even listen."

"Is she insane?"

"Insane enough to be driving over here in a rage right this minute to meet you, David—to somehow make sure that you and I didn't spend all day yesterday corrupting Brian with our disgusting homosexuality."

"Paula's coming here? *Now?*"

"Yes. Right now."

"Whoa. Okay, so, is there anything you want me to do? Want me to hit on her, so she definitely knows I'm straight?"

"No. Listen, David. You're going to hate me."

"Bet I won't."

"Bet you will. I called Kate."

David's mouth just started saying things, while his brain tried to catch up. "*What?* You what? I'm sorry. Why?"

"Oh, David, I *had* to do it. Paula will take Brian away from me in a heartbeat if she thinks I'm having so much as a gay *thought.* So when she was screaming at me about how gay she knows I'm being, I panicked. I told her that you were staying here *with your girlfriend.* And then I called Kate to come over here and pretend to *be* your girlfriend. I'm so, so sorry. I just didn't know what else to do. And I didn't even have time to come to your room and talk to you about it. All I knew was that Kate knows everything she needs to know in order to convince Paula that she's your girlfriend."

"Right. Okay. Right. That does make sense. What did Kate say?"

"She's coming right over."

"*Now?*"

"Yes, now. Paula will be here any moment, David. Will you pretend with Kate to still be her boyfriend, so that she won't take Brian away from me?"

"Are you making all this up? Are we on *Candid Camera?*" When he saw nothing on his friend's face but distress, he said, "I'm sorry. I'm freaking out. But yes, of course, I'm in."

"I'm *so* sorry, David. I was so desperate."

"Don't be sorry. It's not your fault that Paula's who she is. She shouldn't use Brian as a weapon against you. We can do this. Lemme go brush my teeth."

Having dashed back inside his room, David did what he could, as quickly as he could, to look as good as he could. Two minutes later he was back in Jerald's office, trying to remember to breathe deeply. Or at all.

"Thank you for doing this," said Jerald. "I'm sure it won't last long. Oh—I forgot to tell you! If Kate gets here *after* Paula is here, then the story is that Kate's been out in the park, taking pictures. Okay? That's what Kate and I said we'd all say."

"So she knows I'm going to be doing this. Right?"

"Right. She knows."

"She was in the park taking pictures."

"Exactly."

"Good story."

"How do you feel? You ready for this?"

"Absolutely. I even splashed on some cologne. English Leather."

"I smell that."

"Too much?"

"No."

"Too *gay*?"

"No."

"Isn't leather just leather? Why *English*?"

"I don't know."

"I'm so nervous."

"I am too."

"I can't believe Kate's coming here."

When the front door opened, they both started. But it was only Erin.

"Hola, gringos," she said. "What's up?"

"I'm so glad you're here," said Jerald. "Erin, I need you to do me a *huge* favor. Paula and Brian will be here any minute. We're also expecting David's ex-girlfriend, Kate."

David blurted, "We don't know who'll get here first!"

"Okay," said Erin calmly.

"Can you watch the front desk, while we all talk in the house?" Jerald asked.

"Sure. Everything okay?"

After Jerald, talking at lightning speed, had caught Erin up to the minute, she gave a slight shrug. "Okay. No problem."

A white Mercedes-Benz pulled into the motel's parking lot.

"That's Paula," said Jerald.

David gave a low whistle. "Wow. Nice car, Jerald. I sometimes forget how loaded you are. Maybe I *do* wanna be your boyfriend."

"Not the time," said Jerald.

"Okay. But you let me know when is."

"C'mon, let's go inside. Erin, send them in, okay?"

"Can I punch Paula first?" said Erin.

"Yes," said David.

"No," said Jerald. To David, he said, "And you. Stop."

"Done. I got this, baby. It's showtime."

———

"Hi, David!" cried Brian, releasing Paula's hand as he rushed into Jerald's living room. Instead of squatting down and throwing open his arms for the boy, the way he wanted to, David remained standing. Brian crashed into his legs.

"Hi, guy," said David, ruffling the boy's hair. Then he waved to Paula. "Hi, there. You must be Paula. I'm David." He thought Paula pretty, in a fussy, big-haired, overly-braceletted sort of way. Bronzed and polished to a gloss, she looked like a woman who would know her way around a Saks Fifth Avenue store blindfolded.

Dropping a leather purse the size of a bowling ball bag onto Jerald's couch, Paula stood assessing David from over the top of her giant sunglasses. "So you're the person I've been hearing so much about."

"Well, just remember that you can't believe everything you read on the wall of a post office," said David.

Paula looked at Jerald. "What's he talking about?"

David said, "Nothing. It was just a joke. Not a *funny* one, obviously. But they can't all be winners." He felt like he was free falling, and babbling all the way down.

"Hello, Paula," said Jerald. "And hello to *you*, Brian."

Paula sat down on Jerald's couch. "Brian," she said, "come sit over here with Mommy, honey. David, let's you and I have a little chat, shall we? Get to know each other?"

As he took a seat in the easy chair across the coffee table from Paula, David lied. "Sounds great."

"Can I get anyone some tea?" said Jerald.

"Coffee," said Paula.

"Whatever you're having, Jer," said David. Hearing how extremely intimate and gay that sounded, he tried butching up his order. "On second thought, make mine a coffee. I like it black."

"Black it is," said Jerald. "Brian, you wanna come on in the kitchen, and help your daddy make some tea?"

"Okay," said the boy, climbing off the couch.

"Brian, you be careful," said Paula. "I don't want you getting hurt."

Once she and David were alone in the room, Paula said, "So, you're the David that Brian's been talking so much about."

"Am I? He's such a great kid."

"Jerald tells me you have a girlfriend." If Paula's eyes were nail guns, David would have already been bleeding out, while remaining upright in his chair.

"I do have a girlfriend. Why do you ask?"

"Just curious. What's her name?"

"Kate."

"Where is she now?"

"Out in the park taking pictures."

"Is that right? She's a photographer?"

"Yeah. She's great at it."

"How long have you and—I'm sorry, what'd you say her name was?"

"Kate. Her name is Kate." David could feel himself starting to sweat like Porky Pig at a luau.

"How long have you and Kate been a couple?"

"A couple of what? Ha-ha. No, but two years."

"Where did you meet?"

"San Francisco State."

"And how do the two of you know Jerald?"

"Kate used to work with him. I met him a year or so ago."

"And you and Kate live together?"

"Yeah, we do."

"Here at the motel?"

"Sure. Some might think that an odd choice, I know. But Kate and I were both raised by vagabonds. Turns out that, as children, we once met on a flatcar! Funny world, isn't it?"

He laughed. Paula didn't.

"Just kidding," he continued. "Right now we're between places. We were living in Long Beach, but we both missed the city so much we decided to move back. So we thought we'd stay here for a bit, visit with Jerald, see what's what. We'll probably rent a place right around here."

David smiled, and reminded himself to say as little as possible, so as not to trip up Kate when it was her turn to be interrogated by this terror in hoop earrings. And also to keep things as vague and ambiguous as he could, so that Kate might be able to dance around any rock he'd left in the road, rather than trip over it.

Paula said, "Is Kate due back soon? I'd like to meet her, too."

"I expect her back any time now. Once the sun changes from early-morning sun to, you know, regular day sun, she usually stops shooting. Something to do with the shadows."

"Do you wear boxers or briefs?" said Paula.

The audacity of her question caught him off guard, but only for a moment. "Well, I *do* float like a butterfly."

"What? What does that mean?"

"You know, Muhammad Ali?"

Paula looked angrily constipated. "What are you *talking* about?"

"Boxers. Muhammad Ali is a boxer. If I wore briefs, I would have quoted F. Lee Bailey. Get it? Because he's a lawyer."

"Tea time!" said Jerald, coming in from the kitchen, carrying a tray loaded with cups and condiments, with Brian close behind. He set his tray down on the coffee table, and started handing out the cups.

"Here's your coffee, Paula. Careful, it's hot. Sugar's right here. And here's your coffee, David." He shot him a glance. "This is cream, if you change your mind. And here's your juice, Sport!"

Once he'd returned from bringing the tray back into the kitchen, Jerald settled in on the opposite end of the couch from Paula. "So, what have you two been talking about?"

"Just getting to know each other," said Paula.

Brian came and stood beside David's chair, putting his arms on its armrest.

"Hey there, Buster," said David. "What's cookin'?"

Brian thought for a moment, and then, with a big smile, said, "Coffee!" Two of the three adults in the room laughed.

"You're right!" David said.

"Can I sit on your lap?" asked Brian.

"Honey, you leave that man alone," said Paula.

"Oh, no, I don't mind," said David. "It's fine. Here, lemme put my coffee down." Once that was done, Brian climbed up onto his lap.

Just then the door from the office pushed open a bit.

"Knock, knock," came a woman's voice.

Jerald stood up from the couch. "Kate! Come on in!"

Wearing the pair of jeans that David always thought Calvin Klein must have designed just for her, her black leather boots, and a white T-shirt beneath a gray crew neck sweater he'd never seen before, David thought Kate looked much the way a fashion model might if she had decided that it would be fun to torture to death the blithering idiot who had recently been stupid enough to break up with her.

With wide and happy eyes, Kate looked at David. "Hi, baby!" she said.

"Hi, kitty-Kate," said David, twisting a corkscrew through his own heart, since that was a real pet name he used to call her.

Kate crossed to David's chair, bent, and gave him a quick kiss on the cheek. David tried not to pass out, but for a moment wasn't sure he hadn't.

"Brian!" said Jerald. "Guess what I forgot in the kitchen? A cookie for you! I bought the peanut butter kind you like! Want one?"

Brian nodded vigorously at his father.

"Well, come on, then! Let's go get you one!"

Brian scrambled off David's lap. As he and Jerald headed off toward the kitchen, Paula called after them, "Brian, after you get your cookie, come sit here next to Mommy."

Kate stuck out her hand. "You must be Paula," she said. "It's so nice to finally meet you!"

⸻

Forty-five minutes later, Paula had no reason to doubt that David and Kate were a bonafide couple. Her attempt to discover any conspiracy to deceive her concluded when Kate answered her sudden inquiry about David's underwear question with, "David wears boxers. He says that briefs make him feel about the age of that little guy asleep on the couch next to you."

"C'mon now, Paula," said Jerald. "That's enough."

Paula snapped at him, "It's enough when I say it's enough." But then, in a way that struck David as unexpectedly human, she sighed. "I'm sorry if I seem to be acting like a b-word. But if I am, there's a *reason* for it."

"What's wrong?" said Jerald.

Paula reached into her purse for a stick of gum. Unwrapping it, she said, "I've met someone."

"You have?" said Jerald.

"Yes." She bent the gum into her mouth, and gave it a few chomps. "His name is Anthony. We've been seeing each other a few weeks now. The thing is, he wants me to go away with him over the holidays, for a whole month. He wants to take me back East to meet his family, and then he wants us to take a little vacation together in New York. And I'd really love to do all that with him."

"You should!" said Jerald. "That sounds great!"

"*But*," said Paula, "it would mean Brian staying here, from Thanksgiving all the way through till Christmas. And I just don't know if I feel comfortable doing that." She turned her attention to Kate and David. "Do you two know why Jerald and I broke up?"

"I try not to pry," said David.

"Me too," said Kate.

"They know, Paula," said Jerald.

"I wouldn't have even minded what Jerald did—or would have minded *less,* anyway—if it had been with another woman. At least that would have been *natural*. Again, I'm not saying I would have liked it. But at least it wouldn't have been such an unnatural perversion. And I'm sorry if you two feel differently about homosexuality than I do, but that is what it is."

"Paula, please," said Jerald. "Brian's right here."

Paula looked down at the boy lying on the couch between her and Jerald. "He's asleep."

"Maybe Kate and I should leave," offered David.

"I thought you already knew that your friend here is a sicko," said Paula.

David became sharply aware of the fact that gently placing his coffee cup down on the table was preferable to his rocketing the thing straight at Paula's head. So that is what he quietly did.

"Paula, stop," said Jerald. "And listen to me, please, because I know this will interest you. I wasn't going to say anything, because she and I have only just started dating. But I've also met someone."

"*You've* met someone?" said Paula. "Who?"

David and Kate exchanged a quick glance. Jerald reached for the teapot. "Well, like I said, it's a new relationship." He took his time tilting some tea into his cup. "But she's great. Even though we've only been seeing each other for a little while, it's already grown into something that I feel really good about."

"You've met a girl," Paula said flatly. "You."

"Yes, me," said Jerald. "I've told you a million times, Paula, I'm not gay. I tried one thing, *one* time."

"Most guys do that," said David.

"They do," said Kate.

"What's her name?" said Paula.

"Who?"

"This *girl* you've met."

Jerald began stirring his tea, to which he had added nothing. "You know, I'm not even sure whether or not I should—"

Kate piped up. "Oh my God. It's *Lillian*, isn't it? That's who you're talking about, isn't it? I *knew* you guys had a thing going on! I *knew* it! It's Lillian, right?"

Jerald kept his eyes down at his tea. When he looked up again, he was grinning bashfully. "You guessed it."

"Yes I *did!*" said Kate. She was beaming. David pictured her being handed an Oscar. "It's because I saw how you two were talking together when we all went out the other night. And then Lillian *told* me that she'd met someone. But she was all cagey about saying who it was; she said she didn't want to jinx it. But it's *you!* How great is that? You're a lucky guy, Jerald. Lillian is the best."

"You and Lillian, huh?" said David. "That totally makes sense."

"You know this Lillian person too?" Paula asked David.

"Oh, yeah," said David. "Lillian's the best."

"Huh," said Paula. "Well, I'd like to meet her sometime." To Jerald, she said, "Maybe when I drop Brian off next week?"

"Sure, of course, no problem," said Jerald. "I'll make sure she's here."

After Paula and Brian left, Jerald and Kate were animatedly reliving what had just transpired (with David only contributing the occasional colorful comment), when Franklin came in through the office door.

"Hello, all," he said. He lit up. "Kate!"

Kate jumped out of her chair and ran to meet him. "Hi, hi, hi!" she said. Looking beatifically happy, she pressed her face against Franklin's chest as they tightly hugged.

"How *good* to see you again," said Franklin.

"You too!" said Kate. Holding his hands, she said, "Lillian told me that you and Jerald are together. I was so, so happy to hear it."

"You are just the sweetest thing," said Franklin. Then he looked back and forth between her and David. "Wait. Are you two back together?"

"No," said Kate.

"Now, honey, don't be that way," said David. "Ha-ha."

"Stop it," said Kate.

"We're not back together," said David.

"These two were doing me a *huge* favor," said Jerald. "Paula was just here."

"Now *that* I know," said Franklin. "I drove over here from my place, saw Paula's car parked out front, kept on going, and got myself a little breakfast before trying here again."

Taking note of the vibe in the room, he then said, "Will someone please tell me what in the world is going on here?"

———

Once he'd been fully briefed on the situation, Franklin, seated next to Jerald on the couch, put his hand on Jerald's thigh. "Baby, I am absolutely thrilled that Brian might be here from Thanksgiving till Christmas. That is wonderful, wonderful news. But I'm a little concerned about what that means for little ol' me—and for us, you know? If that beautiful child is here, it means that I *can't* be here. I'd have to stay away during our whole first holiday season together."

"No, you wouldn't," said Jerald. "Brian'll just think you're a friend."

"But what if he *doesn't* think just that? Children know romantic love when they see it. What if he intuits what we mean to each other? What if he sees us holding hands for a moment, or something like that? He *will* tell Paula about it. And there's no way *that* turns out well."

"We'll just have to be sure to be discreet when he's around," said Jerald. "We can do that. We *do* do that."

"But we're talking about a whole month, baby. We know that Brian talks to Paula about the people he meets here. What's going to happen when one of the people he talks to her about is *me*? Don't you think Paula is going to want to know about this big effeminate *man* who was here all during the holidays?"

Jerald looked defeated. "No. I don't know. Probably."

"Well, sweetie, who will you say that I am?"

"You could say he's Lillian's brother," said Kate. They all looked at her. "He could be Lillian's brother, from out of town. Since he doesn't know anybody in the area, Lillian's social circle naturally becomes *his* social circle. So, since Lillian's over here all the time to be with her new boyfriend, Franklin could be over here all the time too. He could have started coming over just by way of keeping company with his sister, and struck up his own friendship with Jerald. The two of you are pals! That would explain why, over the Christmas season, Franklin is sometimes here, even when Lillian's not."

They all went from looking at Kate, to looking at each other.

"That seems like it might work," said Jerald.

Looking back at Kate, Franklin said, "It's always the pretty ones who are so diabolical."

Jerald clapped his hands. "I say that's our plan. If Paula ever asks who the devastatingly handsome man was who apparently spent so much time here over the holidays, it's just my girl-friend's brother, Frank!"

"That does sound good," said David.

Jerald said, "Kate, do you think Lillian would be okay with coming over here this Saturday morning, when Paula and Brian will be here, and pretending to be my girlfriend?"

"I'm sure she will," said Kate. "She loves you guys. She doesn't want you to have to break up just because of Paula."

Jerald said, "Great! I'll give her a call, tell her about our plan, and ask her to help us out."

When Kate was ready to leave, David offered to walk her to her car.

"But the car's right outside," said Kate.

"Still," said David, "you never know what kind of people might be staying here."

"Hey!" protested Jerald.

"Sorry. I was actually talking about myself."

"What a surprise," said Kate.

Once they were in the lot and walking the short distance to Lillian's car, David said, "So, when I start writing that big novel of mine, I'm definitely gonna seek you out for plot advice."

"Don't," said Kate sharply.

"What's the matter?"

Kate stopped beside the trunk of Lillian's car. "What do you think is the matter, David?"

"You mean, besides everything that's generally fucked up about me?"

"Are you really not aware of the fact that you just almost got Brian taken away from Jerald?"

"*What*? How's it my fault that Paula's a bitch?"

"That's not your fault. What *is* your fault is that you made Brian fall in love with you."

"*What*? No, I didn't."

"Yes, you did. You know you did. Whenever you're with kids, you do the super, ultra-fun David Finch show. And the kids fall in love with you, exactly the way you know they will."

"What are you talking about? I don't try to make kids fall in love with me. I just have fun with them. That's all it is. Fun."

"Yeah, *you* just have fun. That's great for *you*. But you didn't think about how the fun you were having with Brian might end up impacting his and Jerald's life together, did you? You get so caught up in the moment of what you're doing that you never think of the consequences of what you're doing, of the situations you're creating for yourself and everyone else. You *make* these fucking things happen, and—" She stopped talking, and took a deep breath. "You know what? I'm sorry. Never mind."

"No, don't stop," said David. "Tell me. Please. I know I should know this shit. I just *don't*. You can help me be smarter about this stuff."

"I could, yeah. Except that's not my business anymore, is it? *You're* not my business anymore. So let's change the subject." She pushed her hands into the front pockets of her jeans. "I need to get my wineglasses out of storage for a dinner party at Lillian's."

"Sure. Of course. We can go to the storage place now, if you want. It's just right up the highway." He pointed his thumb toward his room. "Speaking of which, lemme go get your key to the unit."

"Not now. I can't. I'm already late getting Lillian's car back to her."

"I can take you out to the unit tomorrow, if that works."

"Yeah, maybe. Probably not, though. I've got a job interview tomorrow."

"You already have a *job* interview? Where?"

"Downtown."

"What kind of place?"

"It's a business that sells photocopiers."

"Wow! How'd that happen so fast?"

"Through a friend of Lillian's."

"What friend?"

"You don't know him."

David felt his heart skip a beat or ten. "Him?"

"Yes. Him. Male. A guy."

"What guy?"

"I've got to go, David. I'll call you about my wineglasses."

After Kate had driven away, and much louder than anyone talking to themselves in a parking lot should ever say anything, David said, *"What* guy?"

Back inside of his room, David lay down on his bed.

He thought of how often he would lie on his parents' bed as a kid, his chin resting in his hands, and watch his mom as she put on her makeup.

His mother was never so serene as when, seated with perfect posture at her vanity, a glass of wine within easy reach, she was choosing and using whichever items from among her formidable collection of brushes, pencils, powders, lipsticks, lotions, and eyelashes that she knew would serve her best for that moment, for that day, for that night out.

And David was never so quiet as when he was watching her do it.

He was aware that he didn't know much about much. But one thing he did know was that if things kept ripping along the way they certainly had so far in his life, then, before too very long at all, he was going to be a man.

He wasn't exactly sure how beautiful women, lingerie, high heels, lipstick on wineglasses, and perfume touched onto a woman's neck and wrist figured into a man's general awareness of the world, or of himself in that world. But he knew that when he watched his mother seeming to be almost hypnotized by her reflection as she lovingly ministered to her own exquisite features, he was witnessing something that he'd be a fool not to hush up and pay attention to. He might be the moron his father was always telling him he was, but he was smart enough to know when he was learning.

But mostly, he just liked being with his mom when she was unhurriedly enjoying being with herself.

The next day David phoned his mother—which, being mid-morning on a Monday, meant trying her at her office.

"Allied Healing, how may I help you?" answered the woman who worked as a receptionist for the ten or so psychologists and counselors who had offices there.

"Hi, I'm calling for Georgia Wilcox, if she's free?"

"Ms. Wilcox is with a client just now. May I take a message?"

"Yes, could you please let her know that I—that her son David —called, just to say hi, and to maybe see about finalizing our plans for Thanksgiving?"

After a pause, the receptionist's tone switched from Miss Moneypenny to Nurse Ratched. "Oh. I see. I'll give her your message. Goodbye."

"Wait!"

Another pause. "What?"

"Can I give you the number where I can be reached?"

Sounding like he'd asked her if he could crap on her picnic plate, the secretary said, "Fine. What is it?"

After giving her the telephone number to the Surf's front desk, David, by way of clearing up what he was sure was only some kind of misunderstanding, said, "And, again, this is David Finch. Georgia's son."

"I'm aware," came the cold reply. "Is there anything else?"

"No, I—"

She hung up.

Looking wonderingly at his handset, David said, "What the fuck are you so mad at *me* about?"

❧ 9 ❧

THE IDIOT

DAVID WAS SUDDENLY OVERWHELMED BY THE conviction that he shouldn't be where he was—that having walked from the sidewalk up the stairs to the front door of Lillian's Victorian flat was a catastrophic failure of judgment, one sure to abruptly end with Kate taking from his hands the box of her wineglasses he was holding, slamming the door in his face, and then going back inside to enjoy a big laugh with Lillian about what a pathetic dinkwad he is.

"What was I *thinking,* being with that loser?" she'd say.

"Hey, we all make mistakes," he imagined Lillian responding. "Not usually ones *that* horrendous, but we all make them. Now, c'mon. Let's fetch my gun before that sorry sack of shit gets away."

But then, still just standing there, David thought of how absurd it was to fear that Kate would respond negatively to his having interrupted his day—which, for all she knew, was an extremely busy one for him, filled with people he needed to see, and places he needed to go—in order to bring her the glasses that she told him she needed for Lillian's dinner party.

Why *wouldn't* he take the four-mile bus ride from the Surf to

Lillian's house in the Upper Haight in order to bring her the glasses? What option did he have? What was he supposed to do, just let Lillian's party get underway, and *then* have it be discovered that all of the guests were going to have to drink from their cupped hands, because there just weren't any *wineglasses* to be had?

Now *that* would be a dinkwad thing for him to let happen.

And it wasn't like, in the three days since he'd last seen her at Jerald's, he hadn't tried to call Kate to arrange a meeting with her at their storage unit. He had phoned Lillian's three times looking for Kate. And each time no one had picked up.

So he was just doing what any friend would do.

All he had to do now was knock on Lillian's door.

———

The prior three days had not been among David's finest ever. He had mostly spent them holed up in his locked motel room, staring at the television, lolling in the bathtub, and taking drastically varying degrees of interest in the *Playboy* magazine that at some point he snuck out and purchased at Sunset Liquors on nearby Irving Street.

As a kid, one of David's prized possessions was the largest Super Ball manufactured by the Wham-O company—the one that was slightly smaller, but at least ten times harder, than a regular baseball, and contained "50,000 pounds of compressed energy."

David had no idea how one weighed compressed energy. But 50,000 pounds of it sure did seem like a lot.

Sometimes, when he was home alone, David would take his mega-Super Ball out with him into the garage.

He would turn off the garage light, and walk to the center of the open cement floor. He would take a few deep breaths, by way of calming and steeling himself.

And then, using all of the considerable power in his Little League championship-winning pitching arm, he would wind up, and hurl the ball at about a thirty-degree angle against the floor, straight in the direction of the broad and sturdy metal garage door in front of him.

Instantly he would drop to the floor, cover his head, and pray like a madman that the rock-hard projectile now ricocheting at light speed all around him didn't come plowing into him, since that would mean anything from an instant grisly death to a permanent round dent in his body, if they could ever even pry the thing out of his flesh.

Hunkered down in his motel room during the three days before his arrival on Lillian's doorstep, the inside of David's head was like the inside of his garage during those terrifying times with his Super Ball. Except that instead of just one ball wildly rocketing all around him, there were at least a dozen of them, and instead of balls they were questions that, even though he himself had set them in motion, left him, figuratively speaking, crouched on the floor covering his head.

Why had he broken up with Kate?

Why had he pushed her away?

What had she ever done wrong to him—or to *anyone* he knew of?

Why couldn't he love?

Why couldn't he be loved?

What the flying fuck was the *matter* with him?

Why was he always compelled to flee from wherever he was, to a place that not only didn't he know, but that, if he'd only taken a moment to think about it, he would have seen was *bound* to be worse for him than the place he had just been?

Why did he fight his relationship with Kate? Why did he destroy it? Why couldn't he claim it, own it, accept it, honor it, grow it, nurture it? Why couldn't he *believe* in it, the way normal, everyday people believe in the relationships that mean the most to them?

Why did he always have to tear off his own wings?

He had wanted to be a musician. As a kid and into high school, he had practiced both the drums and the guitar—and then, when he was actually pretty *good* at playing them both, had dropped them both.

He had wanted to be an actor. His accomplishments in the National Forensics League were an open door to all of the auditioning opportunities and college scholarships he could have wanted. But instead of taking advantage of those, what did he do? He lived in a probably condemnable flat in a ghetto of East Oakland, always broke and most always stoned.

He wanted to be writer.

All of his life, and always above all, he was going to be a writer.

And how much of his work had he ever submitted *anywhere* for publication?

Exactly, perfectly, and wholly none.

He was going to get an English degree at San Francisco State University.

But then he dropped out.

He was going to be Kate's man.

Then

he

quit

that

too.

And of course he did.

Because he was not capable of doing anything with anything good but quitting it.

Over and over again now, David asked himself why that was, what his indelible, infernal, irreducible problem was—and how ever in the world he was going to *fix* whatever it was, so that if, by some freak miracle, he ever *did* get Kate to come back to him, he wouldn't yet again screw his relationship with her straight into the ground faster than he could say, "Surprise! I'm still a child!"

Where was he *going* with his life?

What was he doing with it?

What in the living hell did he *think* was going to happen to his life when he kicked the finest person he'd ever known out of it—a beautiful person who happened to *love* him, no less?

Did he really think that after he did that, he *wouldn't* end up living in a motel room that would probably have to be burned once he vacated it, or, more likely, was found dead in its bed, a porn magazine open beside him, his broken and abraded dick still in his hand?

After two quick deep breaths, David knocked on Lillian's door.

If messing with Lillian Holly Barnathan was a bad idea, messing with one of her friends was a worse one. So when the tall and Rubenesque African-American woman with close-cropped hair, gold hoop earrings, and oversize tortoiseshell eyeglasses opened her door and saw who it was, she placed a hand on her hip, and stood imperiously regarding David like he was some trifling punk who owed her a lot of money that she knew damn well he hadn't come to repay.

David lamely waved his hand. "Hi, Lillian. Good to see you."

In a tone exactly halfway between bored and contemptuous, Lillian said, "Mm-hmm. Is there something I can help you with, David?"

"Is Kate here?"

"No."

"Do you know where she is?"

"She's at work."

"She got a *job*?" He tried, inexplicably enough, for a little shared affection between them. "Boy, I guess her interview on Monday went really well, right? Girl doesn't waste any time, does she?"

With a look that would have made Shaft blanch with fear, Lillian said, "Not lately, no."

David held out the box. "These are Kate's wineglasses."

Once Lillian had taken them from his arms, he asked, "Do you know where Kate is working?"

"Yes, I do."

"I don't suppose you'd care to share that information with me?"

"I don't suppose I would."

"Okay. Well, anyway, I just wanted to—" But then he couldn't see any reason to continue talking to a closed door.

The next morning, as he sat on a city bus heading downtown, David was barraging himself with questions: *How wrong is it for me to be going to where I think Kate is now working? Am I being crazy right now? Have I become one of those raving maniacs you cross the street in order to avoid? What would I think of someone who was doing what I'm doing right now?* And so on.

Such questions had been hounding him since the moment he had hauled a copy of the San Francisco Yellow Pages out of his nightstand the night before.

These questions did not abate as he let his fingers do the walking down the address of each business listed under *Photocopiers—Sales.*

Their volume did not decrease when he wrote down the

Howard Street address of Office Copy Systems, the only photo-copier sales and service business located downtown.

They kept him awake through much of that night.

That morning, as he looked at himself in the mirror while shaving for the first time in three weeks, the questions in his head reached such a feverish pitch they started randomly bursting from his mouth.

"What am I *doing*?" he said, rinsing off his razor.

"Is there something medically wrong with me?" he asked, buttoning his jeans.

"I think it's safe to say that I now officially qualify as a creep," he said, trying on his third shirt in one minute.

"Is this what happens before you end up on the six o'clock news?" he asked, putting on his shoes, tying them, gathering up his wallet and keys. "Are other Surf guests going to be inter-viewed on TV, where they'll say things like, 'Oh, really? The guy in room 101 did that? Honestly, I'm not surprised. He never eats anything but beef jerky and Hostess cupcakes, which he washes down with booze. And did you notice how his left arm is practi-cally a noodle, while his right arm could be Popeye's? Worst case of *asymmetricus beatoffius* I've ever seen. Why, yes, I am a physician. And speaking as someone whose life is spent tending to the well-being of others, thank God that deviant freak is behind bars. It's about time.'"

Closing and locking his door before hurriedly walking in the direction opposite the Surf's office, David mumbled to himself, "I'd be really lucky right now if someone stopped me."

A few streets away, while gently waving down the driver of the approaching city bus, he said, "I should not be doing this. Someone stop me."

Once seated on the bus and heading downtown, David had a chance to reflect in a more clear-headed way about what exactly he was doing.

I'm not stalking Kate, he thought. *I'm only finding out if a friend of mine works where I think she works. Which makes total sense. What kind of social clod doesn't even know where his own friends are employed?*

But after a pause he murmured to himself, "God, that is such bullshit."

His rational justification for what he was doing continued along, though, almost of its own accord. Because wasn't it, after all, not just important, but imperative, that he always have at the ready the kind of vital information about Kate that could very well prove critical in an emergency? Of course it was. What would happen, for instance, if San Francisco was struck by another of its famously devastating earthquakes? Especially if the quake hit during business hours, which was certainly a possibility?

What would happen *then*? Who would even know where to go to dig Kate out of the rubble?

He, for one, would be damned if he were going to let Kate die in an earthquake, just because he didn't care enough about her to put forth the little bit of effort it took to confirm where she worked.

Not, of course, that Kate ever needed to know that he had ferreted out where she worked. While it was true that, generally speaking, David took exception to the old saying, *What you don't know won't hurt you*—since it had been his experience that what you don't know is actually optimally positioned to knock the bejesus out of you—in this *particular* instance he was perfectly amenable to the idea that not everyone in the world needs to know every single thing that everyone else knows.

For isn't it true, indeed, that discretion is the better part of valor?

He was sure that was true. So he was just being discreet. Some might even say valorous.

He closed his eyes and felt his head jiggling from the bus ride.

———

He thought back to a time when he and Kate had found themselves alone in their college dorm at the beginning of the Thanksgiving break.

They were inside Kate's room, pressing their ears against her door, and speaking in hushed tones.

"I don't hear anything," David whispered. "It sounds like a ghost dorm out there."

"It really does," said Kate.

"I think literally *everyone* has gone home."

"I think you're right."

"Could this entire building really be empty?"

"I think so," said Kate. "I haven't seen anyone in a full day."

"Me neither."

"Maybe the rapture happened."

"That would explain why you're still here. But why would *I* have been left behind?"

Kate quietly punched him.

David whispered, "See? That right there is why you wouldn't make the cut." He stepped back from the door, and stopped whispering. "Okay, seriously now. I think it's time for a recon mission."

"A what?"

"A recon mission. It's a military term. Stands for reconnaissance. Or *reconnoiter*, to the average dork. Don't worry about it."

"Oh, okay, Sergeant Snorkel."

David almost fell over laughing. "Who the fuck is Sergeant *Snorkel*?"

Kate was beaming a smile. "He's the sergeant in the comic strip about the guy in the army. I figured *you'd* know who he is, Gomer."

Anyone anywhere in the dorm building would have heard David's laughter. Once he'd regained himself, he said, "Okay, shhh. No more random hilarity, please. Serious business now. I'm going out there."

"Don't!"

"Why not?"

"It's too soon. We don't want to get caught here if we're not supposed to be here. Let's wait for an hour and then go see."

"An *hour*? What are we gonna do for an hour?"

Kate rolled her eyes. "God, you really *are* a Gomer."

Later that day, David quietly ducked back into Kate's room after the recon mission he'd conducted throughout the building.

"How'd it go?" said Kate.

"There is *no one* out there. We are completely alone in this building. I took the elevator—which is working, by the way—to all twelve floors, and tiptoed real quietly up and down each one. I did not see or hear *anyone*. This whole place is empty, Kate. It's just us."

They stared at each other with only slightly exaggerated gape-jawed wonder.

"Do you think we get to just *stay* here?" said Kate.

"Apparently."

"Whoa." She thought for a moment. "You know what we are?"

"What?"

"We're a couple of toys on the Island of Misfits."

David hugged her. "That's exactly right," he said.

"That's who we are," Kate said into his chest.

Having disembarked from the bus at Market and Second Street, David thought that if he were a genuine basket case—the menacing Travis Bickle of *Taxi Driver* came to his mind—he would have no choice but to immediately walk four blocks down Second Street to Howard Street, and then start looking for Office Copy Systems.

What he told himself, though, was that, rather than Bickle-bonkers, he was nothing more than an enthusiastic citizen of the world, one who, the moment he stepped off the bus, was instantly and deeply enthralled by all the sights and sounds of that particular bustling Friday morning in the very heart of downtown San Francisco—The Golden City, Baghdad by the Bay, Paris of the West, The City That Knows How, and so on.

And all of that was true. David really was gaga over The City.

Also true, as it happened, was that at that moment it was only 10:30. Which meant that he had at *least* an hour to kill before Kate was likely to go on her lunch break.

"Gives me just enough time to put on an Army jacket and grow a mohawk," he mumbled to himself as he gazed up and down the broad and busy Market Street.

When he looked at where he was, rather than toward all the places along Market where he might go, he saw that the bus had dropped him off right in front of Stacey's Bookstore, a two-story Mecca for book lovers far and wide.

He took this as an encouragement. How could any venture that began so auspiciously go wrong?

Inside of Stacey's, David stood before the wall displaying that week's bestselling books. Among them was *Sophie's Choice* by William Styron (during the reading of which Kate had gone through half a box of tissues); Norman Mailer's "nonfiction novel," *The Executioner's Song,* which Kate had found so disturbing that she finally demanded David quit reading aloud to her; and *Jailbird,* which David had devoured because it was by Kurt

Vonnegut, his favorite author after Mark Twain. The only other books on the bestsellers' wall that interested him were Philip Roth's *The Ghost Writer*, and Jerzy Kosinski's *Passion Play*. Having read neither of those, he spent some time browsing through each, hoping, despite his better nature, to stumble upon incontrovertible proof that neither author was all *that* awesome.

But no luck. The prose of each was agonizingly perfect. He put their books back where they belonged.

Before leaving the store one hour later, he purchased a hardbound copy of Dostoevsky's *The Idiot*, since in Long Beach he had ruined his paperback copy by, like an idiot, dropping it in the bathtub he was soaking in at the time.

He was also not unaware of how handy it might be to have with him a big book he could hide behind while he was doing what he was planning on doing next.

***

Sixty minutes later found David sitting at one of the metal table and chair sets evenly distributed across the outdoor public plaza of the stately office building located right across Howard Street from Office Copy Systems. He was situated far enough back from the front edge of the plaza so that, should Kate happen to glance across the street as she happened to be leaving for lunch from the place where she happened to be employed, she would not see him—especially given how engrossed he would suddenly become in his giant new book about an idiot.

At minutes after noon—just as David had nearly chomped off the ends of his fingers cramming a wad of barbecued potato chips into his mouth—the glass front door of Office Copy Systems pulled inward.

And out onto the sidewalk she stepped.

It was her.

It was Kate.

David's heart didn't so much skip a beat as it did pack a month's worth of beats into one colossal slam that almost knocked him over backwards in his chair.

Kate was soon joined by a coterie of coworkers—two of whom, David couldn't help but notice, were of the male variety. He tagged them both as showboaty salesman types; guys who *fix* copy machines—*real* men—don't wear polyester suits from the Struttin' Weasel collection.

Chatting amiably with her new friends and would-be lovers, Kate walked down Howard Street, crossed Second, and then disappeared from view. They were no doubt headed for one of the many eateries on Market Street, where David imagined them all snuggling into a booth together and, throughout their delicious meal, delightedly laughing and kidding and flattering and flirting with one another, because when you are young, good-looking, and gainfully employed downtown in one of the greatest cities on the planet, you're just too fucking happy to act any other way.

That night was not a good one for David. He paced in his motel room; by way of changing the television channel he got up and down from his bed so often he'd have felt better about himself if he'd only stopped to consider how much of a workout he was getting; he paced in his room some more.

Finally, he walked up the highway to Sunset Liquors.

When he entered the grimy little establishment, the old guy seated in his usual spot behind the cash register—whom David thought of as "Bulgarian Lou," since he reminded him of a sweatier, grumpier, and definitely more Bulgarian version of Mary Tyler Moore's boss, Lou Grant—surprised him by greeting him by name.

"Hello, Mr. David."

Discovering that the local purveyor of porn and pints knew him by name was not the boost David could have used just then.

And it was weird that the guy knew his name at all. How did *that* happen?

But as David was yet again showing Lou his driver's license, he knew how.

Trudging back to the Surf with his now-usual paper sack o' guilt, David said to himself, "Mother*fucker*. I have *got* to get my shit together."

———

Over the next two days, getting his shit together was exactly what David tried to do. He endeavored to have himself another healthy weekend, filled with jogging on the beach, eating well, doing yoga, meditating, and writing.

And he actually did some of those things too.

But not nearly as much as he did pretty much everything that is the opposite of those things.

He was too restless. He was too distracted.

He was too waiting to see if he'd see Kate again on Monday.

———

At just after noon on Monday, from the same spot on the plaza where he'd sat before, David did see Kate.

He saw her, with her purse over her shoulder, step out of Office Copy Systems.

Alone, this time.

He saw her look up and down Howard Street.

He saw her spot whomever she was waiting for, and wave.

He saw up the sidewalk, coming toward Kate, returning her

wave, a tall, thin graduate from the James Taylor school of mellow rockin' vibes. Wearing fashionably weathered bell-bottom jeans; brown leather cowboy boots that said, "I rope hearts, baby, not cows"; a long-sleeved, white, gauzy hippie shirt from Ricardo Montalban's Age of Aquarius collection; with shoulder-length dark locks that probably had their own solo number in a local production of *Hair*—this, thought David, could only be the long-awaited love child of Gloria Steinem and Mr. Natural.

Who, David couldn't help but notice, *did* actually look more mature than himself. Mr. Headbobbin' Short Beard probably really *could* play the guitar, or hold the Horny Warrior yoga pose for ten hours straight, or macrame a bong, or whatever the fuck he did when he wasn't giving herbal oil massages to foxy mamas or posing for soft-rock album covers.

While David watched like a hawk from behind *The Idiot,* Patchouli Pat stopped and chatted with Kate, hugged himself to show how sensitively chilly he was, and then, laughing at something Kate said, strolled off with her down the street.

Desperate for distraction, David tried to read his book. But he couldn't seem to make out a single word on the page.

When she got off from work that evening, Kate found David waiting for her on the sidewalk outside.

"What are you doing here?" she said.

He was relieved that she asked it with more concern than anger. "I was wondering if we could talk for a bit."

Kate narrowed her eyes. "How do you know where I work?"

"I'm a loser wank with way too much time on my hands, is how. *Please* can we talk? I won't take up much of your time, I promise."

They held each other's gaze while Kate tried to decide.

"Okay," she said. "But only if we go somewhere warm. It's freezing out here."

———

After David placed two steaming lattes on their table at a nearby cafe, Kate said, "You didn't tell me how you know where I work."

"Well, you told me you had an interview at a place that sold copy machines downtown. So I looked in the Yellow Pages. There was only one business like that downtown."

"You know that really is kind of creepy of you, right?"

"Is it?" David pretended to wonder. "I think the jury's still out on that."

"No, it's not," said Kate. "The jury's in. It's ruled *guilty*."

David laughed. "Okay, could you please try not to be funny?"

"Could you please try not to be Ted Bundy?"

David almost spit out his coffee. "C'mon," he said. "Stop being funny."

"I'm not joking, tragically. What is it you wanted to talk to me about?"

David tried to find the words, couldn't, tried again, failed again, and gave up.

Then he took a deep breath, and said, "You know what? Doing this was stupid of me. I shouldn't have shown up outside your job like a bad penny. It's—I'm being crazy. You're not gonna—I mean, listen: let's just forget all this."

"I'm not gonna what?"

"You're not gonna, well, *like* me, basically. I mean—of course you're not."

"I do like you, David. I love you." She shrugged like it was nothing. "I always will."

"Are you *kidding* me?"

"Of course not."

"Then couldn't we—I mean, isn't it possible for us—?"

"No, it's *not* possible for us. And you promised me you'd never ask me that again."

"I know. I did. I'm sorry. It's just that—"

"David, listen to me. I do love you. But I can't ever be with you again. I changed my whole life so that you and I could be together. I dropped out of college for it. I don't regret our time together. But when you said that you would be with me forever, I believed you. Those words *meant* something to me, David."

"They meant something to me too."

"I'm sure they did. I *know* they did. I know that, in the moment, when you said those words to me, you meant them. The problem is that what's happening in the moment is the only thing that *ever* matters to you. Everything means everything to you *in the moment*. And that passion you have for what's happening in the here and now is fantastic. It's what makes you so much fun to be around. But none of it ever *means* anything, because it never lasts for long. It can't. It's like the future doesn't even exist for you. So you end up not being able to plan anything, because what means everything to you today could mean nothing to you tomorrow."

"C'mon, that's not fair."

"Really? It's not fair for *me* to say that you're incapable of sustaining anything over the long haul—over any haul at all?"

David held up his hands in surrender. "Hey. If you're going to start *rhyming* at me—"

Kate fought it for a moment, and then laughed. She sat back in her chair and reached for her coffee cup. "You are so close to being perfect," she said.

"Then help me get closer to it. Help me figure out what I need to know. You know about psychology stuff. Help me figure out what my problem is with the future. Because I know you're right about that. I know that when I look to the next day, or week, let alone the next year, I just—I don't know—disconnect. Help me understand why."

"You're the one with a psychologist for a mother," said Kate. "You know this kind of thing, for everybody, is all about what happened in their childhood."

David shrugged his shoulders. "But I mean, you know, I was a happy kid."

"Okay," said Kate.

"What?"

"Nothing. I said okay."

"Your lips said okay, but your eyes said, 'Shame on you for lying, lips.'" When he got no response to that, he continued. "Well, I mean, let's face it: my dad, by any measure, *is* a cretin—although, the last time I saw him he was kind of astoundingly non-cretinish. And my mom is—I mean, you know, she's my mom. She's all right."

"Okay."

"*What?*"

"Nothing."

"I'm asking you."

"David, your mother *abandoned* you."

"No, I know. For sure. That wasn't good. But, I mean, things happen to people. Who doesn't have a rough childhood story? My mom did what she had to do. It wasn't *good* that she left the way she did. I'd never say it was. But then she came back, and everything was okay again. Plus, my friends were *everything* to me, Kate. I never really cared what was going on in my house, because every possible second of every day I was *out* of my house, goofing around with my friends. The life I really cared about wasn't happening inside my house."

"Some of it was. Don't you think that having your mom—"

"Look, I know my mom left and everything. But she came back, Kate. She's my mom. She loves me. She thought I was some kind of a genius or something. She encouraged me to write, she taught me to meditate, she bought me a guitar."

And then David flashed on a moment of himself in the seventh grade.

It was a cool and overcast Monday morning. He had just spent the weekend at his mother's house. Guitar case in hand, he was about halfway up the short flight of stairs leading to the door of the portable classroom used for music lessons at his school. Through the wall of the building, he could hear that the class he was due in, Guitar 101, had already begun.

But he couldn't seem to make it up the stairs. Suddenly it was like he was trying to move through molasses. Everything was happening too slowly, and taking way more energy than he had to spend.

He tried lifting his leg up just one more step, but it wouldn't come. Too weak. In what he knew must have looked like comically slow-motion, he helplessly grabbed at the stair railing as he collapsed. He felt his guitar case slipping from his hand, and then listened, as if from far away, as it went bump, bump, bumping down the stairs behind him.

As he crumpled, he lacked even the strength to at least shift his legs such that he might be able to assume a relatively comfortable position on the rough hewn wooden steps. But he was too weak to manage even that. He would lie exactly as he fell.

When the slo-mo fall was over, and the whole side of his face was against the next step up, with his legs folded every which way beneath him, he gazed out at the school's grass playing field. It seemed to go forever. No one was on the field. No one was anywhere to be seen. Everyone was in their first period class. For that, at least, he was grateful. He didn't want anyone to see him looking like some giant broken marionette that someone had just thrown onto the steps.

He closed his eyes, because he had no choice but to.

And then he was back in the coffee shop with Kate.

"What were you just thinking about?" she said.

"Oh, nothing. I mean—it was nothing. I was just remembering this time, when I was in junior high, that I kind of passed out one morning at school."

"You did? Why?"

"I don't know why. That's the thing. I've never known. I had just spent the weekend at my mom's. I think she had taken me straight from her house to school. This was right around when she first came back; I'd probably seen her maybe four times since her return. And I was going up these stairs to my first class, and all of a sudden I just . . . couldn't."

"Couldn't what?"

"Do anything. Like, at all. I couldn't make it up the stairs. I couldn't go to school. I couldn't go home to my dad and Karen. I couldn't be at my mom's, because she and 'Dr. Dan' didn't seem exactly thrilled about having me around. I just couldn't . . . do life. So something in me decided to take me right out of the game. I broke. Suddenly I really *couldn't* do life. One minute I was just a regular kid going up some steps to his class, and the next I was sinking like the Titanic."

Kate looked concerned. "What happened?"

"Next, you mean? I don't know. That's all I remember. I think I just passed out."

"That's not good."

"It wasn't great."

"It sounds like maybe you had a nervous breakdown."

"Maybe. I *was* a pretty nervous kid."

"You had reason to be."

But then David wanted to avoid any more talk about how he had once responded to life by collapsing and falling apart.

On their table was a little glass vase holding two small and drooping flowers. He said, "Yes, but do these flowers have a reason to be *this* dead? Look at these things. They'd make every bee in the world want to commit suicide."

He looked around at the other tables. "What is up with the table decorations in this place? *All* the flowers are dead. It's like a daisy death camp in here. Wouldn't you think that the last thing the owner of a coffee shop would want on all his tables is a vivid reminder of how fleeting perkiness is? Then again, maybe the guy who owns this place is like, 'Nothing says *I need another cup of coffee* like perishing peonies! You know what else we should do? Play *dirges* in here! Let's *scare* people a little! Make 'em feel like a little caffeine is all that's standing between them and the grave! Someone run out and get me a cassette of *Top Ten Dirges*! And I want everyone who works here wearin' black! C'mon, people! Let's sell us some coffee!'"

When he saw that Kate was finding his diversion something less than hilarious, he said, "Sorry. That was stupid. *Top Ten Dirges*. I'm so sure. I don't even know *one* dirge. Do you? Does anybody? Is there an *All Dirges, All The Time* radio station, or anything like that?"

"I don't know."

"What's wrong?"

"Nothing. I was just—nothing."

"What? C'mon."

"It's nothing. But I was wondering, have you talked to your mom since you've been up here?"

"I've called her three or four times. I can't seem to get hold of her. But she'll call me back. She knows I've tried to call her."

"Are you still going over to her house for Thanksgiving?"

"As far as I know, yeah. Are you and Lillian still coming over to Jerald's?"

"We are. Are you planning to be there at all?"

"At Jerald's? I'd like to come by, for sure. But listen, if you'd rather I didn't, it's no problem. I'd totally understand. Besides, my not coming to Jerald's would give me a chance to not get beaten up by Lillian."

Kate laughed. "She doesn't want to beat you up."

"Oh, I'm pretty sure she does. You should have seen her when I brought over your wineglasses. That woman would make Spartacus pee his loincloth. What the heck did you tell her about me?"

"The truth."

"Oh. So I never had a chance with her, then."

"Afraid not. Hey, about Thanksgiving. You and I have some of the same friends. That means you and I have to remain friends. So let's do that. Let's be friends. Friends is *all* we'll be, but we'll be friends. Okay?"

"Yes. Of course. I'd like that. Could you just do me one little favor, though?"

"What?" said Kate.

"Could you never date anyone? *Ever*? In fact, why don't you just go ahead and promise, right now, that until the day comes when you die a lonely *but* spiritually fulfilled little old lady, you will not go on one single date. How's that sound? Good? Great!"

Kate laughed. "I'll think about it."

"And I'll think about what you've said about my childhood. I really will, Kate. Honestly, I think you're right. I think there is stuff—stuff having to do with my mom, and her leaving and all that—that I'm maybe not processing, or even as aware of, as I should be. I can kind of feel, actually, that that's true. So, thank you."

"No problem."

"Well, maybe a *little* problem."

"Maybe just a little," said Kate.

Later that night, before ringing up David's pint of Jack Daniel's, Bulgarian Lou said around his cigar stub, "Cost ya less to buy a fifth."

But David ignored his inner Karen. "That does make sense," he said. "I should do that. But for now, I'll just stick with this. Thank you, though."

Bulgarian Lou shrugged like he was too bored to be bored. "Your money."

As David, purchase in hand, was walking out of the store, he heard the man's voice from behind him.

"See you next time, Dave."

Four days later, at an hour early enough for him to be reasonably certain that his apparent drive to become a truly world-class reclusive derelict wouldn't be derailed by his having to unexpectedly socialize with anyone, David was walking as swiftly as decorum allowed back to the Surf. Cradled in the crook of his arm was a paper sack containing his purchases from Sunset Liquors: beef jerky, sunflower seeds, two Hostess Twinkies, a package of American yellow cheese slices, a small bottle of orange juice, a fifth of Jack Daniel's, and the latest issue of *Penthouse*.

The moment he stepped around the corner of the motel, he saw Jerald and Lillian standing in front of the office. They were holding hands and waving to Paula's Mercedes-Benz as it pulled away from the parking lot.

Jerald and Lillian saw him, too.

Shit! thought David.

"David!" called Jerald. He waved, a broad smile on his face. "Hello!"

"Hey!" said David, returning the wave and continuing to walk forward, since what else could he do? But he was about as ready to interact with others as Bigfoot was ready to debate with William F. Buckley, Jr.

Once he reached the pair waiting for him, David said, "Oh, that's right! Today's the day Paula's gonna come check you guys out! How'd it go? Did the plan *work*?"

"Yes!" said Jerald happily. "We pulled it off! Paula thinks Lillian and I are two peas in a pod. It was pretty obvious she thinks one of those peas isn't the right *color,* of course, because, well, because that's Paula. But she thinks Lillian's my girlfriend!"

"How great!" David had yet to look at Lillian. "Did you tell her all that stuff about Franklin being Lillian's brother?"

"No need. He wasn't here, so why complicate things?"

"Perfect!" said David.

"It *is* perfect!" said Jerald. "Because come this Thursday, I've got Brian for a *month*!" He gave Lillian a big hug. "And it's all because of this Tony-worthy actress right here!"

When released from Jerald's embrace, a smiling Lillian pushed her glasses up on her nose, took a short beat, and then turned to look at David.

"Hello, David," she said coolly.

David knew he looked like a singularly inept fugitive from the law. Sticking out in more directions than the Scarecrow of Oz could point, his hair was on the verge of becoming the least cool dreadlocks ever. He hadn't shaved in many days, which, as he was acutely aware, left him looking less like a bitchin' Marlboro Man and more like an itchin' asthmatic with mange. And he guessed that Tide Clean less accurately described the smell of his clothes than did Tide's Out.

But unless the earth suddenly and mercifully opened up and swallowed him whole, his only choice was to keep broadcasting on Channel Normal.

"Hey, Lillian," he said. "Good to see you again."

For her part, though, it was clear that what Lillian was glad to

186 N. JOHN SHORE, JR.

be seeing was what was poking out of the top of the sack David was holding in his arm.

Back at the liquor store, David had been agonized when he saw that the paper bag Bulgarian Lou had chosen to hold his purchases was inadequately sized for the job. But he hadn't *said* anything about it, because, of course, the man would have understood that what he really meant by, "Could you please use a bigger bag?" was, "Could you please use a bag big enough to hide from view the two tallest things in the bag, being the bottle of booze and the porno magazine?"

And David just could not bring himself to say that. So instead he had stood in suffering silence, while Bulgarian Lou sadistically fitted his latest acquisitions into a bag that inevitably left enough of the whiskey bottle and the magazine peeking over its top to make David, during his whole rapid walk back to the motel, feel like a flagrantly obvious menace to society.

But at least he had the comfort of knowing that it was too early, on this Saturday morning before Thanksgiving, to run into anyone he knew.

And yet, here was Lillian Holly Barnathan, zeroing in on the top of his bag like a hawk on a limping rabbit.

She said, "Whatcha got in the bag there, David?"

"I'm sorry?" said David.

Enunciating meticulously, Lillian said, "What do you have in your bag there, David?"

David acted like the question itself was a pleasant surprise. "Oh! Oh, nothing. Just, you know, supplies. Food. A little orange juice. Magazine to read. Beef jerk—cupcakes. You know, the usual."

He silently thanked God that he had at least made sure the cover of the magazine was facing his chest, rather than the world at large. And also that the cigarette ad on the back cover could have been on any magazine. Still, he knew the likelihood that anyone over the age of nine would know perfectly well what sort of magazine it was, since porno magazines seemed to have entirely cornered the market on pages so thick with gloss they were practically their own supply of lubricant.

"So where's Brian now?" he asked Jerald.

Jerald seemed to be intentionally *not* looking at David's bag, which was somehow worse. "He's inside with Erin. We just stepped out to see Paula off. It's so good to see you, David. It feels like you've disappeared on us lately."

"Me? Nah. I mean, you know, *tempus fugit*, as nobody says anymore, because who speaks Latin? Ha-ha-ha."

Jerald asked affectionately, "What have you been up to lately?" Then he seemed to get real awkward. "I mean, you know, what—"

David said quickly, "Oh, you know—I dunno. Just keepin' busy generally."

"You know what they say about idle hands," said Lillian.

David kept his eyes locked on Jerald.

"Now, David," said Jerald, "don't you keep being such a stranger, okay?" He moved in to hug David, quickly glanced at the bag blocking that move, and instead put his hand on David's bicep. "I worry about ya, buddy. You're coming over for Thanksgiving, right? Lillian and Kate will be here. I know Franklin wants to see you. Brian definitely wants to see you. And Erin and Vicky will be here."

"Vicky?" said David.

"Erin's girlfriend. You haven't met Vicky? Well, see then? Another reason to make sure you come by."

"I'd love to come to your place for Thanksgiving, of course," said David. "I'm also going to my mom's, though."

"Well, what time is her dinner?"

"You know, I *still* don't know what her plans are. I don't even know what time I'm supposed to be there. But whenever it is, maybe I can at least stop by your place after I go to hers? Or before, if she's having hers late?"

"Of course! We'll be eating around six—and I'm sure we'll all be here for hours and hours after that. And before then, too. Just come over anytime at all during the day. Promise you will?"

"I do," said David.

"Good to see you, David," said Lillian, to his bag.

"You too," said David. "Tell Kate I said hi."

Looking David in the eye, she said, "Oh, I will definitely be telling Kate that I saw you today."

That night, frustrated at not yet knowing his plans for Thanksgiving, David phoned his mother at her home.

No answer. So he called her office, where he got her service.

"Could you please let Georgia know that I need her to call me so that we can finalize our plans for Thanksgiving?" he said to the answering machine lady, who, unlike his mom's receptionist, was not one of the three witches from *Macbeth*. "Like, what time I'm supposed to be there, and all that?"

"I'll make sure she gets the message. Is there anything else you'd like to tell her?"

David paused for a moment. "No. That's it. Thank you."

Two nights later, returning to his room after an afternoon spent in bars downtown that had turned into a night spent in bars downtown, that had morphed into a kaleidoscopic jumble of congenial camaraderie and dramatic declarations and loudly whispered confessions and rip-roaring laughter and deafening music and beautiful girls who had everything in the world to recommend them save that they weren't Kate, David found a note slipped beneath his door.

Your mother called. Be at her house on Thanksgiving at 2 p.m. Don't bring any food (she said).

Have fun! See you after? Or before? Or both?

Love you, buddy.

Jerald

LAWN DARTS

ALONE IN THE ELEVATOR ON HIS WAY UP TO HIS mother's three-bedroom condo in the tony Pacific Heights neighborhood of San Francisco, David looked at himself in the mirror that comprised the entire back wall.

He looked like the cover of *Every Mother's Nightmare* magazine.

Then again, along with his standard Levi's, he was wearing, instead of his usual white T-shirt, a *black* T-shirt—and one with a chest pocket, no less.

For him, that was practically formal wear.

He looked down at his shoes, a pair of beige Wallabees that looked like he'd found them in a dumpster at a home for aging cross-country hikers.

But his derelict shoes still worked, and they got him from the elevator to his mother's front door, bringing him face to face with what David thought had to be one of the world's all-time scariest door knockers. Made of solid brass, it was in the shape of a wild-eyed, flaming-maned, long-fanged Balinese lion mask. It looked like the rabid, Satanic cousin of the MGM lion.

He lifted up and let fall the big heavy ring that dangled from the lion's septum. No wonder the thing was always in such a terrible mood.

After waiting a bit, he again lifted and dropped the lion's nose ring.

No answer.

He nose-knocked again.

Nothing.

He wondered if he'd come on the wrong day.

He waited.

He gave Leo one final shot.

When his mother finally pulled open her door, David, who had just turned to leave, spun back around, and said, "Hi, Mom! Happy Thanksgiving! Wow! You look so beautiful!"

Besides all the reasons for which that was always true, Georgia was resplendent in a full-length purple-and-gold silk kaftan, which David immediately pictured being worn by some ancient Egyptian queen as she consulted with her mystic royal astrologer, or by some Druid goddess, as she assured her adoring assemblage that the upcoming harvest would be as bountiful as it was taxable.

"Namaste, my son," said Georgia. With a slow sweep of her hand, a gesture rendered downright majestic by the billowing sleeve of her garment, she said, "Come. You may leave your shoes here, on the *getabako*." Stepping inside her place, David quickly yanked off his wino Wallabees, depositing them on the top shelf of the elegant little two-tiered cupboard just inside the door. It quietly, and even nobly, endured the insult.

Between the Chanel No. 5 sweetly wafting in the air behind her and the optical extravaganza of her gown, David, following his mother through the entryway of her house, found himself halfway between a reverie of nostalgia and a distinct desire to score some weed and go see *Fantasia*.

When they came onto the Carrara marble floor between Georgia's living room on the left and her dining room on the right, David saw that the two of them were alone in the house.

"Where is everybody?" he said.

"What do you mean?"

"I mean, you know, where *is* everybody? Today is Thanksgiving, right? *Is* it? Did I show up here on the wrong day?"

"No, David, you did not show up here on the wrong day."

"Oh. So—I mean, I'm sorry, but weren't you having a whole Thanksgiving thing here today? Did I get that wrong? I sure do *smell* one of your amazing Thanksgiving dinners. I could chew the *air* in here and get full. But why are we the only—"

"Let's sit in the living room," said Georgia. Before entering the room, she stopped at its edge to step out of her purple brocade slippers. Then she walked to her couch, sat down, and unhurriedly reached for the full crystal wine decanter that was waiting on the coffee table before her between two long-stemmed wineglasses.

"Would you like a glass of wine?" she said.

"I would, thank you," said David. "Lemme just hang up my jacket."

Besides the collection of expensive coats and wraps belonging to his mother, David found in her guest closet several men's coats, all of which, at a quick glance, appeared to be the same size.

He nestled his jacket between two of his mother's fur coats, quietly shut the closet door, and headed back into what he always thought of as The White Room.

———

David thinking of his mother's living room as The White Room was anything but imaginative. The whole room was, literally, white.

Its plush wool carpet was white. Its walls, ceiling, and crown molding were white. Its grand suede Chesterfield sofa, and its two matching armchairs, were white. The silk curtains of the floor-to-ceiling window overlooking the San Francisco Bay were white. The Ben Shahn serigraph on the wall next to the window was white (save for the black line drawing of two distorted, big-toothed heads, each of which seemed to be ravishing and devouring the other).

The lacquered credenza holding the stereo equipment? White. The tulip-base speaker stands for Georgia's state-of-the-art Bose 901 speakers? White. The marble Marseilles fireplace mantel? White. The Baroque frame of the massive mirror resting upon and running the entire length of the mantle?

Gold, actually.

So that was different.

Hanging on the wall behind the sofa, directly across from the mantle and mirror, was the standout in the room: a seven feet long, four and a half feet tall lithograph of *Guernica*, in which Picasso famously captured the nightmarish anguish of war using only blacks, whites, and seemingly every shade of gray discernible to the human eye.

Georgia once told David that if she were sitting in just the right spot near the middle of the sofa, and then stood, she would find her reflection in the mirror situated within the monochromatic riot of pain such that the head of *Guernica*'s wildly screaming horse would be just above her own head, while the agonized woman moving upward from her left would appear desperately yearning to tell her something.

"Sometimes I'll move my head just a bit, until the poor soul's lips seem to be touching my ear," Georgia told him. "And I'll stay right there, listening as she sings to me her song of sorrow, which is so deep and full of grief it's almost more than I can bear to hear. But I stay, and I listen to her, because I know that having someone hear and understand her is what she needs more than anything else in the world."

Taking a seat in one of her white suede armchairs, David said to his mother now, "I love this room. It makes me feel like one of the singers in ABBA." He—and only he—laughed a bit. Glass of wine in hand, his mother seemed to be studying him.

"Now, why would you say that, I wonder?" she said cooly.

Like a comedian on stage whose opening joke has tanked, David continued on, hoping and trusting that he would find his groove. "Oh, just because of how white everything in here is. And, you know, ABBA's from Sweden. Where all the snow is." His mother continued to regard him as she might a curiously obtuse lab rat. "So—you know," he continued. "White. Snow. Which of course is how Snow White filled in her name on job applications and the like. Now *there* was a singer. Why she and those dwarfs never put together a music act, I have no idea. *Snow White and Her Singing Dwarfs* would have been the toast of Vegas, don't you think? With Charo as their opening act?"

His mother looked at him stonily.

"No?" he said. "Not Charo? Lola Falana, maybe? Okay, never mind. Stupid idea."

He reached for the glass of wine waiting for him on the coffee table. Where was everybody?

"So, Mom, what's been happening with you? How's everything at your work? I think about that a lot."

"You think about what a lot?"

"About the value of what you do. And what it must mean to you personally. Sometimes I think that what you do must be really taxing for you. Other times I think it must be really rewarding, to help people the way you do. But I guess everything great comes at a cost, right?"

"It certainly does." Georgia took a sip from her glass. "But yes, my work is very rewarding." She turned her gaze out her window at the peaceful jumble of rooftops sloping down toward the Bay, from whose steel-gray waters arose the impossibly majestic Golden Gate Bridge, the tops of its two red-orange towers grown hazy in the gathering fog rolling in from the Pacific.

As if talking mainly, if not exclusively, to herself, Georgia continued. "Every day, I feel inexpressible gratitude for the healing that I am genuinely blessed to be able to facilitate in the lives of others. Teaching people to open themselves up to the power of the universe—playing, as best as I am allowed to, my role as a Bodhisattva in their lives, as a channeler of light into their darkness—is an honor that is always calling me to give thanks to the great, beneficent healer of all."

"So every day is Thanksgiving for you!" The moment David said it, he wished he hadn't. But his mother always put him on such a weird edge that he couldn't seem to go a minute without saying something that came out sounding either simple-minded, disarmingly random, or—as had just happened, which was easily the worst of them all—marginally aggressive.

But instead of the censure he expected, his mother only looked at him benevolently. "If one truly knows oneself, every day is a holiday."

David nodded. "That's true—I imagine. I wouldn't actually know, since I never seem to have any idea what's going on with me. So, for me, every day is more like Groundhog Day. Or Halloween."

"Talk to me," said his mother. "Tell me how your journey is going, young traveler."

"It's going pretty well, I guess." But then David shook his head. "Well, no, actually. To be honest with you, things aren't really going all that great for me lately."

"No?"

"No." He took a sip of his wine. "I broke up with Kate."

"Ah. Good for you."

"No, Mom. My breaking up with Kate was not good for me. God, no. It was awful for me."

Georgia slid back into her clinician mode. "What was it about breaking up with Kate that you found so awful, David?"

"The fact that it *was* so awful. It *is* so awful. It was the stupidest thing I've ever done, Mom, by a very long shot. And that's saying something. It's like I ran myself over with a truck. And I have no idea why I did it. That's the crazy part. I'm *ignorant* as to how I could have broken up with Kate. She's the greatest."

Georgia did a little shrug. "If you say so. She was certainly head over heels in love with you, that was obvious enough. You know, from what you'd told me about her, I expected her to be a real beauty. So when I saw her, I have to say that I was a little disappointed in that regard. I thought she looked a bit, I don't know. Manly."

Once he'd managed not to suddenly spray his mother with wine, David let out a genuine laugh. "*Manly?* I can honestly say that not once, in the course of the approximately ten zillion thoughts I've had about the way Kate looks, has the word *man* ever come to my mind. Except, wait: I did once think, *That girl could turn a gay man straight.*"

From over the top of her wineglass, his mother arched an eyebrow at him.

David sighed. "I'm not gay, Mom."

"Have I said that you are?"

"Yes, actually, you may recall that you once *told* me I'm gay. That time you and I were chatting after my friend Ricky was here?"

"I remember Ricky. I remember all of your friends. You aren't going to try to tell me that Ricky isn't gay, are you?"

"No, Ricky's gay. Ricky's *Cabaret* gay. But I'm the *opposite* of gay, Mom. I'm straight. This is something that you know."

"I also know what you yourself should know by now, son,

which is that people who are conflicted about any particular issue within themselves are always the most defensive about that issue."

"Okay, well, I'm sure that generally—"

"And you do have a lot of gay friends, David."

"Yeah, Mom. I do. For one, I still know a lot of actors and theater people I met in high school when I was doing all that speech stuff. I mean, c'mon. I have friends with freckles and red hair, too. But that doesn't make me Pippi Longstocking."

Georgia didn't laugh—but she did slightly smile. "My God, son. What a wit you have."

Warmed and relaxed by this unexpected breakthrough of the sun, David said, "Well, I learned from the best."

"That reminds me. Have you spoken with your father lately?"

"I saw him right before I left Long Beach. Why?"

Taking an unhurried sip from her glass, Georgia returned to looking out her window. "We'll talk about it later. For now, let's just enjoy our time together."

David silently turned in his chair so that he, too, could look out the window. "I can never get over what a crazy view that is. What a *bridge* that is! Do you know that guys painting the Golden Gate Bridge used to grab seagulls—which I guess just rest on the top of the bridge before flying farther out over the ocean—and slap orange paint right onto their heads? And the birds would fly away—and then there was all this excitement in the bird world about this whole new species of orange-headed seagulls that had been discovered."

He turned back to look at his mom. She appeared not to have heard a word he'd said. He looked back out the window. "True story. Big deal in the bird world."

After a prolonged silence, Georgia said softly, "I cannot tell you how many hours I have sat right here, meditating, reading the *Tao Te Ching*, watching the fog slowly making its way across the water."

David turned back to his mom. "I can imagine. I have no idea how you ever leave that couch. It's such a phenomenal view."

With sagacious serenity, Georgia said, "It's so much more than the view, David. The view is nothing more than a manifestation of the universal *prana*. It's about being inspired by the divine Godhead. It's about merging my consciousness with the source of all consciousness, the source of all knowledge. It's about being filled with a holy bliss that is just—well, words fail me, as they must always in the end."

"Boy, I wish I could make my consciousness merge with the source of all knowledge. I could have really used that in college. Ha-ha. But seriously, I really do hear you. I still have that great copy of the *Tao Te Ching* you gave me for Christmas when I was, what, thirteen?"

"I don't recall."

"But you remember giving it to me, right? I love that book. Do you remember the inscription you wrote me on its inside cover?"

"No. Tell me."

"May all of your knowledge one day become wisdom."

"Ah. Yes."

"Wise words."

"If followed, they are. Have you followed those words, my son? Have you made a practice of turning your knowledge into wisdom?"

"I'm going to have to say no to that. In fact, if anything, I'm pretty sure that each and every day I grow just a little bit stupider."

"Ah. We're back to your breaking up with your girlfriend."

"Well, the truth is that I could use some advice about that, Mom. I really can't make heads or tails of why I did it. I want to win Kate back. But even more than that, I want to understand why I broke up with her in the first place. For the life of me, I cannot understand what my problem is, or was, with committing to Kate. I love her. I *wanted* to commit to her. I *did* commit to her —and then, for no reason that I can understand, I became a wrecking ball that destroyed my relationship with her. I need to understand why I did that."

"I'm not sure that I can help you with that, David."

"I was thinking maybe you *could*. Because you do this sort of thing for a living, right? This is just the kind of problem you help people with, isn't it?"

Georgia smiled knowingly—and then, like a sphinx, only stared at him, and said nothing.

"When I was a kid," David continued, "you always had the quality advice. You know how to see to the heart of things, to really open them up so they make sense. You remember all those conversations we used to have about God and karma and balance and cosmic harmony and all that, right? Well, all that stuff you told me back then really *helped* me, Mom. Through the nightmare of living with Karen and Dad, I meditated. I did a *lot* of yoga. I took Tai Chi and Kung Fu lessons throughout junior high and high school. I burned incense in my room—even though it drove Dad crazy, because he was convinced it meant I was becoming a girl, or something. I read the *Bhagavad Gita* a million times. I read *The Way of Zen; Zen in the Art of Archery; Zen Mind, Beginner's Mind*. I read and did all that stuff. Because it *worked* for me. The same as it still works for me, when I'm not being such a freaked-out basket case that I might as well try to juggle power saws as meditate for more than eight seconds at a time."

"Because you broke up with Kate."

"Because I broke up with Kate. And in doing that, I created a hole for myself that I cannot seem to get out of."

"And you want to know why you created this hole for yourself."

"Yes. I really do."

Georgia took a sip of her wine. Closing her eyes, she settled into a meditation that lasted a full minute or two.

David quietly waited.

Upon opening her eyes, Georgia fixed David with a meaningful look. "The answer to your question, my young seeker, does not lie in understanding why you broke up with Kate."

"No?"

"No. Your challenge is to understand why you believe that you need Kate to be happy. Your karma—which is uniquely your own, as all karma is to all sentient beings still bound to the Wheel of Life—is to discern why it is that you feel you need these relationships. Why are you so dependent upon Kate for your sense of self-worth? What are you missing within yourself that has you searching so desperately outside of yourself? Do you see what I mean, David? Don't ask yourself why you can't commit to this person, or to that person. Ask yourself why you can't let go of your attachment to every person."

After some time spent considering her words, David said, "I do see what you're saying. And you're right. I know I do sometimes look for others to give me what I can really only give myself. But this is different, isn't it? Because this is about love. Real, true love. And isn't love, in and of itself, a different order of—"

Georgia held up her hand. "Stop. That's enough, David. You asked me for my counsel, and I have given it to you. If what I have said to you does not satisfy you, or is not enough for you, then so be it. There is nothing left to be said. Except that I would ask you to promise me one thing."

"Of course."

"When you are alone, and calm, reflect further and deeper upon what I've said to you. Do not question what I've offered you; do not analyze it; do not try to make it any more or less than it is. Just be with my words. Open yourself up to the wisdom that lies within them. Will you do that?"

"I will. I promise. Thank you."

"Oh, we're not quite done working on you today."

"We're not?"

"We are not. I said that I didn't have anything more to say to you concerning the cares and woes in which you now imagine yourself so entangled. And that is true, I don't. But many paths can lead to enlightenment, my son. And one of them—perhaps the greatest one of all—is music." David nodded his agreement. "Lately I've been listening to a record that I'd really like you to hear. Do you feel that you're in a space right now where you can be open to the healing power of music?"

"Music played on *your* stereo? Heck, yes. You could play *The Chipmunks Sing Don Ho* out of your speakers, and before they hit the first chorus of 'Tiny Bubbles,' I'd have golden rays shooting out of my every orifice."

Georgia said curtly, "David, do you mind if I ask you a question?"

"No, of course not."

"Do you write those funny little comments of yours down ahead of time?"

"I'm sorry?"

"Do you write those funny little comments of yours down ahead of time? It's a simple question."

"I'm afraid I don't understand. Are you asking if I write down the things I say *before* I say them—like, the night before? In a journal, or whatever?"

"Yes, that is what I am asking you."

"I don't—I mean, are you being serious?"

"I am being serious, and I think that you know that I am. It's something that a lot of people do, David. Especially those inca-pable of speaking directly from the heart, people who have a hard time connecting honestly, naturally, and productively with others. Writing down things to say ahead of time, and then committing those clever little witticisms and observations to memory, is a common coping mechanism for people who suffer from a wide variety of social affective disorders—especially those with a strong desire to be popular with others."

Sidestepping his mother's less-than-subtle insult of him was made a whole lot easier for David by his immediate fascination with what she'd just told him.

"Are you kidding me?" he said. "That's really a thing people do? Man, you just never know what's going on with people, do you? Are you telling me, for sure, that there are people out there who actually write down on, say, Monday, things they want to say on Tuesday, *memorize* those things, and then, the next day, try to *shoehorn* what they've memorized into a normal, actual conversation that's really happening? Is that true? Because that is just so off-the-charts amazing."

Georgia responded dispassionately. "How interesting that you think so. What is it that you find so amazing about that, David?"

"What about it *isn't* amazing? I can't even imagine someone writing down in a little notebook stuff they're gonna try to jam into a conversation the next day. I would *kill* to see one of those notebooks. The people who write in them must be, like, 'Hmm. Lemme think. *Hitler.* No, too intense. *Infectious diseases.* No, too gross. *Names of craters on the moon.* Good, but I'll save that for a space launch, or maybe an eclipse. *Ways to skin a squirrel.* No. *Dolly Parton.* Yes! People *love* Dolly Parton! That's it! So, let's see, I'll say—oh, I don't know. How about, "Dolly Parton is an excellent singer *and* actress. C'mon, Dolly, leave some talent for someone *else,* why don't you?" Yes! That's the *perfect* thing to say! There's no *way* I'll have to eat lunch alone again tomorrow!'"

His mother's expression was one of marked, and even grave, disapproval. But it was too late to pull David back in from the buoyant water in which he was now almost wildly splashing and playing.

Three factors were contributing to keeping David in that water. The first was his desire to erase from his mother's mind any idea she might have about his being so dysfunctional that he actually wrote down ahead of time things that he wanted to say later. The second was his complete captivation by the idea that there really were people who really did do that. The third was the factor of which he was much less aware than he was the other two, even though it was the strongest of the three. This was his desire to become again the bright and funny boy whom his mother seemed to so often treasure, and even admire, during the two years following her divorce, when she lived alone with him and his sister.

"Have you ever *seen* one of those notebooks, Mom? No? Don't you *want* to? Don't you want to know what's in at least *one* of them? I wonder if the people who write them use any kind of ranking, or a five-star sort of system, to rate their potential contributions to possible upcoming conversations? Or if their would-be comments are maybe divided into subject categories, the way they do on *Jeopardy*—you know: Rock 'n Roll, Famous Capitals, What's On TV, The Sporting Life, Famous Criminals. Do you think? And what's the typical ratio of their comments that do and don't later make it into real-life conversations? Don't you want to *know*? And are comments that don't make it in on Monday tried again, with different people, on Tuesday—and then again on Wednesday? How do they know when a comment is getting too old to use anymore? When does a pithy observation about a current event finally have to be trashed, because its relevance is no more?"

Georgia's expression made clear that, on a five-star rating system, she would give David's excited disquisition one black hole. "Are you through?"

"I'm not sure," said David. "Can I check my notes? Ha! Kidding. I'm done."

It was at that moment when David realized that *he* was a person who planned things he wanted to say ahead of time. He'd sure done it once, anyway—with the joke he'd told his mom about lying but not lying.

"Sorry I went on such a babble-fest," he said. "You go through life thinking everyone is pretty much exactly the same. But the older I get, the more I learn how wrong that is. People *cope*, man, in all kinds of ways."

"They certainly do," said his mother pointedly. Placing her empty wineglass on the coffee table, she stood up from the couch. "It's time for us to eat."

"Oh, is it? But what about the music you were gonna play me?"

"David, I have things to do."

"Oh, shoot. I'm so sorry! Can you at least tell me what album I literally talked myself out of hearing?"

But Georgia only stood, and silently walked out of the room.

David rose from his chair, and ambled over to his mother's white stereo cabinet. There was an album on the turntable. He looked at its label, and saw it was *Diamonds & Rust*, by Joan Baez.

The record's cover was atop the cabinet. He picked it up. Joan Baez, always beautiful and in this photograph beautifully lit by golden candlelight, was now gazing directly at him. Not quite ready for that level of knowing compassion, he turned the cover over. He read the names of the songs on the album's first side.

Diamonds & Rust

Fountain of Sorrow

Never Dreamed You'd Leave in Summer

Children and All That Jazz

Simple Twist of Fate

Walking into his mother's dining room, David enthused, "*Boy*, that smells good." He popped his head into the kitchen adjoining the room. "And I spy on yonder cooling rack that you've made two pies! Pumpkin, and is that apple? Color me salivating!"

Georgia, tending to something in her oven, said nothing.

David saw that both sides of the kitchen sink, and most all of the kitchen's counter space, was filled with dirty pots and pans.

He looked back at the formal dining table, with its eight chairs from what he always imagined as the Henry VIII line of intimidating furniture. Before the middle chair on the far side of the table was a single place setting, missing a plate. Otherwise the long and gleaming cherrywood table was bare.

Looking back into the kitchen, David said, "Can I help set the table?"

Taking a dinner plate out of the oven, Georgia said matter-of-factly, "The table is already set. Go take your place."

David asked tentatively, "At that one setting there? That's for me?"

"Yes, David, that's for you. Go sit down."

So that's what he did.

Georgia set on the placemat before him the plate from the oven, and then returned to the kitchen.

David looked down at what he had to assume was his Thanksgiving meal. On his white plate were maybe three tablespoons of mashed potatoes, even less stuffing, a thin slice of canned cranberry sauce, about a carrot's worth of sliced glazed carrots, and one leg of a Cornish game hen.

He put his hands on his lap. He waited.

Back from the kitchen, Georgia put on the table opposite him her own setting and plate, which had no more food on it than David's. She walked into the living room, returning with the wine carafe and their two empty glasses, which she placed on the table between them.

She took her seat.

"More wine?" she said, spreading her napkin across her lap.

David said, "Sure. Thank you."

After pouring them a half-glass each, Georgia picked up her fork and began to eat.

David quietly lifted his napkin, unfolded it, placed it on his lap, picked up his fork, and started in on a meal he could have eaten in five bites.

Following a moment of deliberation, he chose to begin with the carrots.

He pressed his fork tongs into a slice.

He raised the piece to his mouth.

He chewed it.

He swallowed it.

"The carrots are really good," he said truthfully. "Just delicious."

"Butter and brown sugar makes anything delicious."

"That is true. I once ate an old tennis shoe glazed with butter and brown sugar. It was so good I ordered another one."

During the ensuing quiet David opted for a dab of mashed potatoes.

Also delicious.

He said, "Boy, you really do make the best mashed potatoes. I could totally see how someone would name a whole dance after these."

In the inevitable silence that followed, David said tentatively, "Hey, Mom? So, I mean, what happened to the big Thanksgiving get-together that I thought you were having here? Didn't you say that all your friends and everybody would be coming over today?"

Georgia reached for her wineglass. "I did, yes."

"Well, either every one of your friends has lost a *lot* of weight

—and also has extremely advanced laryngitis—or you and I are the only two people here."

"You and I are the only two people here, David."

"Is everything okay?"

"Everything's fine. Eat your food."

David looked back to his plate, and slowly set about getting just about the only bite possible from his leg of Cornish game hen.

As he sat quietly chewing, he started wondering what kind of games Cornish game hens liked to play.

Hide and go peck?

Simon clucks?

Egg toss?

Duck, Duck, Loser?

Then he imagined a whole flock of the mini-chickens on a vast green field playing lawn darts, having all kinds of feathery fun—until their game came to an abrupt and gory end when one of them paid the ultimate price for not being able to run out of the way with anything near the necessary speed.

He was maybe halfway through his Munchkin-sized meal when Georgia's phone rang. Despite the telephone sitting on its stand in a corner of the room, she rose from the table to take the call on the wall phone in her kitchen. Except when she took advantage of that phone's long cord to step inside her walk-in pantry during the conversation, David couldn't help but overhear most everything she said to whomever was on the other line.

"Yes, I'm still here," she said. "No, it's fine . . . Yes, every-thing's all right . . . No, I'm not worried, it's been okay, although there *was* a bit of a moment there, when . . . Yes, I promise I'll call the police if I need to . . . I'll let you know, but please don't worry. I've been here before . . . Yes, right . . . Just keep them warm in the oven, and as long as you don't let them dry out, they'll be fine . . . And otherwise you're all set there? Everything made it over? .

. . I can't wait to see you all . . . I'll bring them when I come, they turned out perfectly . . . No, I won't . . . Okay, wonderful. And don't worry, okay? I'll see you soon."

David kept his head in a still and downward position, as if he were looking at his plate.

But he wasn't looking at his plate. He wasn't looking at anything.

Everything below his neck was white heat. Everything above it was questions exploding like bombs.

Why did she *hate* him so much?

Why didn't she want him at her house?

Why did she tell her friends that he was so dangerous that she might have to call the *police*?

Why had she moved her Thanksgiving party, for which she'd clearly done all the cooking, to someone else's house? Was that really because of him? Because he was such a huge problem? Because he was such a nightmare? Because he was such an out-of-control animal, such an embarrassing monstrosity, such an abject fucking *disease* that she couldn't stand the thought of exposing any of her friends to him?

Why did she hate him so much?

Georgia came out of the kitchen. She quietly resumed her seat.

David kept his head down.

He heard her resume her eating.

Once again, but this time seemingly of its own volition, his fork was making its way to his plate. After hovering above it for a moment, it found its way down to the cranberry sauce, which required no pressure at all before yielding a wobbly red piece of itself.

When he glanced back up at his mother, he found her staring at him, with what he had always felt was her cruelest expression, the one where she held the arresting features of her arresting face in a state of unperturbed and dispassionate equilibrium, the expression of hers that expressed exactly and perfectly nothing at all—with the possible exception, if you held her gaze long enough, of the intimation that she was now awaiting the inevitable part where you started trying to blame her for your own problems and failings.

He looked back down at his meal.

He moved his fork in for another bite of it.

He heard his mother signal the end of dinner by placing her fork down on her plate.

He quietly put his fork down. He dabbed at his mouth with his napkin. He put his napkin on the table beside his plate.

Choking out the words like he had a noose around his neck, he said, "That was really delicious. Thank you."

When Georgia remained silent, he rose from his chair. He picked up his plate, his napkin, and his silverware. He walked them into the kitchen. The sink was too full to accommodate his plate, so he found a place for it on the countertop as far as possible from the two cooked pies.

He walked out of the kitchen and around the table to where he had been sitting. Georgia was still in her chair, her fingers lightly holding the stem of her wineglass on the table.

David placed his hands on the thick back of his chair. "I guess I'll be on my way," he said. "Before I go, was there something you wanted to tell me about Dad?"

His mother slowly spun her glass a full turn or so, and then looked up at him.

She said, "Your father has had a heart attack. A big one."

It took a moment for David to find his words. "Is he okay?"

"He's fine. He's at home recuperating."

"When did this happen?"

"I don't really know."

"But—I don't understand. I just saw him."

"Well, at some point after seeing you, he had a heart attack. He called me right afterwards, while he was still in the hospital. They did open heart surgery on him. He's been at home recuperating for a week now. He's fine."

"But, I mean—why didn't anyone tell me?"

"I did tell you, David. Just now. And let's try not to overreact, shall we?"

David's vision focused in on his mother's face so fast that everything else went fuzzy and dark. He heard himself speaking very calmly and clearly.

"Mom, you can say a million things about me right now. But one of them cannot be that I have overreacted to anything. I haven't yelled. I haven't raised my voice. I have barely moved. What *has* just happened is that I've learned that my father had a severe heart attack at least a week ago, and that you, my mother, knew about that, but didn't bother to pick up the phone to tell me about it, when I *know* you know that I've been calling you. And the only thing you can think to say to me right now is, 'Let's not overreact'? Does that sound reasonable to you?"

Georgia cocked her head a bit. With a touch of wonderment, she said, "My God. You haven't changed a bit, have you?"

Five seconds later David was on the sidewalk outside of his mother's building, walking away as quickly as he could, breathing heavily, aware of almost nothing.

11

WAVE GOODBYE

HE WAS HALFWAY DOWN THE BLOCK TOWARD HE HAD no idea where when David's memory slammed him back to a time when he was ten years old.

———

It had been weeks since his mother disappeared, since his father had come back home, since his real mother had been replaced by a woman so insane she was incapable of seeing him or his sister as anything but cash flying from her hands.

He is still groggy from having just gotten out of bed. It's seven in the morning on a school day. He's in the fifth grade.

The moment he steps out of his bedroom he knows that something is wrong. For one, the door to his parents' bedroom across the hall is wide open, when, at this time of the morning, it is invariably closed. Also, every lamp and light in their bedroom is turned on, the glow of the bulbs barely discernible in a room already brightened by the sunlight pouring in through its windows. The linens on the bed are in wild disarray. One of the pillows from his dad's side of the bed is on the floor.

The hallway light is on. So is the light in his and Patty's bathroom down the hall. So are the lights in the dining room at the end of the hall.

He momentarily wonders if he's slipped into some version of hell designed just for Karen, one where she has to pay the electric bill for a home in which it's impossible to turn off any of the lights.

He listens to hear if maybe all the faucets in the house are running too. They're not.

"Karen?" he calls. "Mom?" He leans his head inside his parents' bedroom. "Hello?"

Immediately Karen is before him. She's not dressed for work; she's wearing what she calls her "weekend grubbies"—old pants with an old sweatshirt. She has on no makeup, which he has never seen her without. Most startling is his realization in the moment that he's also never seen her not wearing a wig. There's not enough of the hastily brushed, hay-colored hair on her head.

"Your father had a heart attack," she says. "A massive coronary. It happened at two o'clock this morning. I was asleep when I heard a loud crash. I jumped out of bed, and turned on the lamp." She points to the bedroom floor. "That's when I saw him, crawling on his hands and knees right there in front of the closet. His pajama bottoms were down around his knees. He'd been on the john. He was incoherent. I didn't know what to do, so I called an ambulance. They got here, along with a firetruck, and then another fire department car came, and for a while there were even two policemen here. The paramedics put him on a stretcher and carried him right down the hallway, through the dining room, out the front door, and into the ambulance. I followed them to the hospital in my car. I've just come back here to pick up a few things, and now I'm going back to the hospital."

He is having trouble connecting everything that she's saying to real life. "Dad had a heart attack?"

"That's right. You slept through the whole thing. I have no idea how. Patty was awake, but she stayed in her room."

He follows Karen when she moves into the hallway. She stops right outside his bedroom door.

"There were firemen and cops and paramedics all through here," she says. "They were stomping right up and down the hallway, in and out of our bedroom, yelling, hollering, moving things around. And you stayed asleep the whole time."

"Is Dad okay?"

"It's too soon to tell. He's had open heart surgery. They sawed right through his sternum so they could get to his heart. I haven't seen him yet. All I know is that the operation is done, and now I'm going back to the hospital, so that when he wakes up I'll be there."

"Can I come with you?"

"Where?"

"To the hospital."

"No."

He breaks down a bit. *"Please?"*

"No. You go to school today. You can come to the hospital tonight, when he might be ready to see people. Until he's well enough for that, there's no reason for you to be there."

"But I could wait with you. Please let me come."

"No. I'm not going to tell you again."

Her inexplicable refusal of what he so frantically needs weakens him. He leans against his doorframe. "Please, Karen. He's my father."

"Shut up. The last thing I need right now is your lip."

This pulls him upright. Even she can't be so cruel. This has got to be a simple misunderstanding between the two of them.

"I just want to come to the hospital with you," he pleads. "That's all. Don't you think we should all be there?"

And that's when she rushes him.

He takes a fast step backwards.

"Don't you think what you've done already is bad enough?" she says.

"I don't know what you're—"

But she's reaching for his neck. To avoid her grasp he yanks his head backwards. She misses him, but keeps coming. Backpedaling into his bedroom, he turns his head real quick to see behind him. She grabs a big fistful of his pajama top just below his neck and drives him straight backwards, slamming him against the wall.

Holding her face so close he can see the blood vessels in her eyes, she hisses, "You did this, you little fucker. If your father dies, it's you who killed him." She twists his shirt, her knuckles digging hard into his throat. "You understand that? *You* did this. *You* put your father in the hospital. He gave up his life to come back here and save you. And how do you repay him? By being nothing but a *shit* around here, that's how. All you do is complain and bitch and argue about everything. You bring him nothing but trouble and pain. Well, guess what? You got what you wanted. Your father finally had a heart attack. And if he dies, it'll be all your fault. So you just better hope that he lives, do you hear me?"

He cannot talk, breathe, move. He's starting to make gagging noises. His right leg is between her legs, and he sees himself dropping her with a hard knee-slam to her crotch. He's about to do it when she yanks him slightly forward, shoves him back against the wall, releases him, and marches from his room.

Until he hears Karen's car backing out of the driveway and heading down the street, he stays right where he is, his back against the wall. When he starts to move again, he does so very slowly, like he's unsure of how his body works. He has no idea what to do.

Without breaking his long stride, David looked around to take note of where he was for the first time since bolting out of his mother's house. He guessed that he'd already walked half a mile —which left him six or so miles to go before reaching the Surf. That was fine with him. He could walk six miles in his sleep.

But the air was harshly cold, and he'd cut from his mother's house without stopping to get his jacket. He thought grimly of how it could be worse. He could have forgotten to grab his shoes off the fucking *getabako*.

Like a dog instinctively making his way home, David weaved his way through Pacific Heights, Japantown, the Fillmore, the Haight. All along the way he saw people celebrating Thanksgiving with their family and friends. He saw them through the windows of their homes, feasting and laughing. He saw them at opened doors, greeting one another with hugs and cries of joy. He saw them emerging from their cars, some holding babies, some holding hands, some holding the food they'd brought for everyone to share.

Except for sometimes pulling up short to let a car go by, hopping into the street to get around a cluster of people gathered on the sidewalk, and once stopping to kick a ball back to some children from whom it had gotten away, David didn't stop moving on his way to the ocean, to the Surf, to the Thanksgiving gathering waiting for him at Jerald's.

———

As he was approaching Golden Gate Park's panhandle, the memory came to him of the time when he and Patty, together, had first seen their mother after her return from her disappearance. Early on a Sunday afternoon, Georgia had picked the two of them up so she could take them out to lunch at a buffet-style restaurant.

David had never been to any restaurant where, rather than ordering at a counter, or sitting around waiting for a waiter, you were free to walk up, slide your tray along right in front of the food, stop before anything you saw that looked delicious, and then take however much of that deliciousness you wanted.

The moment he grasped the system was the moment David failed to grasp why there were any other kinds of restaurants in the world at all.

"I can't believe this is *allowed*," he whispered to Patty as the two of them were cruising the offerings.

Plates filled and back at their table, he and Patty took a seat on either side of their mom. The round banquet table Georgia had chosen for them to eat at was covered with a white linen tablecloth. It was near the restaurant's front door. The other seven chairs placed around their table were empty.

The space inside of Sammy's Smorgasbord was large enough to hold three or four of the smaller stores with which it shared a strip mall. The glass front of the restaurant looked to David like it went on forever.

The three of them were nearly the only customers in the place, a lone trio of diners on the edge of a veritable sea of big round tables identical to theirs.

But only two of the three of them were eating. Georgia had not visited the buffet. It was obvious enough to her children that she had no intention of doing so. Less obvious to them was why.

Neither David nor Patty had any idea what their mother was thinking or feeling, because she had barely spoken a word to either of them since seeing them together for the first time in two years.

Sitting motionless in her seat, Georgia was wearing a black short-sleeved turtleneck, a tight black knee-length skirt, charcoal hose, and black pumps. Her dark hair was perfectly coiffed, her deep red lipstick impeccably applied, her porcelain skin luminescent. Even inside the restaurant, she had not taken off her sunglasses. Her hands were frozen atop the black patent leather handbag on her lap.

David was so agog over seeing his mother for only the second time since her return that he could barely breathe. And though he knew Patty would rather swallow a live toad than admit it to him, he could tell she was feeling the same way about her mom being right there beside her, after all that time.

Georgia's unbroken muteness, however, was affecting David's excitement over being with her in about the same way his excitement over being on a Ferris wheel would be affected by it violently lurching to a stop just as his car had reached its highest point.

It was also rendering Patty so feverishly uncomfortable that she had begun joking and laughing with, of all people, him.

It was dizzying for David, he and his sister drowning together as they were, each acting as a life preserver for the other.

"What'd you get to eat?" he asked Patty. He was in such a state that he was barely aware of what was on his own plate, beyond that most of it seemed to be some shade of yellow.

"Fried chicken!" answered Patty. He had never seen her so manic, so scared.

Jabbing his fork in the air toward Patty's plate, he enthused, "What's that green stuff there?"

"Creamed *spinach*!"

Their audience of one remained a statue.

"Oh, wow!" answered David. Looking down at his plate, he jabbed his fork into something, anything, that he found there. "I got *this* stuff!" He held the glob up in the air. "Macaroni and cheese!"

"Me too! I got some of that too!"

"Isn't it *great*? Don't you love macaroni and cheese? I could eat it all day! Sometimes I *do*!"

"It goes so well with creamed spinach! Did you get any creamed spinach?"

"No! But I *love* creamed spinach! How did I not see it? I'm Popeye's biggest fan!"

Patty actually laughed at his joke. "You can have some of mine!" Her forkful of spinach was halfway through the air toward his plate when their mother spoke.

"You kids handle yourselves disgracefully," she said.

Patty's fork stopped mid-flight.

"It's really unbelievable," Georgia continued. "I wouldn't have thought it possible, but the both of you are even more immature than I remember."

After a moment, Patty's fork began its slow and slightly shaky descent back to her plate.

David kept his eyes on the tablecloth. The muscles all around his jaw had seized up hard.

"And it's appalling how divorced both of you are from your feelings."

Peripherally, David could see that Patty was remaining as motionless as he has become.

Georgia went silent again.

Time at their table seemed to stand perfectly still.

Finally, and moving slowly, David began poking at his food with his fork. He shot a quick glance up at Patty.

Head bowed, the hair that had fallen on either side of her face had become her veil, her curtain, her shield.

He continued pushing his food around. Keeping his eyes nowhere but on his plate, he said, "Some of the desserts up there looked pretty good."

His mother gave a short burst of exasperation, and rose from her chair. "You two take all the time you need to finish the mountains of food you took. I'll be waiting in the van."

He and Patty were both staring into their plates when he

heard from behind him the same whooshing sound of air he'd heard when they had first pulled open the restaurant's glass front door.

He finally broke the long silence between him and his sister, by saying, in the slow, goofy voice of a village idiot, "So, can I still try some of that creamy spinach?"

But when Patty looked up she was glaring at him, her eyes and face swollen and red. Furiously, she whispered, "Shut up. You just shut your mouth right now."

Then she bolted up out of her chair and stormed past him.

Staring at the white tablecloth, he heard once again, like it was the only sound anywhere in the world, the rushing air of the door as it opened into the outside world, and then closed shut again.

———

David became aware of the smell of the ocean at the same time he thought that Lincoln Way, which runs along the southern border of Golden Gate Park, had a lot more traffic on it than he wanted to be around. So he went across Lincoln and down a few blocks to Irving Street, which runs parallel to Lincoln all the way to the Great Highway. He turned right on Irving, and began the straight three-mile walk to the Pacific, to the Surf.

Somewhere behind the low and heavy gray sky, the sun was setting. In an hour the evening's dimming light would be gone altogether.

Wearing only jeans and a T-shirt had left David so cold his face felt like a sheet of ice—with a leaky faucet jutting from its middle. His nose dripping nonstop was a problem with no solution, since by then his tee had become so soaked from the roiling fog that it couldn't possibly absorb one more drop of anything. So he continuously used the back of his hand to wipe the clear, dangling goo from his nose, more to be at least momentarily free of its tickling than to enhance his appearance. How he looked was hardly the main thing on his mind just then.

He was cognizant of almost nothing beyond that he was freezing, it was nearly dark, and he was all alone on a long street of businesses, every one of which was closed for Thanksgiving.

David shot right past them all, walking fast, his long strong legs nearly chewing up the sidewalk.

Ray's Color TV & Radio Service.

Parker's Stationary and Office Supplies.

Merrill's Dance Studio: DISCO, WALTZ, CHA CHA, SWING.

The La Fuente Club.

Gifts by Harry.

Rosalie's Unisex Salon.

Galletti Bros Shoe Service.

Anchor Cafe: Breakfast All Day.

Golden Gate Photo Center. Everything Photographic.

And then, just as he was approaching a cross street, he stopped.

He was breathing hard.

He closed his eyes.

Out of nowhere, and out of everywhere, the thundering truth rolled over him.

His mother had never really come back.

She had never returned.

For two years he had waited until time had no meaning, had cried himself dry, had prayed so furiously for his mother to come home he thought he'd made God cover his ears.

Always and everywhere he looked for a sign that she had either been where he was, or would be where he was going—that, through this enigmatic message, or that coded signal, or by all of the cryptic markings that he was always seeing everywhere, his mother was attempting to reach him, to communicate with him, to tell him that she was still there, still near, still watching and loving him. Still with him. All he had to do in order to know that as a fact, instead of a hope, was to break the cipher of the communiques that he was sure she was forever sending him, and which he believed might come in the form of just about anything: graffiti on a wall; carvings in a fence, a tree, a picnic table; a piece of ribbon caught in a chain-link fence; in hand signals given by people who pretended to be paying him no mind as they drove by him in their cars.

But no matter how hard he tried, he always failed to comprehend what it was his mother was trying to tell him. So he fervently begged the sky, or trees that he found himself sitting beneath, or the spirits of birds passing overhead, to bring him a message from his mother that was just a little more obvious, a little more clear, something he could grasp, something someone even as stupid as he could understand. On countless nights his fevered desperation to know what had happened to his mom possessed him while he slept, so that he would awaken in the morning to find himself on the floor beside his bed, his body contorted into some impossible position, sore beyond moving, bleeding from the cuts and scrapes he'd received from his metal bed frame on his way down, or through hours of fitfully thrashing about on his bedroom's shag carpet. Eyes then open, he would lie there, registering all of the places he was freshly hurt, filled with the conviction that it still couldn't be, that she still couldn't *really* have simply walked out on him—or, at the very least, that she couldn't have walked out on him permanently, since that could only mean that she didn't love him.

And she did, he knew. His mother loved him very much. Of that he had no doubt.

He was her boy. Her son. Her baby. Her pumpkin. Her sweet pea. Her Charlie Brown. Her cowboy.

His mother loved him, and had not left him forever.

She would come back to him—and soon. Any day. Today. Today would be the day.

He lived and breathed that certainty, every second of every minute of every hour of every day, for two years.

And then, one afternoon, out of nowhere, the miracle that refused to happen actually happened.

"Your mother is back," his father said. "She wants to see you tomorrow afternoon."

And it was true.

She was back.

She was there again.

She was alive.

She was home.

And he had run toward her, as fast as his legs could carry him. And he had done that again. And then again, and again, and again. And yet he never seemed to draw any closer to the only thing in the world he wanted. With her purse in one hand, and a glass of wine in her other, his mother impassively watched him as he kept striving to reach her, his arms thrown open because of course she would hug him, of course she would pull him into her bosom, of course she would not keep receding away from him so that he could never reach her, never embrace her, never again know her love.

And now, all these years later, here he was, having just run toward her one more time.

And now, all these years later, here he was, no closer to her than he had been when he first stepped into her shiny new Volkswagen van.

Because she wasn't really there on that day, either.

She wasn't there the day she'd taken him and Patty to lunch.

She wasn't there any of the times that he'd slept over at her house.

She had never come back.

She had never returned to him.

———

David opened his eyes.

He was glad there was no one around to see him bent over, his hands on his knees, the dangling snot.

He straightened up. He wiped his nose.

He turned toward the sea again.

He walked again.

———

Hyde Leather and Brass Works.

Perry's Gallery and Frames Unlimited.

G. Barranza Cigar Shop.

Jade Palace Restaurant.

Ceccato Insurance.

Molly's Children's Store.

Tapes 'n' Stuff, The Auto Stereo Store.

Good Neighbor Pharmacy.

Sunset Liquors, its red blinking sign sending out the message that it was open, open, open.

When he reached the highway and the sea brooding in the darkness just beyond it, he turned right. He was two blocks from the Surf.

Getting to his room, so that he could change and clean himself up before joining his friends for the holiday, meant passing by the wooden fence outside of Jerald's. Seeing that the curtain of Jerald's sliding glass door was pulled open, he stepped across the patch of lawn, and looked through the fence slats.

The inside of Jerald's home looked like a live Norman Rockwell painting. The party had just arrived at that happily chaotic, all-hands-on-deck moment when it was time for the food to be transferred from the kitchen to the dining table. Everything was movement, anticipation, cooperation, happiness—and then, coming from the kitchen, carrying napkins and silverware and taking David's breath away, was Kate.

Facing toward him, Kate began setting the table.

A brown-skinned, dark-haired little girl in a pretty red dress ran up to her. She wanted to help. Kate smiled and seemed to ask the child a question, which she answered by holding up her little hands, fingers spread wide. Kate inspected her hands, said something merry to the beaming child, and then transferred into her helper's hands some of the flatware she was holding. Now a team, the two of them set to work.

From the direction of the kitchen Jerald appeared, carrying a casserole. He set his dish on the table and then waited for Franklin, who had followed him in, to place a gravy bowl just so beside it. With their backs to David, the pair then stood side by side, their shoulders very nearly, but not quite, touching. Kate looked up from her work, smiled, and said something to them. Franklin turned and went back into the kitchen. Jerald was stopped from following him by Brian, who came running up to tell his father something he clearly felt was important. Jerald bent to listen accordingly, and then stood and threw back his head, laughing a laugh that made it all the way outside to where David stood watching. Both Kate and her little partner stopped what they were doing to watch their delight. Jerald took hold of Brian's shoulders, and said something that made the boy clap joyfully before he spun and bolted off for the kitchen, followed by his grinning dad.

As Brian and Jerald were exiting the dining area, Erin came into it. She placed the big red bowl she was holding down on the table. A boy about Brian's age ran across the living room behind her. Entering the scene from that same room came Lillian, smiling and holding a glass of wine. She said something to Erin, who laughed. A woman who David guessed was Erin's girlfriend, Vicky, walked in from the kitchen, finding a place on the table for the foil-covered baking dish she brought with her.

Having finished their task, Kate and her able assistant, now on the side of the table closest to David, looked at one another, as if questioning how they might next be useful. They seemed to be exchanging thoughts on the matter, when the little girl suddenly, and with great affection, hugged Kate, who hugged her back, and leaned down to kiss the top of her head.

David stepped away from the fence.

He walked back over the grass.

He faced Jerald's house again.

Behind him was the crashing, infinitely indifferent ocean.

To his left was the solid darkness of Golden Gate Park, and the cliffs and tangled wildness of Lands End stretching northward along the coast.

To his right was Irving Street, and Sunset Liquors.

With the neck of his T-shirt, he dabbed at his nose.

Looking down at the ground, he then turned and headed right.

———

David walked on the wet sand closest to the pounding, hissing ocean. Through the impending complete darkness he could still just make out heaps of seaweed randomly strewn along the beach, and here and there the looming silhouette of an immense piece of contorted, otherworldly driftwood. Sand birds, nearly invisible in the blackness, scurried away, leaving behind nothing but their high-pitched squeals of protest.

He walked and he walked along the shore, and at some point

dropped to his knees and cried for his mother, who was gone forever.

In drier sand up the beach from the water, he lay down and curled himself around that infinite hollowness.

He stayed there for a while.

And then, back on his feet, he continued walking down by the shoreline.

He'd gone another mile or so along the water when, in a voice that started softly and quickly grew louder, he began raging against his mother.

And then he was screaming at the top of his lungs, as if Georgia were standing in the darkness before him.

"Why did you leave?" he roared. "What did I ever do wrong? When did I ever show you anything but love? *Never!* I *always* loved you! I *always* treated you right! You *know* that! You know I've always been good to you!"

He begged, "What is your *problem* with me, Mom? What on earth is your fucking problem with me?"

He waited for any other answer besides the sound of the ocean.

Nothing else came, of course.

He didn't know what his mother's problem with him was.

He didn't know why she had left.

He didn't even know why she had come back. She'd never told him that.

She'd never told him anything about any of it.

He knew almost nothing about her.

"How the fuck *could* I know anything?" he screamed into the darkness. "Who the fuck am I? God? Freud? What the *fuck* do I know? And even if I *did* know what makes you the bitch that you are, Mom, what good would that do me? *What would it change?*"

He stood unevenly on the sand, his hands on his knees, breathing hard.

Behind him the ocean slammed and thundered its indecipherable answers.

He stood straight again.

After a time, he resumed his walk.

He felt more clear than perhaps he ever had in his life.

His mother was the way that she was, and that's all there was to it.

That was where that story, for him anyway, had to end. That's where it *did* end. He just had to accept that fact.

He walked along silently for a long time before saying aloud, "And it's not like anyone's gonna mistake the rest of my family for the fucking Waltons."

All of his life before he moved out of his house in Cupertino had been defined by nothing so much as his father's unrelenting anger and disgust with him—and that was when the man paid him any attention at all.

If she knew she could get away with it, his sister would strangle him to death with a lei.

"Oh, and then there's my *stepmother!*" he cried. "Even the *Grimm* brothers would be like, 'We gotta dial that bitch *back*. Even *we* can't be that grim!'"

The cold, wet darkness pressed in around him like a numbing shroud.

He kept walking.

Another mile or so further down the coast, it came to him that all of the questions then roiling through his mind came down to exactly one: What, finally, was he going to *do* in response to his simply and finally accepting that his family really and truly was exactly the way he knew them to be?

Ultimately, immediately, and permanently, what was he going to do about—that is, how was he going to be able to contentedly *live* with—the absolutely indisputable fact that his mother and his sister would *much* prefer that he drop dead than otherwise, while his father would or wouldn't prefer that, depending upon how much of an inconvenience it would mean for him?

How were those horrendous core realities about his life ever going to be okay with him? How was knowing that he isn't, never was, and never would be loved by any member of his family ever going to *not* have the effect of keeping him crazy, miserable, and forever desperate for something foundationally comforting that he could simply never have?

He knew that he was broken. Now he knew that the only person in the world who was ever going to fix him was him.

But how? What was he supposed to *do*?

Through the pitch-darkness, he trudged his way back up to where the sand was as dry as the fog ever allowed it to be. He turned to face the ocean, pulled from his back pocket the pint of Jack Daniel's he'd bought at Sunset Liquors after spying on Thanksgiving at Jerald's, and sat.

He cracked open the bottle. He took a sip, waited a bit, and took another.

Then he capped the bottle, set it in the sand between his crossed legs, and wiggled his hips around till he was good and settled in. He rolled his shoulders all the way forward, pulled them back, and blocked from his mind most of his awareness of how insanely freezing he was.

He tensed every muscle in his body as hard as he could, held it, released, and then settled himself one last time.

He started breathing deeply and evenly, slowly filling and then emptying his diaphragm rather than his lungs.

A minute later he was still as a mountain.

———

Sometime later David opened his eyes.

He had his answer.

He knew what he needed to do in the face of the truth that he would never receive any love from his mother, father, or sister.

He needed to let them all go.

He needed to fully and finally emotionally detach from them, separate from them, wave goodbye to them, and never look back.

If he wanted to cease being the ball in their endless game of Kick the Youngest, all he had to do was call it a day, and walk away.

Which was exactly what they wanted him to do anyway. It wasn't like any of the three of them had ever been subtle about their desire for him to beat the quickest possible exit from their lives. He'd always just been too slow, or too naive, or just too *nice* to pick up on their constant avalanche of hints.

But now, finally, he'd gotten their message.

He took in and let loose a long and deeply felt sigh. He straightened his legs out before him.

It was over. His life with his family was over.

Not that it had ever really *begun*.

But there it was.

He thought about how there had never really been a Finch family. He, at least, had never known it to be anything but him and three assholes (or four, if he included Karen—or *five*, if he counted Dipshit Dan), none of whom seemed to like anyone else in the group more or less than they did him.

Me and Some Assholes. He decided, right then and there, that if he ever wrote his memoir, that would be its title.

He stood up stiffly, held his bottle out in a toast to the ocean, and said, "Here's to throwing your own party."

As savagely harsh as it was, it was the best sip of alcohol he'd ever tasted.

With the delight of a man newly liberated from a heavy weight he'd been carrying his whole life, David practically skipped back down to where the sand was firm and moist.

Maybe fifty steps into his arm-swinging walk along the shore-line, he stopped.

For a long time he did not move.

And then he said aloud, "Kate, too."

He sighed again.

And then again.

But he knew what he knew.

Done had to be done.

So Kate too.

He turned to face the thundering ocean.

Though it was so dark that technically it made no difference, he closed his eyes.

He imagined him and Kate hugging, hard, like they would never let each other go.

And then he let her go.

He watched her walk away from him, toward the water, and then upon the waves, ever receding, looking back at him no more.

He took two steps toward her, stopping at the very edge of the sea.

He opened his eyes.

He let the hand that was waving goodbye to her drop to his side.

On his third step back into his walk, the sand dropped out from underneath him so far that his right leg was instantly submerged up to his hip. He got out, "What the f—?" before being slammed backwards by a frigid wall of ocean.

As he went under, two things flashed through David's mind. The first was that he was sitting on his left leg the same as if he'd folded it under his butt on purpose—so it wasn't going to break. The second was that he did not want to get dragged out to sea when the wave that was now threatening to drown him receded. So when the water rushing over him slowed to a stop before beginning its flow the other way, he stiffened his body, with all of his might pushed his right foot against whatever there was of the outer wall of the hole into which he'd fallen, and tried as hard as he could to keep his back flat against every last bit of the sand beneath it.

It worked.

The water pressing down on him went away, leaving him again surrounded only by life-giving air.

Not that there was any time to revel in that. With all possible haste, David fought his way out of the sinkhole from hell, and then wildly scrambled up the beach far enough to be certain that the next wave couldn't catch him.

Once he stopped running, he found that he could not catch his breath.

Furiously gulping for air, he bent to put his hands on his knees.

Now he was coughing out ocean water through his mouth and nose.

Standing failed him, and he fell to the sand.

He rolled onto his side.

He vomited pure brine—and then did it again, and then coughed until he was sure he was going to leave at least one of his lungs right there in the sand.

It took all of his might to pull himself up onto his hands and knees. The water rained down off him.

When maintaining even that position became too much for him, he chose trying to stand over collapsing face down in the sand, and possibly never rising again.

Once standing, with his hands on his knees, he was shaking uncontrollably, and certain that if he tried standing any straighter he would pass out.

His teeth weren't just chattering, but violently banging together. This somehow made him want to at least try to stand up straight. But doing so would mean bringing the front of his freezing wet shirt, now dangling off his chest and stomach, back into full contact with his skin. And fuck that.

So while staying bent at the waist, and with his hands shaking like wild birds tethered to his wrists, he slowly reached behind him, and then started dragging his T-shirt over his head. Once it was off of him, he dropped the shirt to the sand, and then very, very slowly started moving himself into the closest thing to a standing position it was possible for him to achieve.

He was so cold that even the slightest movement felt like it had to be his last. Despite that, and vibrating like a short-circuiting robot, he felt his back pocket for his wallet, and then his front pocket for his motel key. Both were there. The bottle in his other back pocket was also there, miraculously unbroken. He pictured himself found dead the next morning, with half a busted bottle of Jack Daniel's sticking out of his frozen butt cheek.

But that wasn't happening. Too bad, he thought. At least then he'd be dead.

Okay, okay, he told himself, *I've got to move.*

Between where he was, and the hot bath and room heater waiting for him back at the Surf, he guessed there was at least three miles of ice-cold, pitch-black, fog-laden beach for him to get across.

On wildly unsteady legs, he started making his way home, this time staying up in the sand that was drier and safely away from the water, even if its mushy softness did make walking that much harder.

He had traversed all of maybe twenty feet when he realized that trying to ignore the sand and salt that were scourging his lower body generally, and his crotch in particular, was like trying to ignore his balls while dangling them in a tank full of piranhas.

"Come the fuck *on!*" he screamed—but with the kind of hoarseness perhaps only achievable through the prolonged vomiting of ocean water.

Struggling to get his violently shaking fingers to control themselves, he finally got his Levi's unbuttoned. He started to slide them down his legs.

It was only then that he realized that he had roughly the same chance of successfully removing his pants while standing up with his shoes on as he had of spontaneously combusting.

Silently muttering every curse word known to the English language, he slowly pushed his jeans down past his literally knocking knees. As carefully as he could possibly manage it, he then sat down in the sand.

Reaching over his bunched-up pants, he tried to untie his Wallabees, tried again, revived his cursing, tried yet again, made it his mission in life to hunt down the inventor of the shoelace and strangle him with a motherfucking shoelace, promised his fingers that if they ceased their spastic jittering, and got serious about untying his shoes, he would, once he got home, reward them with a pair of fur-lined, electrically warmed gloves that he would never, ever take off, and finally managed to pry his infernal shoes and socks off his feet.

After what felt like an eternity in a very cold hell, David was back on his feet, his rolled-up jeans in one hand, his T-shirt in his other. He was naked to the world, save for his paisley boxer shorts, and his shoes and socks—which, as horrible as it had been to wrestle them back onto his feet, were necessary for saving him from doing what, given his luck, he surely would, which was slice the bottom of his foot on a broken bottle, or maybe a beer can pull-tab, which would then surely bring Jaws himself flying out of the ocean at him to finish the job that his great pal, the ocean, had so inexplicably left undone.

Some twenty hobbling feet later, David stopped one more time.

Panting, he wondered if perhaps he was actually asleep back in his motel room, having the kind of dream that, once he awoke, would compel him to seek out, or, if need be, invent himself, a drug that would one-hundred percent guarantee that he would never, ever fall asleep again.

But, no. Teeth in dreams don't play the ear-splitting castanets, the way his were.

So then he got down to doing what he had halted in order to do, which was to bend over, and remove his boxers, because they, like his pants before them, had enough salt and sand embedded in them to, in very short order, give him the crotch of a Ken doll.

If only, before beginning his final disrobement, he had remembered his very recent lesson in how impossible it is to remove one's pants—boxers included—over one's wet Wallabees.

When his naked ass slammed onto the sand, David obliterated what was left of his voice.

And now he had cold, damp sand in places where he imagined his future mortician going, "Holy shit! How'd he get sand *there?*"

Having managed to wrangle off his boxers, and to then stand up again, David tried brushing the sand off his body. This brought him everything that is the opposite of relief.

He thought of wading into the water to rinse the sand away.

Then he rasped at the ocean, "Oh, you'd like that, wouldn't you?"

If the ocean cared one way or another, it didn't let on.

Feeling somehow *more* naked wearing shoes and socks than he would have felt wearing nothing at all, he shook some wet locks of hair from off his face, wiped his nose with his boxers, almost broke down in tears from the pain of the grit against the last shreds of skin left on the end of his nose, and, walking like a nude Grandpa McCoy with an advanced case of diaper rash, started forward.

He prayed that he would bump into exactly no one. Although that's literally what he would have to do in order for anyone to get a look at him. He was walking through darkness so absolute that each step only seemed to bring him to where he already was.

He imagined things he might say to anyone whom he did suddenly smack up against. Might as well be prepared.

"Me?" he said hoarsely. "Oh, I'm just having some fun seeing how minuscule my dick can get. See it? You don't? I win!"

Then he tried, "If you've got a map, go ahead and open it up. I'll just shine my full moon on it, so you can see."

Then, "Say there, friend. I don't suppose you happen to have anything you could use to kill me with, do you? Oh, you only have a can opener? Well, you know what? That'll work. You just have to get started, and then really stick with it. Would you mind?"

———

By the time he spotted the faint glow of the Surf Motel sign, David didn't care if Charlie and all three of his angels saw him naked.

So far not a single soul had seen him at all. But the chances of that lucky streak holding long enough for him to make it all the way across the freeway and into his room were not, he knew, winning.

So once he reached the beach directly across from the Surf, and while still back far enough toward the water to be hidden by the darkness, he stopped.

It took an insane amount of time, and no small amount of suffering, but eventually David was once again wearing his drenched, freezing, sand-caked clothes.

Moving like the Tin Woodsman if Dorothy had found nothing in his oilcan but sawdust, David started shuffling up the beach toward the Great Highway, toward the Surf, toward warmth, and heat, and heat, and warmth, and, he prayed to God, more heat.

———————

As he moved closer to the Surf, David saw that Thanksgiving at Jerald's house hadn't ended yet. His place was all lit up. Lillian and Erin's cars were still in the lot.

David walked a detour far around Jerald's place, and then crept his way back.

Finally, he found himself standing at the door of his room.

He already had his room key in his hand. There was no reason to think it wouldn't work. But when it did—when his doorknob gave and turned—he almost broke down crying.

He stepped inside, quickly closing the door behind him.

The perfect quietness of the room made a screaming ring that hurt his ears.

But he got over that pain real quick.

Without turning on any light, he made sure that the curtains and blinds of his window were completely shut.

Then, moving as slowly as necessary to save whatever was left of his ransacked skin, David got himself naked one more time.

Then he made his way through the darkness of his room, and into his bathroom.

He quietly closed the bathroom door. He flipped on the light.

Immediately he gasped, and covered his eyes with his hands.

Once his eyes had adjusted to the light, he lowered his hands. Then he looked at himself in the mirror of his bathroom sink.

"Motherfucker," he whispered.

He could hardly believe that he was looking at the same

person he'd looked at earlier that day in the elevator at his mother's house.

And it wasn't just because of all he had been through since then.

There was something more going on.

He looked into his own eyes, and kept looking into them, until he understood.

He didn't appear to be the same person who had gone to his mother's house for Thanksgiving that day, because he wasn't that person anymore.

An hour later David was lying face down in his bed, sleeping like one exceptionally clean corpse.

Two hours later, he was throwing off his blankets. He jumped from his bed, and then flipped on the light switch by the door.

From his scalp to his toes, he was soaking wet.

"What *is* it with me and water?" he said.

He felt his sheets and pillowcase. They were also wet.

He went into the bathroom, and dried himself off with his least soggy towel. He was rubbing his hair dry when he became so dizzy that he had to lean on the bathroom counter for support.

"What the hell?" he said to the sink.

Once the worst of his dizziness had passed, he made his unsteady way back to his bed. He sat down. After remaining motionless for a while, he became aware of the fact that he wasn't so much breathing as he was panting.

That struck him as pretty odd.

"And what's up with this *dizzy* shit?" he said. "Go home, Gillespie!" Then he imagined Dizzy Gillespie, famously bent horn in hand, begrudgingly leaving his room.

"Wait!" he said. "I was kidding! Come back! I've got salt peanuts!"

That cracked him up. "Musicians love it when you reference their songs," he said. "Dizzy didn't, apparently. But it's hard to predict the *real* artists."

His voice sounded weird to him. Then he thought that he definitely needed to lie down again. So he climbed back onto his bed, and started patting all around on the thing, searching for any place that might be drier than the rest of it.

"Come on, now," he said. "Help me out here, bed. I'd do it for you, if you'd just been mugged, as I happened to have been earlier tonight, by Neptune."

He found a strip along one side of the bed that seemed dry enough.

He had only just reclined, when he rose again, saying, "Curse you, Apollo! And also your electric minions!"

He turned off his room light. Then he got back into bed, and, before his head hit his dampened pillow, dropped into a feverish sleep, where he dreamed that no matter what he did, or how hard he tried, he could not stop himself from being helplessly dragged back out to sea.

12

DEVIL'S GRIP

EARLY THE NEXT MORNING, DAVID ROSE UNSTEADILY from his bed, flipped on his room light, and quickly sat back down again.

"Standing not good," he murmured. "I am not in good standing. With standing."

When he had a little chuckle at that, it felt like his head had exploded.

"Whoa, whoa, whoa," he winced. "Okay, something's maybe not *rotten*, but is definitely amiss in the state of me. Body check time. I'm clammy. Is that the word? *Clammy?* It probably is, since everything unpleasant is connected to the ocean. Exhibit A are the massive raw welts in every horrendously inconvenient place on my person, since I'm fresh off the worst Poseidon Adventure *ever*. I'm also definitely light-headed. Either that, or someone came into my room last night, got me high, and left. And that could only be the work of Tinker Bell's stoner cousin, the Toot Fairy."

The pain in his head cut his laughter extremely short. "Ow! Mother*fucker*! Okay, buddy, remember: laughing is out. Only tragedy from now on. Think misery, David. Doom and gloom. Speaking of gloom, let's see what's happening outside."

He parted his closed curtains just enough to peek between them. "Oh, look. So foggy you wouldn't see the sun coming to attack the earth. What a surprise." He turned his attention to the parking lot. "In other news, I see that Lillian's car is gone."

"Party's over," he said, letting the curtain fall shut. He turned to his room again, and said, "Okay, I have *got* to figure out what's going on with this bed." He started feeling all around his sheets. "Shit. These are really wet. Not just clammy, Sammy, but drenched. Not *ocean* drenched, but a lot wetter than they should be. That's not good. It means there'll be no hanging out the ole Do Not Disturb sign for me today."

He dropped into a sitting position on the bed. "Which, let's face it, is probably for the best. It's definitely time for me to get some clean towels in here—and also, now, some clean sheets and pillowcases, since these right here have been seriously suckified by my unsavory salty seepage. Because I have a fever. Or I broke a fever, or mangled a fever, or whatever the fuck. Who am I, Marcus Welby?"

He looked about his room.

"Holy cow. It's like someone locked a rabid werewolf in here. I can't let Jerald or Erin see that I've turned their beautiful room into a Dungeon of the Doomed. Domain of the Depraved. Dwelling of the Damned. Domicile of the Demented. Digs of the Deranged.

"The point is, I really need to clean this place up. Pronto, Tonto."

So, pushing through his light-headedness, David started in doing all of the things in his room that needed doing if he stood even a chance of fooling Jerald, Erin, or anyone else in the world into thinking that he wasn't the sort of person who lived the way he very obviously did.

A half hour later, now sweating profusely, David dropped into his desk chair, took out a pen and pad, and started writing.

Hi, Erin or Jerald. I hope you had a wonderful Thanksgiving. I am extremely sorry to have missed all the fun here yesterday. I was at my mother's house, having pretty much no fun at all, to be honest.

If you would just leave me some linens and towels, I would appreciate it very much. Please don't bother making my bed; I can do that. (And I'd like to! Is there any pleasure greater than folding your own hospital corners? If there is, please don't tell me about it. I can take only so much stimulation.)

Sorry about the moisture content of my sheets and pillowcases. Before you scream and run away, do rest assured that it's naught but sweat. (Not that sweat isn't fully gross. It definitely is—which is just one of the reasons why I, for one, refuse to exercise. It's the right thing to not do.)

I broke a fever last night; when I awaked (awoke? had woken?) got up this morning, sheety dampness reigned.

If you want to just leave all my linens for me to burn at a later date, please do.

Thanks again for all. You're the best. See you soon.

Leaving the note on his clutter-free desktop, along with a ten-dollar bill that he first painstakingly dried over his heating unit, David headed out of his room to go find a bite or two thousand to eat. He was famished. As he stepped back into his room to find a place for the Do Not Disturb sign he had slipped off his door-knob, he saw that his hand was shaking.

Upon returning from his Paul Bunyanesque breakfast at the Anchor Cafe: Breakfast All Day, David found his room thoroughly clean—made bed, new towels and all. His note and the money were gone.

Wonderingly looking around the place, he said, "Wow, Dorothy was right. There *is* no place like your motel room. But holy crap, it's hot in here." He crossed to his room heater, which he assumed Erin or Jerald had either left running or only recently turned off. But it didn't seem to have been turned on at all.

"That's weird," he said, peeling off his shirt.

David spent the day in his room, watching television shows he couldn't seem to track, and feeling alternately too hot, too cold, too fidgety, and too loopy. He also developed a cough that rapidly progressed to the point where it was clear to him that his lungs weren't going to be satisfied until he was wearing them draped around his neck.

By late that afternoon he was wondering if he should actually be worried about how long and hard he kept coughing, especially given the great wads of lumpy green goo he had started hacking up.

But he concluded what he always did in such matters, which is that there was nothing too much for him to worry about.

He figured that whatever was wrong with him, he'd get over it.

He always got over it.

When he awoke the next morning from a long and restless night, it took David a while to remember where he was. After sitting up in his bed too quickly, he had to wait, wincing, while his head pieced itself back together.

Before he had the chance to lie back down on his bed, he was thrown back down onto it by a cough that felt like a mule was kicking his head and chest.

When the near demolishment of his rib cage had finally ended, he groaned and rolled onto his back. But being in that position only launched him into another fit of coughing, this one so protracted and violent that it left him shaking, moaning, and once again covered in sweat.

He turned over onto his side, curled himself into a ball, and more or less passed out.

When next he opened his eyes, he didn't dare move his head, for fear that doing so would hurt like hell or trigger another coughing jag. But after mumbling, "All right, I can do this," he cautiously pushed himself into an upright position.

For a long moment he then held himself perfectly still.

"Okay, good," he said. "Victory is mine. Relatively speaking." He slowly scooted to the edge of the bed. "Good Neighbor Pharmacy, here I come." Tentatively, he stood up. "Because, as we all know, good neighbors have good drugs. And good drugs are what I need right now."

Eventually David was standing just inside his door, fully dressed, and ready to venture into the world.

"Medicine, here I come," he muttered.

The problem, though, was that, for the life of him, he could not find his room key. Which made no sense to him at all, since he *knew* the thing was on him somewhere.

"C'mon now, key, help me out here," he said, patting and burrowing his hands into what was rapidly beginning to seem like an infinite number of pockets in his clothes. "Come out, come out, wherever you are. I promise I'll buy you a ring. No, not *that* kind of ring. Key ring, not ring for key. I like you just fine—

you're a great key—but what would the courts say? Please go from lost to found now. I need drugs. Don't hold me back."

But he had exhausted all of his pockets.

It was no use. "So you've really left me," he said defeatedly.

The thought of keys finally deciding they had to run away from home made him so sad that he started crying a little.

But then he put a quick stop to that. "C'mon, Dave. This isn't King fucking Lear here. It's a room key. Get it together. You know what you need. NyQuil! That's the goal! Get that goal, son!"

Thusly roused, he resolutely pulled open his door, stepped outside, and firmly closed the door behind him. "My fate is my own!" he said.

But right away he sensed that somehow it wasn't quite.

Something was wrong. He just couldn't put his finger on what it was.

"Fuck!" he muttered. "My key." With hands that seemed to him as if they were moving in slow-motion, he searched everywhere through his pockets. When he was sure that he'd checked every last one of them at least three times, he gave up.

"I'm locked out," he said dejectedly.

He tried the doorknob, because one never knows. It was locked. "Of course it is," he mumbled.

Despite the chilly day, David felt himself rapidly growing warm—and then so warm that, for a moment, he feared that he might actually melt.

As fundamentally uncooperative—and as *yellow*—as it was being, the closed door to his room seemed to be offering him some cool relief.

So he leaned his forehead against it.

The door was cool as a cucumber.

Just what the doctor ordered, he thought.

As he was resting his head against it, David began to wonder if maybe he and the door would merge, if the atoms giving the cool, dry door its form and substance wouldn't intermingle with the atoms of his warm head, so that ultimately a phenomenon would occur that wasn't really extraordinary at all, since all things really *are* all other things, which to him at that moment meant that it was entirely feasible, if not altogether likely, that the next time he opened his eyes he would find himself standing on the other side of the door, having just passed through it. Once that happened, he would be free to continue searching for his room key, since the key might, after all, still come in handy, should he ever again care to enter or exit his door in the usual way.

David thought how almost bizarre it would be if he *didn't* slowly and smoothly pass through the door. He was sure that doing so would take nothing more from him than a little applied atomic interaction.

He decided to get serious about giving that a go.

He thought: *Matter, meet mind.*

With closed eyes, he laser-beamed all of his powers of concentration on the very singular spot where he could already feel his forehead and the door merging into one.

He slowed his breathing way, way down.

Ever so slightly he pressed his forehead forward, activating the intermingling of the door's essence with his own.

And sure enough, he felt the door starting to give way.

This was really going to happen.

It was happening.

"David?"

David's eyes popped open. It took him a moment. "Door?"

"David, are you all right?"

Keeping his forehead on the door, David rotated his head just enough to see Jerald standing beside him.

"Hi, Jerald," he said.

"What's going on, buddy?"

"I'm trying to merge with the door." He could see from Jerald's expression that right then might be an excellent time to conclude that experiment. Lifting off the door what suddenly felt to him like his shockingly heavy head, David said, "But that can wait." He then became acutely aware that carrying on a normal conversation was going to take considerably more energy than he happened to have on him at the moment.

Still, he wanted to give congenial conversing the ole college try. You just don't quit on your friends.

"How was your Thanksgiving, Jer?"

"It was great. But we missed you! You never made it over."

"I know. I'm sorry. But you know what? I sure made it *under*, if you know what I mean."

But Jerald didn't seem to.

"The ocean," David explained. "Thanksgiving night, the ocean stopped being the friendly place where Flipper freely frolics—whoa, that's a hard one to say!—and instead became a common *thug*, who attacks people like me, who are only innocently trying to say goodbye to the love of their whole entire life, who is also their soulmate."

Jerald smiled uneasily. "I'm not sure—"

"A wave hit me. I was standing on the beach, and a wave came out of nowhere, and flattened me like the wettest, most maniacal steamroller ever. I almost *drowned*. It was terrible. I'm never talking to the ocean again. Is it *hot* in here?"

Jerald looked concerned. "We're outside."

"But are you really hot?"

"I can't say that I am. But you look like you're burning up. C'mon, David. Let's get you inside your room."

"Oh," said David, suddenly doleful. "That, right there, is the dream."

"What is?"

"Going inside my room."

"I don't understand. Why can't we go in your room?"

"Because my *key* is somewhere in there. And without some righteously conscious concentration, I have to tell you that our situation here may be hopeless." He flipped himself around, put his back against the door, and started sliding downward. "Let's have a seat, okay?"

But Jerald cut that plan short by taking hold of David's arm.

"No?" said David.

"Well, maybe just not out here. Let's get you inside, okay? Erin told me that you weren't feeling well."

"*Boy*, did Erin—or you, if it was you?—clean my room. If it was you, thank you. It's weird to have a friend clean your room, but these are pretty special circumstances, aren't they? But thank you for what you did. If it was Erin, thank her. Because it was *amazing*, coming home to that. But listen, I'm okay. I was just on my way to the drugstore. They have all the stuff there."

"I'll go to the drugstore for you. Right now, let's just get you into bed, okay?"

David passively stood aside while Jerald opened his door using a key from the ring he pulled from his pocket.

"You are the key *master*," said David. "Do you ever find the responsibility overwhelming?"

Jerald chuckled. "Sometimes I do, actually."

"I'm sorry!"

"I don't *now*," said Jerald. "You know I'm always glad to see you." He pushed open the door. "Now, c'mon. You shouldn't be up."

"You're right. I probably shouldn't be the answer to Bugs Bunny's favorite question." David stepped into his room, said, "Honey! I'm home!" and then sat on the edge of his bed, the better to remove his shoes. But the rounding of his back triggered in him a sky-blackening blitzkrieg of a cough.

About halfway through his coughing jag, David found himself

trying not to topple off the bed onto the floor. But his dizziness had clearly come to win, so down he went—or would have, if Jerald hadn't intervened by trying to guide him back onto the bed. But knowing that sitting would only make his coughing worse, David, still hacking away like a drowning madman, waved Jerald off, and stood with his hands on his knees. And then his cough found a whole new intensity, so he strapped in hard, and rode the bucking bronco of his lungs until the beast threw him, kicked him, stomped on his chest, and left him with just enough strength to wish he were dead.

Gently helping to lower his friend back onto his bed, Jerald said, "My God, David. You are one sick puppy." He put his hand on David's forehead. "You're burning up. We need to get you to a doctor."

David slowly tipped over onto his side. "I don't need a doctor. Thanks, though. You're so sweet. But I just need to rest here for a while."

Jerald picked up the phone, and dialed a number. Keeping his eyes locked on David, he then said, "Hi, Kate? It's me." When David widened his eyes and started to sit up, Jerald hushed him back down. "Listen, I've got David here. He is sick as a dog. He needs to see a doctor, and I mean now. I'm stuck at the front desk, and Erin's not here. Are you free to come drive him to UCSF? You are? Wonderful. Yeah, he really needs it. I found him outside, talking to his door."

"It's not quite that simple," said David.

"Yes," said Jerald. "Just come to his room, 101. The door will be open. Okay, thanks again. See you soon." Jerald hung up the phone.

"David, Kate is coming to take you to the clinic, okay? Right now I've got to get back to the front desk. But I'll try to come back here at least one more time before she arrives."

David did his best to sit up straight. He succeeded, too, in a slumpy sort of way.

He couldn't seem to think, though. He asked Jerald, "Kate's coming here? *Again*? Is that what's happening?"

"That's what's happening."

"I saw her less when I lived with her."

"She's going to drive you to the doctor's. Now, you just wait right here for her, okay?"

"Okay," said David. "I will. Thank you. You're such a good friend. I'll wait for Kate. Which rhymes. But that's not important."

Jerald sat on the bed to give David a hug. "I'll see you soon, buddy."

Once in Jerald's arms, David started to weep.

"Oh, you poor thing," said Jerald. "You've got the fever dramas."

"No, I don't," said David in teary defensiveness. "It's *nice* to be hugged."

"Yes, it is," said Jerald. He ran his hand up and down David's arm. "Are you okay?"

"I am," said David, wiping his eyes. "Sorry. Go. I'm fine. It'll be good to see Kate. It's been so *long*."

David smiled. "All right, then. Sit tight, buddy, and we'll get you fixed up in no time."

A few moments after Jerald closed the door, David started maneuvering his way off the bed. He'd be a monkey's uncle, he thought, if he was going to let Kate see him looking like an actual monkey's uncle.

With more wobbling than he would have preferred, David made it into the bathroom. With his hands on the sink counter for support, he stared at himself in the mirror.

"Yep," he said. "That's my face."

Then he had to pull in a quick and deep breath, because another hurricane of coughing was upon him.

When the latest tsunami finally receded, David, through blurry eyes, saw so much dark phlegm in the sink it looked like the Incredible Blob had given birth in there.

Still bent at the waist, David used hot water to help all the repulsive mess make it down the drain.

Remaining in the general shape of a boomerang, he thoroughly washed his hands. The very last thing in the world he wanted to do was make Kate sick.

And then, when he went to straighten himself up, he found that he couldn't.

He waited a puzzled beat, staring helplessly at the white floor.

Next he found that he could, in fact, straighten himself up, but only if he moved as slowly as he'd ever moved in his life. So that is what he did.

And when he had achieved a vertical position, he discovered a new thing that he could not do.

Breathe.

He couldn't breathe.

His lungs weren't allowing for the intake of any air.

Instantly David calmed himself, and rather than trying to gulp in air, he attempted, as slowly and evenly as possible, to take in whatever air he could.

He found that what felt like a micro-thin strip along the very top of his lungs was still operational, and would still allow him to take in tiny, shallow breaths—which, if he did it rapidly enough, seemed to be staving off his suffocation.

Slowly putting out his hand until it came onto the counter for support, David, while being careful to remain perfectly still, breathed in and out as rapidly as he could. He could feel how pale he'd become, and how much he was sweating. He wanted to sit down, on the toilet or the side of the bathtub, but was terrified of moving.

At some point he heard Kate call his name from the other room.

He managed to wrap his fingers around an empty drinking glass near him on the counter. He lightly tapped the glass up and down on the tile.

Kate came around the corner toward the bathroom, saw him, and stopped.

Very precisely coordinating his breathing with his speaking, David whispered, "Having. Trouble. Breathing."

Kate ran to him. "C'mon," she said, carefully taking his arm.

At a snail's pace, they walked out of the bathroom, through and out of his room, and then across the parking lot to Lillian's car.

As Kate drove them to the University of California at San Francisco Medical Center, exactly two things were in David's mind: by what a very slight margin his quickened panting was keeping him alive, and how completely, utterly, and eternally he loved Kate.

When they reached the hospital admittance desk, everything started happening so fast that to David it was literally a blur. Kate didn't seem to get out anything more than, "Hello, I—" before a white-coated doctor was standing beside him, and then supporting him as he almost collapsed onto the floor.

Next he was on a gurney that was slightly inclined at the back and was speeding through a hallway until, after a sharp left turn, it stopped inside a curtained cubicle.

The doctor who'd caught him at the front desk was standing beside his gurney.

He bent to bring his face close to David's. He looked friendly.

"David," he said, "I need you to listen to me."

Still shallowly panting as fast as he could, David nodded that he was.

"You have what's called Devil's Grip. That means that your right lung has collapsed. That means that you are going to have to do something, and do it now. Are you listening to me?"

David nodded again. He definitely was.

"You *have* to breathe in, pal. You have to force air down into your lung, so that your lung opens back up. When you do that, it's gonna hurt like hell. But you have to push through the pain. If you yourself don't force air into it, your lung will stay shut. And that means you'll lose that lung, David. So you have to do this, right now. Do you understand?"

David nodded. Figuring there was no time like the present, he tried to fully inhale.

Once he realized that he hadn't quite lost consciousness, David, locking his eyes hard onto the doctor's, firmly shook his head no. There had to be some kind of mistake here. No way on earth was he simply inhaling. What he had just experienced wasn't "pain." He had slammed into something unimaginably hard, heavy, and sharp as an ax. You "pushed through" that like you pushed through a mountain of solid granite.

"Listen to me," said the doctor. "This isn't like normal breathing. This is something you're gonna have to just will your way through. It's going to hurt more than anything you've ever felt before. Medically, we know it's one of the worst pains a person can feel. But you have to do it anyway. Do you hear me? You have to. You've got about one minute to fill your lung with air before it seals itself shut. You do not want that to happen. You've got to save yourself here, David. You've got to breathe in hard, all the way, and you've got to do it right now. Okay?"

As he nodded yes, David's eyes filled with tears at how honest the doctor was being with him, at how deeply he clearly wanted him to be all right.

"Okay, my man. Get this done. I'll see ya on the other side."

The doctor stepped around the curtain, leaving David alone.

At first David tried to finesse the inhale. Maybe the doctor was wrong, and by exercising all possible control he could pull air into his lungs evenly, gradually, naturally.

He held short one of his mini-breaths, and began his slower, deeper inhalation.

Instantly he felt the same explosive pain he felt the last time he tried that. It felt like his lungs had been slammed between two massive plates of iron.

And now he had less than one minute.

And no thought could help him now, so he hurled his shoulders back and threw his chest out and opened his mouth as wide as possible so that he could all at once pull in all of the oxygen in the world.

What happened after that would forever remain a blank for him.

———

It was the middle of that night when David groggily regained consciousness.

He was in a hospital bed with, he managed to make out, an intravenous tube plugged into the top of his right hand.

His was the only bed in his room.

The relief that washed over him when he realized that he was breathing normally caused him to let out one quick and deep sob.

———

Later that morning, David awoke to find Kate watching him from a visitor's chair near the foot of his bed.

"Hey," he said hoarsely. "It's you."

Kate rose and came to the side of his bed. She looked worried. "How are you feeling?"

"Good. How long have you been here?"

"Not long. Visiting hours just started."

"It's so nice of you to be here."

"Of course I'm here. I've been worried about you. Hearing how you had to do that inhalation was just—" She looked down at her hands for a long moment before meeting his eyes again. "How was that?"

He gave a slight shrug. "I don't really know. I think I blacked out. But apparently I did it. So that was good."

"The doctor told me they gave you a bunch of antibiotics throughout the night, because you had a huge infection in your lungs."

"I did? That's what it was?"

"Well, technically, I guess it's called Devil's Grip."

David smiled. "I know. I couldn't believe it. I was like, but of *course* that's what it's called."

Concernedly, Kate asked, "What happened to you Thanksgiving night? Jerald said something about your almost drowning in the ocean?"

"No. I mean, sort of. I got hit by a wave. But I was okay."

"Did you go to your mom's for Thanksgiving?"

"Yeah." He looked down at the faded little blue flowers on his hospital gown. "I didn't stay at her place for too long."

"How was seeing her?"

"Well, let's just say that you knew my mom better after two visits with her than I've ever known her."

Tenderly, Kate asked, "What happened?"

"I mean, I wasn't comfortable at her house, to say the

least. It was just bad, basically. So I left there and walked home. I ended up out on the beach across from Jerald's. I was thinking about a lot of things. I was just walking along, and went pretty far, actually, sort of living through everything I was thinking about, and it was so dark that I couldn't see a foot in front of me, and the next thing I know I've stepped into this big *hole* in the sand, right down by the water, and then this *wave* comes out of nowhere, and just flattens me. Thing almost did drown me, to tell you the truth. And after that I walked home."

"You must have been *freezing* out there. No wonder you got sick. What time did this happen?"

"I dunno. Pretty late."

"How late? Were we still at Jerald's when you got back?"

"Yeah."

Kate looked concerned. "Why didn't you come over?"

"I would have. I *should* have. I'm sorry I didn't. It's just that by the time I got back there, I was so soaked—and so, so miserable. All I could think of was taking a hot bath. So I did that, and afterward just sort of passed out in my room."

As she stared him in the eye, Kate seemed to want to say something. David waited to hear whatever it was. But then she gazed down at her hands, looked back up at him, and said, "They're releasing you today."

"They are? For sure?"

"That's what they told me. At two o'clock. Do you feel well enough for that?"

David nodded. "I guess so. I'll just have to take some antibiotics for a week or so, right?"

"For ten days."

"Sounds doable. What's the matter?"

"I'm a little bit concerned that the reason they're releasing you so soon is because you don't have insurance."

"Well, if the problem is an infection, and I've got antibiotics for it, that seems okay. Right?"

"I'm worried that it wasn't just an infection. You were *really* sick, David. I was with you when you checked in. They didn't even find out if you *had* insurance before they wheeled you back. Do you know how sick you have to be—how *scared* they have to be—for them to start treating you before they know if you have insurance?"

"Maybe if they beat *Devil's Grip*, they get to bill God directly."

Kate caught a sudden sob that almost escaped from deep in her chest. "I thought you were dying."

"I know. I wasn't."

"You were. I saw the face of the doctor and the nurse when they rushed you back. And I saw how they looked at each other, too. *They* thought you were dying."

David took her hand. "I'm okay," he said.

"Listen to me, David. You need to tell me if you really feel well enough to go home today. Because if you don't, I'm going to make them keep you here. Okay?"

"Okay. I really feel good enough to go home. I can tell the antibiotics have worked great. If I'm going home with the same stuff they've given me here, I'm all set."

Kate slipped her hand from his. "And how's your breathing? How do your lungs feel?"

"Amazing, to tell you the truth. Look." David took a slow, deep breath. Too deep, as it turned out; he launched into a raucous coughing fit.

When his coughing was over, and he'd fallen back upon his pillows, he found Kate looking at him gravely. "Book me here for a week," he said.

"Okay," she said seriously.

"No. I'm kidding. Kate, I'm fine. I still have some congestion in my chest, of course. But that's all it is. I promise you, I wouldn't go home today if I didn't feel one hundred percent up to it."

She kept her eyes on his for as long as it took her to know that he was telling the truth.

"Okay," she said. "I'll be here at two o'clock to pick you up."

"No, please don't. You don't have to come take me home. You've done more than enough for me already. You saved my life, Kate. Believe me, that's enough. I'm happy to take a cab home. It's not like that takes any effort. You sit; they drive. Easy-peasy."

She turned and walked back to her chair. She lifted her purse, slung it over her shoulder, and in a voice that David knew signaled the end of all debate, said, "I'm coming back at two to pick you up. Try not to *drown* or anything between now and then. Okay?"

"Oh, like it's so *easy* to avoid drowning," said David.

"You know, for most people it is."

"I'm not most people."

"Gee, there's a news flash. I'll see ya at two."

13

THE OTHER SIDE

IN HIS MOTEL ROOM LATER THAT AFTERNOON, DAVID was reclining on his bed, pillows behind his back, watching Kate as she straightened up his room.

"This is a serious *When Worlds Collide* moment for me," he said.

Kate stopped folding one of his white T-shirts to look at him. "Whaddaya mean?"

"You. In my room. It's too weird. It's like pushing a shopping cart around K-Mart, and suddenly bumping into the Queen of England. If the queen was a super fox, that is."

"Are you insinuating that the queen—*my* queen—isn't super foxy?"

"No! She is. In a cold, unattainable, supreme ruler kind of way. But enough about my mom."

If Kate thought that was a funny joke, she gave no indication of it. She only placed his T-shirt atop the short stack of the others she had folded, and tucked them all into his dresser drawer. Then she came over to his bed.

"How are you feeling? Do you need another pillow behind your back?"

"No, I'm comfortable. Thank you."

"Okay." She went back to ordering the wads of clothes in his dresser.

"And thank you for not taking one of these pillows when you had the chance to, and suffocating me with it," he said. "It's not like I could have fought back. And no judge who knew our story would find you guilty."

"Guilty? I'd be named Citizen of the Year."

When David was done with the coughing fit that cut short his laughter, he said, "Oh, man. Didn't you used to be *nice?*"

But Kate, who had come to stand beside him while he coughed, looked worried. "Are you all right?"

"Oh, yeah. I am. I think laughing's good for me. It helps clear some shit out, grossly enough. So you just keep right on being Henny Youngman."

"Are you sure you're okay? You look a little pale."

"I'm fine. Really. It's nothing."

When she placed her hand on his forehead to check his temperature, David had to exert considerable internal effort to stop himself from unreservedly swooning.

"You feel warm," said Kate.

"Do I? I feel okay."

"Are you hungry?"

"Am I ever not?"

"I'm gonna go to the drugstore and pick up your prescription. I'll also stop off at the grocery store, and get you some food. Is there anything you'd like to eat or drink? Any snacks, or anything like that you can think of?"

"No, nothing. I'm fine. Kate, you don't have to do any of that stuff. I've got enough food to last until I can go to the store myself—or I can take a cab to the store, or Jerald can pick me up whatever I need. And I can get my own prescription. It's not that far a walk. You don't have to do any of this for me, okay?"

But Kate's expression made it clear that he was succeeding only in exasperating her. "Is there anything special you want from the store?"

"Okay, fine. Be that way. And since you're apparently insisting, as it happens there *is* something I'm craving. A Yoo-hoo."

"A what?"

"A Yoo-hoo. They're kind of like chocolate milk—but aren't, somehow. They come in bottles, and have a yellow label?"

"Oh, right. Yoo-hoo."

"I'd love one of those."

"Okay. Anything else?"

"That's it. Just a Yoo-hoo, you."

In short order Kate had her purse on her shoulder, her car keys in her hand, and was placing a piece of paper on his nightstand, right beside his phone.

"This is a list of all the phone numbers you might need. I wrote down the number for the doctor who was in charge of you, my work number, Lillian's home number, Erin's home number, and Jerald's number. I don't know your mom's number, so I didn't add that. But you might want to."

"I don't."

"Promise me you won't lose this list."

"Promise."

"Good. I'll be back in an hour or so. You stay right here and rest, okay? I can tell you're not feeling well. You're talking slow, like you do when you've got a fever. So don't go running around outside, or whatever. You're fighting a serious infection. You need to take it easy."

"I will. Man, I wish *you* were my mom."

Kate stared at him for a beat. "Since you're sick, I'm gonna let that go."

"Please do."

"I'll be back soon."

The moment Kate pulled the door shut, David closed his eyes, and let his head fall back onto his pillows.

"Oh, Lord, *please* make her fall in love with me again," he murmured. Then he opened his eyes. "Okay, fine. There's only so much you can do, miracle-wise. I get it. Well, could you at least keep me from saying things that would creep out Norman Bates? I would *really* appreciate that, God. Thank you."

When Kate returned to his room some time later, she was carrying two brown paper Safeway bags filled with groceries. David saw a couple of red and white Kentucky Fried Chicken sacks protruding from the top of one of the bags.

"Oh my God! You brought me groceries *and* KFC? "How have you never won some kind of major humanitarian award?"

"I wake up every morning asking myself the same question."

"That stuff's all rigged, man. *Boy*, that smells good."

"I figured you might want something warm to eat." Having set the grocery bags down on the counter, Kate handed David one of the KFC bags.

"You're right about warm food," he said. "Plus, fried chicken in bed! This is *so* worth having almost croaked for." He opened the sack, and jammed his whole face into its top. "Macaroni and cheese!" he called to the deliciously wafting food below. "And coleslaw!" He brought his face back out into reality. "Thank you, thank you, thank you, Kate."

"You're welcome."

"You're gonna eat with me, right?"

"Yeah, lemme put away this stuff first."

David scrunched closed the top of his sack, and watched as

Kate unpacked and put away all the food she'd brought him: milk, two boxes of breakfast cereal, peanut butter, jam, a loaf of bread, muffins, cream cheese, cheddar cheese, chips, yogurts, bottled juices, canned sardines, tuna, salami, and crackers. And also a big bunch of green grapes.

"Grapes!" he said. "My favorite!"

She held up a bag of pistachios. "I also got you these."

"My favorite nuts that I'm not attached to!"

"Oh, God, you *are* feeling better," said Kate.

"And you got me two packs of Yoo-hoo! That is *eight* Yoo-hoos! You know what this means, don't you, Kate?"

"What?"

"It means that, right now, Florence Nightingale is looking down at you from heaven, and thinking, 'Why, the *nerve* of that missy! Who does she think she is—*me*?'"

Kate laughed. "I've got another bag in the car. Be right back."

She returned with another grocery bag, this one filled with everything a person could want to take with them on a picnic: disposable plates, cups, bowls, dining utensils, and so on.

"My gosh," said David. "You are nothing if not thorough."

"Can't eat with your hands. Well, *you* can. But you shouldn't."

As she unpacked all of his new supplies, he said, "Are you sure about that? Because in many cultures, you know, eating with your hands isn't just proper, it's mandatory. They say that visitors to such lands really, really miss soup. But that's travel for you. When I'm crazy hungry, like I am right now, I take it one step further. I eat with both my feet."

"Because . . . ?"

"Because it's four times faster! I've done it before. Yes, the other people at the table were disgusted. But I'd finished my whole meal by the time they were done unfolding their napkins. Losers."

"Well, however you're gonna eat, please start without me. I'll join you in just a sec." David watched as she folded up the three now-empty grocery bags, and then slipped them into the narrow space between the fridge and the wall of its enclosure. "In case you need these for anything," she said.

"Have you ever considered becoming an in-home healthcare provider? I will hire you for that job right now. The pay is all the fried chicken that's left over once I've attacked all of it with my face. I will also let you choose what we watch on TV, for up to one full hour a day. When can you start?"

Ignoring him, Kate opened her purse, and pulled out a plain little white bag, out of which she took an orange pill bottle.

"Here are your antibiotics," she said. "Take one of these every six hours, just like it says on the label. The pharmacist said to be *sure* to take these on a full stomach. If you don't, it's gonna upset your stomach. Now, I'm putting these *right here* on the night-stand, okay?"

"Okay. Thank you. You're amazing."

"You take one of these every six hours."

"Got it."

"On a full stomach."

"Let's get me one of those right now. It's chow time, yes?"

"Yes," said Kate. Grabbing her own bag of KFC, she sat down at David's desk.

Pulling the food and napkins out of his bag, David said, "You wanna watch TV? It's almost time for one of the greatest shows in the history of staring at a box."

"What show?"

"*Walt Disney's Wonderful World of Color.*"

"No, thanks."

"Are you sure? Tonight's showing is part two of *The Love Bug*. Which is set right here in San Francisco."

Digging a fork into her coleslaw, Kate said, "No, thanks."

"How can you say no to a movie about a quirky speedster Volkswagen named Herbie, who has a mind of his own, and also some deeply disturbing psychological problems?"

"Herbie had psychological problems?"

David had to wait till he swallowed to answer. "Are you kidding me? He almost committed suicide."

"I don't remember that."

"You blocked it out of your mind because it was so traumatic. When he thinks Dean Jones has abandoned him, ol' Herb takes off on a psychotic rampage through Chinatown. He plows *right* through a Chinese New Year's parade—and *then* attempts to jump off the Golden Gate Bridge. How psycho is that?"

"Oh, that's right! I forgot about that part."

"I wish I could. I still wake up screaming sometimes."

"It's probably best we don't watch it, then."

"I think you're right. Life's traumatic enough without inviting into your brain the same people who basically made a snuff film of Bambi's mom."

"And Old Yeller."

"And Old Yeller!"

"Disney's the worst," said Kate.

"It really *is*," said David. "How have I never before realized that something that I thought was really nurturing and great for me as a kid, was actually—oh, that's right. I was raised by Cruella."

"That would do it," said Kate.

Having cleaned up after their meal, Kate stood looking down at David, her hands on her hips. "Are you okay?" she asked.

"I am. A little tired, but fine."

"Okay. I'm gonna go now. You get some sleep. Don't forget you've got these numbers right here by your phone."

"I won't."

"And don't forget to take your pill tomorrow morning *after* you've eaten breakfast."

"Eat pill for breakfast. Got it."

"Stop it. I'm serious. You're just gonna stay here and take it easy, right? You're not gonna go walking around the beach in the middle of the night, or anything extremely stupid like that. Right?"

"You can count on that. I'm never going to the beach again. The ocean is clearly a demonic nutjob who can't be trusted. But the point is, I'll stay right here. I've got the TV, my medicine, and, thanks to you, so much food that, right after you leave, I'm gonna turn this room into a 7-Eleven. The next time you see me, I'll be a fat, successful businessman with bedsores because he never gets out of bed."

"That sounds perfect. Now tomorrow, during the day, Jerald and Erin will stop by to check up on you, and tomorrow night after work I'll come by and do the same. If you want me to bring anything with me when I come, call me at work and let me know. Promise you'll do that?"

"Promise."

"How's your temperature? Do you feel warm at all?"

"Not too much, no."

"Let me check." She laid her palm against David's forehead, and then softly pressed the back of her hand to his cheek. "You feel okay. So, okay, I'm gonna go. I'll see you tomorrow night."

David stared at his door for a long time after Kate closed it. He listened to her walking through the lot, and then getting into her car. He heard her car door slam shut, and then the engine start. He heard her car back up, shift gears, and then slowly head out of the parking lot. She turned right on the highway, and then was gone, back to Lillian's and her job and her new friends and the whole rich life of hers that had nothing whatsoever to do with him.

It's unlikely that there was a record for how much time one person had ever spent looking at the inside of a closed door. But if such a record did exist, David broke it that night.

The next night, David prepared himself for Kate's visit like the two of them were going on a date. By the time she knocked on his door, he was sitting up against his headboard, atop his perfectly made bed, feeling nearly as groomed as James Bond. He was even wearing a clean button-down shirt, even if it was so wrinkled it looked like a major origami experiment gone catastrophically wrong.

"Come in!" he called in a voice disastrously close to Minnie Mouse's. "Jesus," he murmured to himself.

And sure enough, in came Kate.

There she was.

Right there in his room again. Looking bright-eyed, well-dressed, and unmistakably happy.

"Hey, there," he said, inexplicably channeling Li'l Abner. Telling himself to calm down, he nailed his landing in the non-crazy-sounding zone with his, "How are you?"

"Good," said Kate, closing the door behind her. "How are *you*?"

"Good. Better."

She dropped her purse onto his desk chair. "You're really feeling better?"

"I really am."

"Did you take your pills?"

"On the clock."

"And always after you'd eaten?"

"There was no time today when I *hadn't* just eaten. So, yes."

"Good," she said. "Speaking of eating." She held up the big Taco Bell bag she'd come in with. "You hungry?"

"Taco Bell!" said David. "Yes, I am starving. Seriously. It's been absolute *minutes* since I ate."

"Cool," she said.

As she was unwrapping their food, and putting it on the paper plates she found where she'd left them the day before, Kate said, "I swung by the pharmacy, and got you a thermometer and some aspirin." She stopped what she was doing and went back to her purse, from which she lifted a small paper bag. "I don't know how I forgot to buy you these yesterday. You need to know what your temperature is—and if it gets even slightly high, you need to take two or three aspirin right away to lower it. I'm putting these right here next to your medicine. Take your temperature tomorrow at least a couple of times over the course of the day. Okay?"

"Okay."

"Do you promise you will?"

"I promise. And thank you. *So* much."

This time Kate sat cross-legged on the bed with him as they ate. "Did Jerald or Erin come over today?"

"They both did. Erin brought me some new towels and washcloths. And then Jerald came by around two."

"How was your time with him?"

"Great, like always. Your plan for them really *worked*, Kate. Paula's gone for the next month. It's so great for Jerald not to have to worry for that whole time about her suddenly appearing at his place. And having Brian with him all the way till Christmas puts him in heaven."

"He and Franklin seemed really happy at Thanksgiving," said Kate. She then looked at David curiously. "What is it?"

"Oh, nothing."

"Tell me."

"No, it's stupid. It's just that—well, I saw them."

"Saw who?"

"Jerald and Franklin."

"When?"

"On Thanksgiving. Right before you all ate dinner."

"How did you see that?"

"In the same way any wino Peeping Tom would."

"What are you talking about? What happened?"

David related how he'd watched a few minutes of her Thanksgiving night through Jerald's fence.

"Why didn't you come inside?" Kate asked. "Why'd you go to the beach instead?"

"I don't know. I should have come in. I wanted to. But, well, let's just say I wasn't in a very happy place just then."

Kate's voice got soft. "What happened at your mother's house?"

"Oh, it was just—it was nothing."

"C'mon. Tell me."

"Are you sure?"

"Of course I'm sure."

"Okay."

———

Right after revisiting the part of his story about his mom's intimation to her friends that he was a dangerous threat, David

EVERYWHERE SHE'S NOT   269

stopped for a moment. Then he said, "I don't understand why she would tell such a vicious lie about me. Do you?"

"I think I might, yeah."

"Really? Tell me, please. Because that is a complete mystery to me."

"I think it's because your mom is an actual, clinical narcissist. And, like all narcissists, she *must* have everyone believe that she's perfect. And there are only two people in the world who know what bullshit that is."

"Who?"

"You and Patty."

"Why us?"

"Because you two know what she did. David, she *abandoned* her children. She walked out on you two, without any explanation at all. That's about as far from being perfect as you can get. It's the total opposite of having your shit together. Do you think she wants the crowd *she* hangs out with to know she did that?"

"I don't think they'd think it was all that big a deal."

"*Everybody* would think it's a huge deal, David. *Nobody* would be okay with that. It's such a heartless thing to do, that it makes her a freak. That's a real problem for her. And that makes *you* a real problem for her, because you're a witness to who she really is. There's no *way* she can have you at her big Thanksgiving dinner, with all of her enlightened highbrow friends."

"But she *invited* me there."

"Yeah, when you were in Long Beach. When there was no way you were going to actually show up there."

"Oh. Right."

"But suddenly you were in the city, calling her all the time. And then you really *were* coming to her party. That didn't leave her a lot of choices."

For a long and silent while, David experienced the truth of

Kate's words, which explained so much that had always been a mystery to him.

Finally, he said, "She was never going to choose me or Patty over what she needed people to think about her, was she?"

Kate said softly, "No, I don't think she was."

David thought some more. "And she never will, will she?"

"Probably not."

"Well—shit," David murmured.

After some silence, Kate said, "Are you all right?"

Talking brought David back to something a lot closer to the moment at hand. "Yeah. Yes. I am. I mean—yeah." Looking into Kate's eyes, and feeling almost detached from his body, he spoke slowly. "You know, when I was out on the beach on Thanksgiving night, one of the big things I thought was that I'll never know why my mom has always treated me as coldly as she has ever since she came back. And now I do know why. That's so huge. And the reason I know that now is because of you. So—thank you. So much. I know one thing I'll *never* know is where you get your gift for figuring things like this out."

"It's always easier to see that stuff in someone else's life."

"I guess." There was another long pause, during which David mainly looked down at the bedspread. Then, looking back up at Kate, he said, "Okay, so the bottom line here—as far as I'm concerned, as far as her relationship with *me* goes—is that my mom is, and is apparently always going to be, just an ungodly bitch."

"I hate to say it, but I think it's true."

"I *like* to say it because it's true." Quickly gathering together a couple of empty burrito wrappers, he pressed them into a tight ball. "You know what the last thing she said to me was—on *Thanksgiving*?"

"What?"

"She told me that two weeks ago, my dad had a massive heart attack."

"*What?* Is he okay?"

"Apparently he is. I guess he's back at home now, recuperating."

"When did—? I don't understand."

"Neither did I."

"Why didn't anyone call you?"

"You tell me—oh, that's right, you *have* told me. I mean, I get why my dad or Karen couldn't call me: I haven't contacted them since I got here, so they don't know how to reach me. But for the whole two weeks that I was here, and leaving messages for my mom, she *knew* it had happened. My dad called her while he was still in the hospital. I'm calling her, she *knows* that he's had a heart attack, and she just doesn't return my calls."

"Oh, David. I'm so sorry. Have you called your father?"

"No. I thought I would today, but for some reason I couldn't bring myself to do it. It's so stupid. I should have called him. I'll definitely call him tomorrow."

"Are you okay?"

David nodded. "Yeah. Of course. I've got my pills. I've got all the wonderful food you brought me. You're still talking to me. Jerald and Erin came by today. And, perhaps most wonderfully, I went the whole day without *once* getting almost drowned by the ocean. So I'm super-okay."

Kate's smile was all sadness and compassion. "You're going to call your father tomorrow?"

"Yeah, I will."

"You don't have to, you know."

"I know. And I really appreciate you saying that. But the last time I saw him, after I returned the car to those guys, he was pretty good to me."

"Was he really?"

"He was. It was pretty weird. He gave me, like, *dad* advice. It was actually pretty solid stuff. I liked it. It actually helped me. But I was also, like, 'Who the fuck *are* you, and what did you do with my father?' Maybe his regret over having been nice to me is why he had a heart attack."

"What kind of advice did he give you?"

David hesitated just a moment before doing his best to gracefully steer around that open manhole. "Oh, nothing. Just, you know, general stuff."

"You don't want to talk about it?"

"Nah. I mean, you know, maybe not tonight."

After looking at him curiously for a moment, Kate said, "Okay. Well, see how you feel tomorrow about calling him. *Mostly* just keep taking it easy, though. Okay? Don't stress yourself at all. And do *not* stop taking your antibiotics."

"I won't. I know you're not supposed to do that."

"You're *really* not supposed to do that."

"I know you're not. And I won't. Promise."

"Good." Kate got off the bed. "If you're okay, then I'm gonna go now. I'll come by here again tomorrow after work, just to check in with you. I'll bring us something to eat again."

"Thank you, Kate. Seriously, man. I don't know how to thank you for—for everything."

"You don't have to thank me," said Kate.

"No, I do," said David. "I'm really—" And then he knew enough to say nothing more.

"I'll see you tomorrow night," said Kate.

———

The following night, Kate found David in a pensive but distracted mood. After an assessment of his health, some general small talk, and a dinner courtesy of McDonald's, she asked him, "What's going on with you tonight?"

"I'm sorry. I know I'm being weird. It's just—I called my dad today."

"How'd that go?"

David took a deep breath. "Well, he told me that he knew where my mom was the whole time she was gone."

"*What*? Are you kidding? Where *was* she?"

"The same place she was when she came back: living in San Jose with Dr. Dan. She was being his muse, or whatever, while he wrote his big best-selling book. The entire time that I had no idea where she was, she was only, like, twelve miles away."

"This is unbelievable."

David nodded. "I've spent the whole day—and may spend my whole life—not believing it."

"Did your dad say why he didn't tell you where she was?"

"He said it was because he thought that it would be less painful for me to think that my mom had just disappeared, than it would be for me to know that she was nearby, but just didn't want to see me."

Kate was silent for a while.

"Wow," she said.

"I know."

"So—how do you feel?"

"Honestly? Shocked. One thing is that it ended up making me feel sorry for my dad. I don't think he made the right decision; I think I'd have rather known where my mom was. But he made the call that he thought was best. And, either way, it couldn't have been an easy choice for him to make."

"Yeah, you're right. He was in a really awful position."

"He was. I was thinking about my dad today—about him lying on his bed in his house in Sherman Oaks, recuperating from his heart attack, the same as he was after his heart attack back in Cupertino. When that first heart attack happened, I had no idea how to take care of him when he came back from the hospital. Not that I was *supposed* to take care of him or anything. I was ten."

"How long had your mom been gone?"

"A month. Maybe two, at most. But, you know, *he* was back, and that was still basically blowing my mind. I remember looking into his bedroom, and seeing him in there, lying on his bed, and feeling so unbelievably helpless. I couldn't think of *anything* I could do to make him feel one bit better. It was the worst feeling."

"That is the worst feeling," said Kate. "As you know, my mom was so out of it. And there was never anything I could do about it. I couldn't fix her. I couldn't heal her. No matter what I did, or how hard I tried, I couldn't make her better. I thought that if I could make her happy, or something, she would stop drinking. But I could never seem to make her happy at all, much less happy enough to quit drinking. And, just like you said, all I ever really felt was helpless. Helpless and overwhelmed." She looked down at her lap, and began smoothing her long skirt. "And so now, I'm sort of, I don't know—a compulsive caretaker. As you may have noticed."

"Well, that's definitely been to my benefit. But you're not compulsive about it. You're not compulsive about anything." He said what he said next before he could stop himself. "You're perfect."

Quickly looking back up at him, Kate said curtly, "No, I'm not."

"Yes, you are." And then David's horses knocked down their gate, and started trotting in the open field. "Kate, look, I know this is the kind of thing I'm not supposed to say, so that it won't seem like I'm trying to win you back or anything. But let's just chalk this up to a fever, okay?"

"No, David—"

"Yes. I'm sorry, but yes. I don't know how *not* to say this to you—and it's really not that big a thing *to* say. But the fact of the matter is that I think you're perfect. I think that, because you *are* perfect. If nothing else good ever happens to you in your life, you can always know that at least one person in this world thinks about you the way every person wants *someone* to think about them, which is that they are absolutely, one hundred percent perfect. Not crazy, Georgia-style perfect, obviously; I'm talking about actually, truly perfect. I thought you were perfect the moment I met you, and I've felt that way every day since. I haven't *done* well with the fact that I feel that way about you, to say the least. But I do feel that way about you. I always have. I always will."

Kate had kept her head down the whole time David was talking. Now she looked up at him. "That's not anything I want to hear, David. How is it good for me that you think I'm perfect? Because I'm *not* perfect. No one is. And your thinking I'm perfect only means that you care more about your *idea* of who I am, than you do about who I really am. That doesn't do a thing for me. It only makes me feel really lonely. I don't need someone who thinks I'm perfect. I need someone who loves the things about me that *aren't* perfect. We're supposed to be *friends*, David. A friend isn't someone who can't or won't see you for who you really are."

Now it was David's turn to fall silent.

"You know I'm still your friend," he said. "I hope you know that, anyway."

"Well, then don't tell me I'm perfect. Just don't ever say that to me."

"I'm sorry. I just meant—well, honestly, what I wanted to most essentially communicate to you is that I think you are really, really *keen*."

She laughed a bit. "That's a little more like it."

"I do know what you mean. I heard you. I'm not trying to superimpose over you anything that hides or denies who you are."

"Okay. Good."

"We're okay?"

"We're okay."

"Are you coming back here tomorrow night?"

"I don't know. I want you to have something warm to eat. But I may have something else going on tomorrow night. If I do come, I'll probably just swing by with some food, and be on my way."

And then the horses of David's that had begun trotting started to gallop—and pretty wildly.

"Don't, Kate. Don't just swing by. Come here, and then don't leave. Ever. Look at this room. It's so nice. There's a parking lot right outside the door. You park, you walk right in, you're here. All the plumbing in the bathroom works. There's a TV! That's not a walk-in closet, but you could go in there and *lean* pretty well. There's a liquor store *right up the street*. I'm not proud of this, but I practically already have a line of credit there. And they sell *food* there, too—if you're not too picky, and consider preservatives a food group. And the rent here is basically the same as an apartment."

"Stop it, David."

But it was too late. The stampede was on.

"Listen, I made a crazy, *crazy* mistake leaving you, and it's been torturing me ever since. I know I blew it, absolutely. But isn't there any way that you can imagine letting me *un*blow it? Letting me fix it?"

He stopped—and then started again, much slower this time. "Is there just no way for you and I to maybe get back together again? I love you so, so much."

"David, no. Okay? No. What you're asking isn't fair. It's not right. It's great that you love me, I guess. But I don't trust you. I *can't* trust you. How can I? You don't even know why you broke up with me. So why would I think that you wouldn't break up with me again? I'd have to be an idiot to put myself back in that position."

David looked down at his lap.

Every one of her words was like a lightning bolt striking dead one more of his running horses.

Now it was just silence.

Which it was clearly up to him to break.

He looked up at her, and just trusted that whatever came out of his mouth wouldn't be too bad.

He said, "You did hear the part, didn't you, about my having a line of credit at the liquor store?"

Kate reached for an empty cheeseburger wrapper, balled it up, and threw it at him. David caught it in midair, and threw it back at her.

He missed her by a mile.

All throughout the next day, David tried to ignore his jittery anguish over having strapped on his idiot wings the night before, and flown much too close to the sun of Kate. But the more he tried to tell himself that everything was still copacetic between them, the more anxiously he seemed to find himself watching the clock, and wondering if she would or wouldn't come by that night.

At just after six o'clock that night there was a knock on his door—and after calling from his bed, "Come on in!" David had his answer.

278 N. JOHN SHORE, JR.

"Jerald!" he said. "It's good to see you. Except I'm sad to see you."

Closing the door behind him, Jerald said, "Was it something I said?"

"No. It's someone you're not. Which is Kate."

"Well, you certainly have me there. I am not beautiful Kate."

"I see that you *are*, however, bearing a plate with an extremely delicious-looking sandwich on it. If that sandwich is for me, then you are officially forgiven for not being Kate. If it's not for me, then you officially have a talent for torturing people, and should immediately apply for a job at the CIA."

"Ha!" said Jerald. Handing David the plate, he said, "Kate called me about a half hour ago to say she wasn't coming by tonight. She asked me to look in on you, and to feed you. And *voila:* me, with a ham and swiss on rye."

"Oh my gosh, you did not have to do this. This is so monumentally kind of you. Thank you."

"Don't be silly. I wanted to come by anyway, and see how you're doing."

"I feel all better. I still have to finish the antibiotics, but that's about it. Hey, wanna Yoo-hoo? Or anything else you see on the table there, or find in the fridge? Help yourself, of course."

"You have so much food! I love it."

"Did Kate say anything else?"

Jerald looked around the room real quick. "About what?"

"About why she didn't come over tonight."

"I'm sorry—what?"

David looked at Jerald suspiciously. "Did Kate say anything about why she didn't come over here tonight?"

Jerald started to sit on the edge of the desk, but then stood up straight again. Brushing nothing that David could see off the front of his pants, he said, "No, I don't think she said anything about that."

"Oh, c'mon. If you were Pinocchio, your nose would have just jabbed out my eye."

"I really don't remember if she said anything else."

"You do."

"I don't."

"You do."

"It's *possible* that she said something about going to see Al Jarreau tonight."

"Al Jarreau? *Tonight?*"

"Yes."

"Kate *loves* Al Jarreau."

"I know she does. I'm sorry."

"Who's she going with?"

Jerald busied himself trying to open a bottle of Yoo-hoo. "I'm sorry—what did you say?"

"If you want to be a real boy, Jerald, you have to tell the truth. Who is Kate going with to see Al Jarreau?"

"Oh, that." Jerald took a sip of his Yoo-hoo. "It's just some guy she used to know. He teaches photography at State."

David felt his insides freeze. He was sure he knew who Kate's mystery date was. When they had first gotten together back at State, she had mentioned to David how she'd recently "had coffee a couple of times" with one of her photography teachers, a mustachioed, Rugged Joe type of guy in his mid-thirties. He was a staff photographer at *The San Francisco Chronicle,* and had made a point of just about trying to break David's hand the time Kate had introduced the two of them after class one day.

"Goddamn it," said David. "Isn't there a law against teachers dating their ex-students?"

"There certainly should be," said Jerald.

"No shit. It should be punishable by death."

"Hey, why don't you come have your sandwich at my place? Brian would love to see you. And we've got ice cream!"

"How is Brian? I'm so sorry I didn't ask sooner."

"He's the best. Come see him, if you're up to it. You're not contagious anymore."

"I know, but no, thank you. I'll see him soon. For tonight, I think I'll just stay here and slowly gnaw off the inside of my face."

"Well, if you're determined to stay here alone tonight, then promise me one thing."

"Done. What is it?"

"That you'll come visit me tomorrow. Come over at one o'clock. Franklin's coming over then, Brian will be taking his nap, and the three of us can enjoy some tea and company together. Will you come?"

"I will."

"Do you promise? *Promise* promise?"

"I promise promise."

"Good. And I also want you to promise me that you won't spend tonight thinking about Kate."

"Why would I think about Kate? What, because she's out on a date with a guy I *know* she likes, and who's super accomplished in the field she loves the most, the field she *had* chosen for herself before she left it behind to let me completely derail her life? You're suggesting that I shouldn't think about the fact that tonight Kate's going to see one of the world's best jazz singers— with the best photojournalist in the city? While the most impressive things I have on my résumé are that I can lift really heavy boxes over my head, and make a bong out of just about anything? Don't think about any of *that*, you mean?"

"Yes. Right. Don't think about all of that."

David shrugged. "I don't even know why I would. And I'll tell you why I wouldn't. Because I'm not the one who's gonna miss *Mork and Mindy* tonight. Kate'll be at some dilapidated college auditorium, getting sonically tortured by that caterwauling

Anthony Newley wannabe while swatting away the developer-stained paws of a pretentious poseur, while I will be here, in the comfort of this marvelously cozy room, chuckling up a storm at the spectacularly unique and almost disturbingly manic comic stylings of one Robin Williams. What in the world could possibly be better than that? Why would I waste even a single moment of a night like that thinking about Kate?"

"I can see that you won't," said Jerald. "I don't know what I was thinking." He sat on the bed and hugged David. "I love you, buddy."

"I love you too."

"You *sure* you won't come over tonight?"

"I'm sure. And I'm sure you'd rather I didn't."

"You're wrong. We'd love to have you."

"No, you wouldn't. There's no way I'd be fit company."

Two hours later, David, his hands jammed deep into his pockets, was determinedly walking on Irving Street through the cold night, away from the Surf and toward his mother's house.

He had no idea what he was going to do or say once he reached his mom's. He didn't even know if she'd be home. He hadn't called her before leaving his room.

"Not that she'd answer her goddamn phone anyway," he murmured.

While he might not have known exactly what it was, David knew that he needed to say something important to his mother, something big, something cathartic—something that included the fact that during her missing two years, she was not in an ashram in India being the chosen disciple of a revered guru, as she had always hinted that she was, but was, rather, living in fucking San

Jose, doing nothing loftier than hiding from her own two children.

Not long into his trek up Irving, David realized that unless he wanted to arrive at his mom's house pale, weak, and wheezing, he should stop walking as if he were training for the next Olympics, especially given that the way to her house was all various grades of uphill. So he cut to one street over, and was soon enough sitting aboard one of the N-Judah electric streetcars, rumbling, herky-jerky throwbacks that since 1928 had been sluggishly trundling passengers to all kinds of places across San Francisco to which they should or should not have been going.

After transferring from the N-Judah to a city bus, and then walking twelve blocks, David, who from the moment he stepped out of his room had been passionately murmuring aloud at least some of what he intended to say to his mother, found himself standing in the darkness across the street from her building.

He looked up at the window that he knew to be the one over her kitchen sink.

The lights in her kitchen were on. So were the lights in her living room.

She was home.

And then his mother was at the window—but only for a moment before being joined by a man whom David did not recognize.

The man and his mother exchanged a quick kiss. Then the man walked away again, back toward the dining room and the White Room.

As soon as she was alone, Georgia looked straight at the window, which the lights of her kitchen were rendering useful to her as a mirror.

David could see that she was leaning over the sink to get a closer view of her face. She traced a little finger first along the outer edge of her bottom lip, and then on either side of her open mouth. She looked to see that her perfect teeth were nothing but white. Finally, she ran her fingers through her hair, until it looked precisely the right amount of blowsily carefree.

And David became a boy again, silently watching his mother tending to her makeup.

But this time, for the first time, he was watching her from the other side of the mirror.

When she was finished touching herself up, his mother left the window, disappearing from his view.

David stood there a while.

As he turned and started walking back to the Surf, he said, "Done."

❧ 14 ❧

OUT AND OUT

Shortly after one o'clock the following afternoon, David stepped into the office of the Surf Motel to find Jerald behind the counter, restocking his postcards.

"David! You came! And what perfect timing. Brian's taking his nap, Franklin's lounging about inside, and I have water on for tea."

"You are the host on the coast with most to boast," said David.

Jerald placed both hands flat atop the counter, and let his jaw drop open. "Did you just make that up?"

In a dull monotone, David said, "No. I write down interesting and clever things to say ahead of time, and then say them later. In this way do I appear spontaneously witty and socially adept." Switching back to his regular, non-automaton self, he added, "Do you know that's actually a real thing that some people do?"

"Is it really? Well, if that's what you did, it was time well spent. I am flat-out going to steal that rhyme you just said for my brochures."

"Okay by me. But who can say how my lawyers will react?

Those guys are animals. They—" David started at the sound of the office door opening behind him.

"Paula!" Jerald exclaimed.

David turned around to look—and right there in the office, with Franklin *lounging about* just on the other side of Jerald's door —was Paula, in a cropped rabbit-fur jacket, white skin-tight bell-bottoms, and suede platform ankle boots. Her giant, bronze-framed sunglasses were pushing her golden hair back into a fore-head-featuring mane. She was radiating disheveled distress.

If David hadn't pulled his hand away in the nick of time, Paula would have crushed it with the black-and-silver behemoth of a purse she threw down onto the counter.

"Tony broke up with me!" she said. "Last night, after dinner— after this big, lavish *dinner*—we're in our hotel room, getting ready to go to *bed* if you can believe it, and he tells me, with no warning or *anything*, that it's not working out between us. Just like that. All of a sudden we're not *working out*."

David stepped into the gap left by Jerald's loss for words. "That's terrible," he said.

"Goddamn right it's terrible. I swear, he may as well have just kicked me in the stomach. I met his whole *family*."

"So you're back?" said Jerald.

On that dime Paula's mood turned from disconsolate to angry. "Do you see me standing here? Of *course* I'm back. Can we get out of this *office,* please?"

"Yes, of course," said Jerald. Then he more or less yelled, "Come inside, Paula!" David shot a quick glance at Paula. She didn't seem to have noticed Jerald's sudden decibel increase.

"Well, I'm gonna let you two be," said David. "Jer, we'll have tea later. It's good to see you, Paula."

"Where are you going?" said Paula. "Come inside with us. I want you to. Maybe you'll learn something about how *not* to treat your girlfriend."

With something less than pep, David said, "Oh. Well, okay. That sounds good."

Jerald hastily opened the door to his place maybe two inches. "Come on in, Paula!" he exclaimed.

"Jesus, I'm right here," said Paula, yanking her purse off the counter. "What's the matter with you?"

Jerald said, "I'll go make some tea," and ducked behind the door.

"Mmm, tea," said David. He casually leaned on the countertop between Paula and the way around the countertop. "Did you and Tony enjoy drinking tea together?"

"What the hell are you talking about?" said Paula. When she strode around him, rather extravagantly flipping her hair as she went by, David resisted his desire to stick out his foot and send her flying.

When, fast behind Paula, he stepped into Jerald's house, David quickly glanced about, and saw Franklin exactly nowhere. He was just closing the door behind him, when Jerald came flying out of the kitchen, calling, "Water's on for tea!"

"Great!" said David. He wondered if maybe Franklin had ducked into the kitchen. If so, the only way he wasn't at that moment simply standing there in plain sight was if he were triple or quadruple-jointed, and had managed to fold himself into a cabinet, or maybe in the crisper drawer in the fridge. Maybe he was down the hall, in Jerald's bedroom. Maybe he'd shot out the sliding glass door and hopped the fence around the small patio, the whole of which was now visible, since the curtains were pulled all the way back. He definitely wasn't *on* the patio. David pictured Franklin running on the beach, his shimmering kimono flowing in the air behind him.

Paula groaned and flopped down on the couch. "Where's Brian?"

"He's taking a nap," said Jerald. "Lemme just go peek in on him real quick."

David took a seat in one of the chairs across the coffee table from Paula. "That's too bad about Tony."

"Do ya *think*?" snapped Paula.

David bit his tongue to stop himself from saying, "No, what I meant is that it's too bad he didn't murder you in your sleep."

Jerald returned from his quick trip down the hall. "The little guy's out like a light," he said.

"Where's your girlfriend?" Paula asked Jerald testily.

"She's at work right now." Jerald folded his arms across his chest. "She's a social worker." He unfolded his arms, and then folded them again. "Now, what kind of tea would you two like?"

"What is the matter with you?" said Paula. "Why are you so jumpy?"

"Me? I don't know. I've had some of that Red Zinger tea you like so much. And I can see why you do; it's delicious! But I think it has caffeine in it. It's not supposed to. But I think it does. Anyway, would you like some of that?"

Paula leaned back on the couch, and closed her eyes. "I don't care."

"David?" Jerald asked. He took advantage of Paula's closed eyes to pop a quick expression at David indicating that, as far as he knew, Franklin had vanished into thin air.

David replied with an instant manic-fear face, but then said calmly, "I'll have whatever you're having."

When Jerald scurried off to make the tea, Paula opened her eyes. Fixing them on David, she said, "And where's *your* girlfriend? What's her name again?"

"Kate. She's at work."

"She got a job?"

"Yeah."

"Where?"

"Place downtown that sells and services photocopiers."

Already bored, Paula began rummaging around inside of her purse, finally pulling out a tissue.

"I just cannot *believe* this happened to me," she said, dabbing at the corners of her eyes. "I guess Tony just couldn't figure out, *before* we traveled together halfway across the country to visit his lunatic family, that I just wasn't the girl for him. Either that, or he'd just been *lying* the whole time up till then. I guess I'll never know which it was."

"Some guys just don't know what they want," David said. "So they ruin what they have."

"Gee, really, Phil Donahue? Could you tell me something I *don't* know?"

"I doubt it," said David.

Jerald came back from the kitchen carrying a loaded tea tray. "Here we go," he said, setting the tray down on the coffee table.

"That was fast," said Paula.

"It really was," said David.

"Well, it's still steeping. Seeping?" Jerald looked at David. "You're the writer. Does tea steep, or seep? I seem to have forgotten which it is."

"Does it matter?" said Paula.

"Not really," said Jerald, sitting in the other chair across the table from Paula.

"Tea steeps," said David. "Gross wounds seep."

"Nice," said Paula.

"Sorry," said David. "I guess it's true that tea bags seep as they steep. That *is* confusing."

"Sugar, Paula?" said Jerald.

Paula pushed herself back on the couch so that she was sitting more upright, folded her arms, and crossed one leg over the other. Wiggling her foot so furiously that David feared her shoe might come flying right off her foot and brain one of them, she said, "You know what it is? You know what the problem is?" When neither Jerald nor David seemed to, she said, "It's that no man wants a single mother."

"Oh, I don't think that's true," said Jerald, spinning his spoon around in his steaming cup so fast David imagined a mini-hurricane starting in there.

"Then you don't know what you're talking about," said Paula. "Trust me. Guys hear you have a kid, and they run like you told them you have VD."

Jerald protectively glanced toward the hallway. In a low voice, he said, "Oh, that's not true, Paula. Anyone who meets Brian knows right away how lucky they'd be to have him in their life."

"That's for sure," said David.

"Oh, really? So you're saying that if Kate had a kid when you first met her, it wouldn't have stopped you from wanting to get involved with her?"

"It wouldn't have," said David.

Paula scoffed. "Easy for you to say now."

"It *definitely* wouldn't have if that kid was Brian," said David.

"Well, I guess I'm just really unlucky, then, aren't I?" said Paula. "I guess I just don't know how to find the right kind of man, do I?" She looked pointedly at Jerald. "*Do* I?"

"This tea is *so* good," said David. "What kind is this, Jer?"

"Darjeeling," said Jerald.

David pretended to ponder his answer. "Hmm. Darjeeling. Isn't that the name of the star of that really big burlesque club on Broadway? Darjeeling Glitterbuns?"

"That's *right!*" said Jerald, playing along. "And now she has a *tea* named after her!"

"Oh, you two are a riot," said Paula. "I swear, that's all men care about, sex and jokes. That's it. Oh, and eating. Sex, jokes, and eating. That *is* all men care about."

"That's not true," said Jerald.

"Yeah, that's not true," said David. "There's also sports."

Paula picked up a pillow, mashed it against her face, and screamed. When she was done doing that, Jerald said, "Talk to us about what's happened, Paula. You'll feel better if you do."

"He's right," said David.

"Okay, fine," said Paula. About ten minutes later, as she was well into her histrionic evisceration of men in general, and of "Tony Baloney" in particular, a sleepy-eyed Brian emerged from his bedroom. Paula called the boy over to her, and made a great show of hugging and kissing him, pulling him onto the couch so that he could sit beside her, and peppering him with five questions for every one he had a chance to even begin to answer. Then she went right back into her tirade against men.

Jerald gently interrupted her. "Paula, maybe we should wait until Brian's not here to hear this."

"Why?" said Paula testily. "He has no idea what I'm talking about. Watch. Brian, sweetheart, do you have any idea what Mommy is talking about?" Brian shook his head no. "See? He doesn't understand. Because we're adults having an adult conversation, Jerald. Brian's not an adult, in case you haven't noticed."

"No, but he's not a baby anymore, either. And besides, I just think the *tone* we use around him should probably—"

"Oh, *stop* it," Paula snapped. "If *you've* got a problem with my tone, Jerald, just say so. But don't try to blame your problems on Brian. Anyway, I have to go. I just wanted to come by to tell you that I'm home now." She kissed Brian on the head, pinched him on his cheek, and vigorously mussed up his hair. "Mommy's leaving now, precious. But I'll see you soon, okay, honey? Do you want to walk Mommy to her car? With Daddy? So that we can talk about what we're going to do with you on Christmas?"

Jerald said, "Paula, I—"

"Oh, don't worry, I'm not gonna interfere with your precious Christmas." Standing up from the couch, she lifted her purse, and said, "I just thought I might come by here on Christmas morning, if that's not asking too much. C'mon, Jerald. Walk me and Brian out to the car."

David rose from his chair. "Bye, Paula. Good to see you again."

"Brian and I will be right back," Jerald said to David. On the trio's way out of the office door, Jerald turned around so he was facing David, and did a quick "What Is Happening!?" face. David returned the expression, adding a shrug.

David had just heard the three of them exit the front office for the parking lot, when he saw the door of Jerald's coat closet, located between the office door and the hallway leading to Jerald and Brian's bedroom, slowly opening up. Franklin's head came poking out.

"There you are!" David whisper-screamed.

"They're gone, right?" Franklin whispered back.

"Yes. They're gone. Oh my gosh! How *are* you?"

Stepping from the closet, Franklin said in a soft voice, "Feeling a tad claustrophobic at the moment." By way of stretching his legs, he took a few giant steps around the living room. Then he sat, straight-backed, on a chair at the dining room table.

"It's so nice to sit down," he said.

David sat next to him at the table. "You were in there that *whole time?*"

"What choice did I have? I was sitting on the couch when I heard Paula talking in the office. I *panicked*. I couldn't remember our plan about how I'm supposed to be Lillian's brother from out of town. I mean, I *could* have remembered it—but my mind went blank. All I could think was where to *hide*. So into the closet I went. Which is *not* a place I am comfortable being, either metaphorically or literally. I especially don't like being in *that* closet. It's not exactly a walk-in."

"No! It's tiny! You must have been so uncomfortable in there!"

"I *was*." He leaned forward and arched his back. "I couldn't stand straight in there. Or move at *all*, basically. It was not easy." He reached out his long arm, and lightly slapped David's shoulder. And your Darjeeling *Glitterbuns* did *not* make it any easier on me in there, I can tell you that. I swear, I about bit a hole through my bottom lip trying not to laugh."

"I am *so* sorry!"

"Oh, don't be. Believe me, I needed the comic relief." Settling his gaze on the middle of the dining table, Franklin grew pensive. After a while, he said sadly, "That was not an easy conversation to overhear."

David studied Franklin's face. "No," he said softly. "I guess it wouldn't have been."

Just then, Jerald and Brian came back through the door. When he saw Franklin sitting at the dining table, Jerald stopped in his tracks.

Waving his fingers in the air, Franklin said, "Hello, you two."

"Hi, Franklin!" called Brian.

"Hello, little man," said Franklin affectionately.

Looking puzzled and relieved, Jerald said, "Happy to see you, Franklin."

"Happy to be seen," said Franklin.

"Brian, you wanna watch some TV?" said Jerald.

"Yeah!" cried Brian. "Cartoons!"

"Okay. Just for a half hour, though."

As Brian turned to run toward the corner of the room given over to two bean bag chairs and a television set, Jerald crossed to Franklin. "Where *were* you?" he whispered.

"Guess," said Franklin.

"*Where?*"

"In the closet."

Jerald swiveled his head to look at the enclosure in question. "Not in *that* closet!"

"In that closet."

"But it's so *small*."

"It seems that way from the outside," said Franklin. "But it's funny. Once you're inside of it, it's even smaller."

"Oh my God," Jerald said. "I am *so* sorry."

"Dad!" called Brian, who was looking at a television showing nothing but gray hissing fuzz. "Come do the TV so I can see it!"

"Be right there, Sport!"

When he was done manipulating the rabbit-ear antenna atop his TV set until the gray snow finally became *Sesame Street*, Jerald came and sat across the table from Franklin. Speaking in a voice low enough to ensure that Brian wouldn't overhear him, he said to Franklin, "Poor *baby*. What *happened*?"

After Franklin told him how he'd hid and then stayed hidden, Jerald said, "Franklin, I am so, *so* sorry."

Reaching across the table to take Jerald's hand, Franklin said, "It's not your fault." Quickly glancing over at Brian, he pulled his hand back. But then he looked at Brian again, and this time kept his gaze on the boy for a long time.

When Franklin turned back to Jerald, his eyes were moist. "It's not your fault," he whispered.

Jerald offered Franklin both of his hands on the tabletop, palms up. When Franklin, looking down at Jerald's hands with a somber sadness, remained still, Jerald's eyes also filled with tears. He slowly pulled his hands back.

David stood up from his chair and went over to Brian. "Hey, buddy. I feel like going over to the park, maybe playing on the playground. You wanna come with? Maybe get a hot dog from the hot dog guy?"

"Yeah!" cried Brian. "Can I go, Dad?"

Jerald had just finished dabbing his eyes dry with a napkin he'd taken from its holder on the table.

"You bet, son," he said, adjusting his glasses.

"C'mon, Bry," said David. "Let's get your coat and shoes. It's cold outside." When Brian dashed off for his bedroom, David followed him down the hallway.

———

When David and Brian returned to the living room a few minutes later, they were all zipped up and ready to go.

"We'll be at the children's playground," said David.

After a beat, Jerald broke eye contact with Franklin. "Have a good time, you two."

"We will," said David. "See you soon."

"See you soon," said Jerald.

When Franklin saw David walking across the room toward him, he stood from his chair. As the two men hugged, David said, "Love you."

"I love you too," Franklin whispered.

———

About an hour later, while he was sitting on a bench in the park watching Brian running around and playing with the other kids on the playground, David spotted Jerald walking toward him over a grass-covered rise in the middle distance, his hands stuffed deeply into the pockets of his gray wool overcoat, a long maroon scarf tied loosely about his neck.

When he reached the bench and sat down beside him, David saw that his friend had been crying.

Jerald, keeping his hands in his pockets, leaned back on the bench, extending his legs before him. He and David silently watched the children play.

After a time, and without turning his head, Jerald said, "Franklin and I broke up."

It took David a while to find the only words he could. "I am so sorry."

Pulling a white handkerchief from his coat pocket, Jerald wiped his eyes under his glasses, and dabbed his nose. "It had to happen. And I should have realized it sooner. We can fool Brian for now, but how long is that going to last? And even if we could make it last, what kind of message would I be sending to him? I can't live a lie in front of my own son. And Franklin is anything but a liar. One of the things that makes him such an amazing person is how honestly he lives his life."

"Dad!" called Brian. He was sitting with a cluster of companions, all of whom were busily excavating in the sand. He waved at his father. By way of returning the greeting, Jerald smiled and shook the ends of his scarf in the air before him.

Watching Brian for a bit after the boy had returned to his play, Jerald said, "I love Franklin, with everything I have. And he loves me the same way. But I can't risk losing my son. And as long as Paula holds Brian over my head the way she does, that risk will be a part of my everyday life. I'll always have to lie. I'll always have to pretend to be someone I'm not." He wiped away a tear that was streaming down his cheek. "In one way or another, Franklin was always going to be running back into the fucking closet."

David gently rubbed circles around Jerald's upper back. "I'm so sorry," he said. "This shouldn't be happening."

"No, it shouldn't. But it is. And it's going to be happening for a while."

After a long moment, David said, "So what now?"

Jerald breathed deeply. "So now I stay single. Now I make the focus of my life being the best father to Brian I can be. I provide him the safest and most nourishing environment that I can. And the only way for me to do that is to stay single. So that's what I'll do."

"I can't bear to think of you as lonely."

"I'm not too crazy about it myself. But what choice do I have? The thing to remember is that I won't have to live alone forever. This is one of those instances where I trust in the healing power of time. Things do change. People change. Paula grew up with parents who believed what everyone else she knew believed, which is that being gay is a sin. That's all she's ever known or been taught. But now she lives here. Things aren't like that here. So maybe her opinions on gay people will change. Also, right now, Paula's really unhappy. She's not in any kind of romantic relationship. Maybe when she finds someone of her own, she'll stop punishing me the way she does. And even if she doesn't change one bit, in ten or so years, Brian'll be old enough to think for himself. I just need to wait until he gets through all his young and formative years. And that won't be all that long from now. I just need to make sure I'm with him the whole time."

"It's so moving that you would sacrifice so much for your son."

"It's nothing any normal parent wouldn't do. Or isn't supposed to do, anyway. If you're a parent, you're not supposed to choose yourself over your children."

"A lot of parents don't seem to know that," said David. "Or maybe they do know it, but want to pretend like they don't. That way, they don't have to really commit to doing anything that they don't actually want to do."

"I think that happens a lot," said Jerald. "Of course it does. We all want to keep all of our options open, all the time. But that's not what it means to be an adult. Being an adult means choosing a lane, and then staying in that lane."

A silent minute or two later, Jerald sighed. "Speaking of responsibilities, it's time for me to get back to the motel."

But the two continued watching the children at play.

"So your new life is beginning," said David.

"As of right now," said Jerald. He stood up from the bench. "Brian! C'mon, little man. It's time for us to go home."

———

Once the three of them had walked back to the motel, David gave Brian a quick hug goodbye, and then hugged Jerald a little longer, and a lot tighter. He also waved to Erin, who was in the office behind the desk.

After that he went back to his room.

He sat on the edge of his bed.

And he stayed sitting there, thinking about Jerald, Franklin, Brian, and Paula.

He thought about his mother, his father, his sister.

He thought about Kate.

He thought about love. About all that love is, about all that artfully masquerades as love.

He thought about what those who want the truest kind of love must be prepared to sacrifice in order to have and keep that love.

———

He scooted over to the nightstand, picked up the phone, and dialed.

When Lillian answered, he asked if Kate were there.

She was.

"Hello?" said Kate.

"Hi, Kate. It's me, David."

"Yeah, I know. It's me, Kate. We've met."

"I know. But I always feel like I have to say who I am, or the other person just won't know, or won't be sure. It's just . . . phones. They're so weird."

"No, they're not."

"Oh my God. You're impossible."

"And yet you've called me. Why, again?"

"Because I'm hoping that you and I can get together some-time. Just to talk. For five minutes, max."

"Why? What about?"

"Nothing. I mean, everything, really. Just—it's about me, basi-cally. And you. And us."

"There is no us, David."

"I know."

"You don't seem to."

"I do, I promise. Okay? I promise. There's no us. I get that. But Kate, there is you. And there's me. And when you and me *were* an us, the weak link in that us was me. And I've never been able to understand why that is—what is actually the *matter* with me. Well, now I do. It's not pretty, but at least I know what is— or what *has* been—wrong with me. And all I want to do is tell you what I've discovered about that. Not so that you'll take me back—I promise. But just so you'll know that I know why I did what I did to our relationship. And I feel like if I can tell you that, then I can properly apologize to you. And I would *really* like to do that. So, again, I'm just wondering if we can get together sometime. Five minutes is all I need to say to you what I want to say."

Kate was silent.

Then she was silent some more.

Then she said, "Talk to me in a month."

"I'm sorry?"

"Talk to me in a month. If what you've got to say is real, then it'll be real in a month. I know you, David. Stuff that feels huge to you one moment can mean nothing to you the next."

"Ouch."

"Am I wrong?"

"Yes."

"Am I?"

"Yes."

"David."

"No."

"Then talk to me in a month. Let's see if you're still feeling as strongly then about whatever you're feeling now. Okay?"

"No, sorry. You blew it. Now I have to come over there right this minute."

"Goodbye."

"I'm kidding! Gosh, remember when you used to have a sense of humor?"

"Yeah. Gee, I wonder where *that* went?"

"Got me. Anyway, seriously. Yes. I hear you. A month from now will be just fine. Thank you. So, let's see. One month from today would be—wow. That's New Year's Eve."

"It's also a Monday."

"How do you just know that?"

"Because I'm looking at a calendar on Lillian's fridge. Let's do the day before."

"Perfect."

"Okay. So we'll meet at the Bandshell, at one o'clock, on December thirtieth. Sound good?"

"That sounds great. I—"

"I'll see you then," said Kate, hanging up.

David started off the following day by checking in on Jerald. He found his friend sitting alone at his dining table, having just finished breakfast with Brian, who was off playing in his bedroom.

"How are you?" said David, putting his hand on Jerald's shoulder.

Jerald sighed and placed his hand atop David's. "I'm fine. I miss you-know-who."

"Of course you do."

"I've been making a list of all the things that need tending to around the motel."

"Oh?" said David, taking a seat. "That seems really productive."

"I actually do look forward to checking some of these things off my to-do list."

"Speaking of making things better, I've been thinking that the time has come for me to get a job. As much as I love getting paid by the state of California to do nothing but test the viscosity and breakdown rate of various lubricants on my wang, if I don't rejoin the real world pretty soon, I am not going to be fit to be in it."

"That sounds like a positive thing. Where are you thinking of applying for a job?"

"I thought I'd try City Lights and Stacey's."

"Oh, that's such a great idea—especially for a writer. Those are both such great bookstores. I *love* Stacey's."

"Me too. And I feel like I have a better chance of getting a job there than I do at City Lights. I don't think Allen Ginsberg is hip enough to get a job at City Lights. So I thought I'd try Stacey's first. The only thing is, Stacey's is three blocks from where Kate works."

"So?"

"So I was thinking maybe I *shouldn't* get a job there. So that it doesn't seem like I'm, you know, *Eyes of Laura Mars*-ing her."

Jerald laughed. "I don't think you have to worry about that.

Half the jobs in the city are downtown. It'd be hard to find a job that's *not* within rock-throwing distance of Kate's job. Besides, she's not going to work there forever. She'll move on to something else."

"Good point. Especially given that she's probably already engaged to Joe 'Lemme Take A Picture Of You With Al Jarreau.'"

"Stop that. You have no idea what Kate's relationship is with that guy."

"I know what it *isn't*."

"What are you talking about?"

"I have no idea. I'm insane." David took a deep breath. "But sanity is my goal. So it's settled. I'm gonna go shave, wrangle my hair into submission, put on my least wrinkled clothes, try not to strangle myself to death putting on my only necktie, and then take the bus to Stacey's, and ask them if they're doing any hiring."

"Good for you," said Jerald. "Take the tiger by the tail."

"Speaking of which, kind of, I called Kate last night."

"You did? How'd that go?"

"Well enough. We're getting together in a month."

"Why a month?"

"I have something I want to tell her, and she wants me to wait a month before I do, in case my feelings about what I want to tell her change."

"What do you want to tell her?"

"Why I screwed up my relationship with her."

"Oh. Can you tell *me* why you did that?"

"You don't want to know."

"But I do."

"It's a bit of a story, and I *will* bore you with it sometime."

"I'm sure I wouldn't find it boring, David."

"Well, maybe not, because you're such a sweet person. But,

believe me, it's nothing exceptional. Or—I don't know. Maybe it is, a little."

"I'm sure it is."

"Well, the point is that Kate has agreed to meet with me in a month, so that I can tell her what I did wrong in our relationship, why I did it, and why exactly I'm sorry that I did it. And after that, maybe we can at least be friends."

"That sounds really good."

"I feel so stupid and selfish talking to you about me and Kate, right after what's happened between you and Franklin. I'm sorry."

"Why? Don't be silly. I still want *you* to be happy."

"And I want you to be happy. And I *might* be happy yet. But how can you ever be?"

"Because I'm human. And because sometimes happiness just takes time."

"It takes too much time, if you ask me."

"Me too."

"Jerald, are we gonna be all right, you think? I mean— honestly, I just feel so lost sometimes."

"So do I, buddy. Everybody does sometimes."

"But do you think that you and I are—I don't know—each in a story that has a happy ending?"

"I think that's up to us. We all write our own story, don't we?"

"I guess."

"I *know*. And if we want our story to be a happy one, then we have to make that happen for ourselves."

David fell silent for a while. Then he said, "I think that you are one-hundred percent right about that."

❧ 15 ❧

I HATE YOU

On a cold, overcast afternoon one month later, David stood in an open-air plaza in Golden Gate Park, facing an orderly sea of green wooden benches. Just behind him was the majestic stage known as the Bandshell.

Being nearly the only person on the plaza, he was free to sit wherever he chose. He picked a bench in the center section of the audience seats, toward the rear. This felt like a good, natural spot for him: definitely in the middle of the action—but humble about it. *There*, but not showy. Focused, but not obsessed.

Or something like that. He really had no idea. He couldn't think.

As he sat down upon its surprising coldness, he put on the bench beside him the Christmas gift he'd brought there for Kate. It was a just-published behemoth of a book, titled, *Henri Cartier-Bresson: Photographer*, showcasing the work of Kate's all-time favorite photographer.

He gazed at the ornate cement stage. Its key feature was a massive, forward-facing bowl, flanked on either side by Roman columns supporting a promenade that offered a very short walk with a very great view.

He imagined, on the stage itself, a toga-wearing Caesar, belting out an opera. Next he imagined Oedipus the King, stumbling around, freshly blinded and bellowing his grief, while behind him a Greek chorus stood intoning about the inevitability of chaos and destruction, and also slipping in a choice tip here and there for removing bloodstains from a royal tunic.

"Woe be unto the man self-blinded by his own pride and arrogance, for his downfall is imminent!" he saw the choir soberly chanting. "Some baking soda and salt will probably do the trick there. But take care not to scrub, oh mighty King! Pat dry only!"

He was laughing a bit over that when he saw Kate, walking toward him in her blue jeans, her green down jacket, and her hiking boots.

He waved to her. At the same time, barely moving his lips, he rapidly and quietly said, "I love you, I love you, marry me, marry me."

When she was close enough to hear him, he switched to, "Hi!"

"Hi," said Kate. She walked down the row he was in, and took a seat beside him. "How are you?"

"Good. Fine. I mean, you know. Alive. I'm glad you came. I thought maybe you'd, you know, come to your senses, and not."

"And yet, here I am."

"Lucky me!" Then he turned to pick up the weighty slab beside him. "Speaking of Christmas, I bought you a little gift. And by 'little,' I mean you'll need a wheelbarrow to get it home. Here you go. It's called *The Christmas Workout*."

"It's so *heavy*," said Kate.

"That's the whole idea. It only *looks* gift-wrapped, by the way. That's part of its cleverness. It's really just a weight. The idea is that you lug it around, to help burn off those extra holiday calories. I lost four pounds just bringing it here. So I can vouch for it. Merry Christmas."

"Aw. You never did know what to get me."

David laughed. "That is so not true! Have you forgotten the authentic, all-weather Nehru jacket I bought you, with all the awesome little *mirrors* sewn into it?"

"No, I can't say that I've forgotten that, as hard as I've tried to. Do you want me to open this now?"

David shrugged. "Whatever you'd like. But sure."

Once she had unwrapped her present enough to see what it was, she said, "Oh, *wow*! You *really* shouldn't have." Reverentially flipping through the glossy black-and-white images, she said, "I read about this book. God, Bresson is just so amazing. This is really kind of you, David. Thank you."

"Of course. And listen, I know it's maybe a little weird that I got you a Christmas present. But when I saw it at work, I had to pick up a copy for you."

Kate gently closed the book. "At work? Did you get a job?"

"Oh, right. Sorry. Yes, I am now employed."

"You are?"

David laughed. "Could you try not to find that *quite* so astonishing?"

"Where do you work?"

"At Stacey's Bookstore."

"*Really?*"

"Cross my heart, and hope to figure out how to continue collecting unemployment. I work in shipping and receiving, Monday through Friday, eight to five. It's beyond great. And, unlike all the clerks who work in the actual store—known by us in the bookstore biz as the *sales area*—I don't have to wear a tie, or shave, or get dressed up in any way. I get to remain my normal hobo-looking self."

"That's really great, David. Loving books the way you do, you must feel like you died and went to job heaven."

"I honestly do. I kind of can't believe I work there. In other news, I got a little one-bedroom apartment, on Leavenworth between Pine and Bush."

"Really? You're not at the Surf anymore?"

"I'm not. It's the end of an era."

Kate lifted the book and wrapping paper off her lap, and set them down on the bench beside her. "Boy. That's a lot of changes, right?"

David shrugged. "I guess so. The *main* thing is that I moved inland. Less chance of getting ambushed by the ocean."

"Good plan. Hey, how's your father doing?"

"He's good, thanks for asking. Seems all healed up. Back at work."

"Good." After a pause, Kate said, "So. You wanted to talk to me."

"I did. And I appreciate your letting me."

But suddenly he wasn't sure how to begin what he'd come to say. He looked back up at the stage. It was as empty as empty gets. He looked back at Kate. Waiting for him to start, she brushed back the stray pieces of her hair the wind was playing across her face.

Breathing deeply, David said, "When I broke up with you, I had no idea why I did it. You had good ideas at the time for why —and if I'd listened to you then, we might still be together. Because what you said about that was right: I was bothered—and, as it turns out, a whole lot more bothered than I knew—by the fact that I wasn't financially supporting us the way I wanted to, or felt that I should. I just felt like such a loser during that whole time. But that's not the reason I broke up with you. Two and a half grueling months after that insanity, I am here to tell you why I did that. Ready?"

"Sure," said Kate.

"I turned you into my mother."

Kate let a silent moment go by. Then she said, "That's not good."

"It was definitely not good. Because it meant that I was sure that you would do what she did."

"Leave you."

"Leave me. That's what you would do. That's what I thought, because in my world that's what happens. The people I love leave me. I loved my father. He left. I loved my mother. She left. I loved you. Of *course* you were going to leave. So I exercised the only control I had over the inevitability of that happening, and let swing that wrecking ball myself."

He looked away long enough to wipe the tears that had come to his eyes. "My life has been pure regret since then. The thing is, I didn't just think you were going to break up with me. I *knew* you were. I knew it in my bones. Because no woman I really love can ever love me back. That's just the truth of my life. Very early on, and in no uncertain terms, I learned that I'm just not lovable. I wasn't lovable enough for my own *mother* to stay with me. And even when she came back—which, in my mind, she'd maybe done to give me one more try, to see if while she was away I hadn't become someone she could love—she only seemed to hate me more. She rejected me more in the years after she returned than it felt like she had during the two years she was gone. At least when she was gone, I didn't *know* that she couldn't stand to be around me. But when she was back, man, there was no doubt about that."

He leaned his head back, and watched for a moment the perfectly still blanket of light gray clouds hanging so low in the sky.

"Anyway," he said, "the upshot of everything that happened to me when I was a kid is that it made me deeply, profoundly, and permanently ashamed to be me. I was ashamed to be someone whom no one could love—at least, not anyone who knew me well. That's the thing about having your parents so completely reject you that they just can't abide living in the same house as you anymore. Those are your *parents*. Your parents *know* you. They *really* know you. So if they decide you're unlovable, then you are definitely unlovable. Because who can't even get their own *parents* to love them? Who can't get their own *mom* to love them?

"And when you're a kid, and you learn that you're unlovable, it makes you two things. It makes you ashamed, and it makes you angry."

"That's right," said Kate.

"You're angry, because at your most core, animal level, you're, like, *What is so reprehensible about me? Fuck you. I* am *lovable.* But mostly, you're ashamed. The anger is so deep inside you, you don't even realize it's there. But the shame? The shame you know. The shame is like your skin. It's with you, covering you, all the time. Your shame is who you are.

"But the thing about shame is, you can hide it. You can disguise your shame. You can *pretend* it right off the center stage of your life. You can basically *will* your shame out of your mind. And that works. You can get away with that. You can, that is, until you love someone as much as you've ever loved anyone in your life. And then you've got a problem. Because loving someone means letting them get to know you. And you know that once the person you love gets to know you, they are going to learn your deepest and darkest secret, which is that you are anathema to the very idea of love. They're going to learn what you already know, which is that wherever you are is a place where love cannot be.

"And that's what happened to us in Long Beach. It's *easy* for me to feel shame. I'm a walking shame trap, always ready to trip. My shame just *waits* in the wings for a chance to take center stage again. And when my job started failing us, that's exactly what it did. I immediately dropped right back into my shame hole.

"And what happens next? When I'm feeling ashamed, and embarrassed, and generally hyper-vulnerable to the idea that I'm not lovable—what happens?"

"I leave."

"Exactly. Every morning you grab your keys, and you grab your purse, and you say, 'Bye, I'll be back soon.' And you leave. You walk out the door. And when you do that, everything inside of me screams—in such harmony with everything I know and am that I don't even *hear* it—that you're never going to come back. Because what's out there in the world is *obviously* going to be more appealing to you than the useless jerk-off back at your house, who's probably gonna just stay on the couch all day, watching television, and eating fucking Cocoa Puffs.

"Out in the world, you can have a great life for yourself. But at home, the only life you've got is with me. So of *course* you're going to choose a life away from home. It's such a no-brainer."

David leaned forward, and stared down at the packed dirt near his feet. "It's so fucking stupid," he said. "The wiring for your whole system gets set up for you when you're a kid. And that's it. That's who you become. I let myself destroy us, just because I couldn't get the needle on the record of my life to play a song different than the only recording I'd ever heard."

When he looked back at Kate, he saw tears running down her face.

"But I'm the same way," she said. "You aren't the only one. I feel ashamed. I feel afraid. I think I'm unlovable. I couldn't save my mother. She didn't love me enough to choose me over a bottle of gin. She didn't care what that asshole she married did to me. We're the *same*, David. That's why we were together. That was the whole *point* of us: we were a couple of misfits on the Island of Misfits." She started to sob. "We had each other. We were supposed to be a team.

"And then you kicked me off the team. You left me all by myself again."

When David moved to put his arms around her, Kate hit him away. "No. Fuck you."

"Please," David said desperately. "I'm sorry. I'm so sorry. I shouldn't have left you. It's the worst thing I've ever done, and it's tortured me every single day since I did it."

"I don't care! Your pain is not my problem! Your solution to your pain is not my problem! I'm glad you've got clarity on why you suddenly and out of nowhere fucking *ditched* me like you did —which, by the way, was basically the same way your mother ditched you."

"Oh, God, you're right. You're right. I never even thought of that."

"Okay, well, now you know that you treated me just as shittily as your mother treated you. Good for you."

He barely choked out the word, *No*.

"But your learning about *you* doesn't do anything for me, does it? Your understanding about why you broke up with me might help *you* out, but why the fuck am I supposed to care about that? I don't. That's your business. You've been hurt, David. You feel no one can love you. Well, you made sure I *knew* that no one could love me, didn't you?" Her eyes were ablaze with fury and pain.

"I did," said David. "I did. I am so sorry."

"I was braver than you, David. I did what you didn't have the nerve to do. I trusted—despite everything that had happened to me—that love is possible. That love is real. That love can make everything good.

"I trusted *you*, David."

"I know you did. I know. And you *are* braver than me, Kate. I was so blinded by my past, that I couldn't see my present—let alone my future. When all I had to do, to claim as my own the whole new life you had already given me, was look at you. Only see you. Only listen to you. Only trust that you would listen to me—that I didn't have to *manage* our relationship, in the hopes of hiding the truth of what a loser I am. Because all you ever wanted was for us to be a couple of losers together."

"That's right," said Kate. "But that didn't happen. Instead, you made my worst nightmare come true. You proved to me that my biggest fear was right, which is that my own happiness absolutely cannot be trusted. That the moment I relax, the moment I think love is real, it will disappear. Everything will just come apart again. And I'll be left alone again."

And then she was crying too hard to talk.

David slid to her side. He went to put his arm around her, but stopped himself, gently putting his hand on her back.

Still sobbing, she fell against him.

"I hate you," she said into his chest.

When he wrapped his arm around her shoulders, she collapsed further into him.

Holding her tight, he said, "I can work with that."

ABOUT THE AUTHOR

N. John Shore, Jr. is a long-time magazine and newspaper writer who has edited and ghostwritten several fiction and non-fiction bestselling books. In 2014, in order to start writing *Everywhere She's Not*, he put on hiatus his personal blog, which since 2007 had been among the most read blogs in the country (receiving views upwards of 300,000 views a month).

From April 2016 to November 2017 John penned, for The Asheville Citizen-Times, *Ashes to Asheville*, the first real-time serial novel ever published on the website of a major daily newspaper. With the conclusion of *Ashes* he started writing for the *Citizen-Times* his popular advice column, *Ask John*.

Everywhere She's Not is John's first (non-serialized) novel.

For first updates about his next book, subscribe to John's free (and ad-free) monthly newsletter at:
johnshore.com

facebook.com/NJohnShoreJr
twitter.com/johnshore

CPSIA information can be obtained
at www.ICGtesting.com
Printed in the USA
JSHW021441180819
1095JS00003B/5